CATCH

Simon Robson was born in 1966 and grew up in Wiltshire. After graduating from RADA he worked extensively in the theatre, and his play *The Ghost Train Tattoo* was produced at The Manchester Royal Exchange in 2000. His first book, *The Separate Heart and Other Stories*, was shortlisted for the Frank O'Connor Award in 2007.

ALSO BY SIMON ROBSON

The Separate Heart

SIMON ROBSON

Catch

A Novel

VINTAGE BOOKS
London

Published by Vintage 2011

2 4 6 8 10 9 7 5 3 1

Simon Robson received a grant from the Authors' Foundation, which
is administered by The Society of Authors, to whom he would like to
express his gratitude

First published in Great Britain in 2010 by
Jonathan Cape

Vintage
Random House, 20 Vauxhall Bridge Road,
London SW1V 2SA

www.vintage-books.co.uk

Addresses for companies within The Random House Group Limited
can be found at: www.randomhouse.co.uk/offices.htm

The Random House Group Limited Reg. No. 954009

A CIP catalogue record for this book
is available from the British Library

ISBN 9780099547082

The Random House Group Limited supports The Forest
Stewardship Council (FSC), the leading international forest
certification organisation. All our titles that are printed on
Greenpeace approved FSC certified paper carry the FSC logo.

To Sophie

It had rained in the night. From the eaves and from the ends of the branches that reached higher than the roof came the steady drip of rainwater: the last evidence of what had been committed in darkness, now submitted to a daylight jury. Richer for their night-time misdemeanours, the drops of water refracted the dull December-morning light into something brighter and made of themselves a more luxurious company than their accomplices that had fallen first as rain; they made a heavy, lazy patter on the windowsill.

Alone in her bed, Catharine watched the ceiling and imagined what was being finished outside; the last business of the night. It was nice to guess. Nice to think of what she had not seen or heard herself, but whose epilogue she had caught, a drama she might now reconstitute in her own head, subject to her own sense of what was most pleasing. Besides, it was marvellous to be reminded that there were unwitnessed phenomena still – like the chanced-upon communication of dreams betrayed by the whisperings and flickering eyelids of a sleeping partner. That there were changes and revolutions, sustaining rituals and the regular, therapeutic husbandry of Nature, that must still take place under cover of darkness. Alongside which she was superfluous.

As Catharine lay there, the ceiling above her as white and pleasurable as winter mist, she wondered how far her superfluity went. She took pleasure in the idea of her unimportance beside the cleansing downpour. Her bed was warm with only her warmth. How far might she extrapolate her unimportance? To the meadows below the cottage, certainly now covered in a sheet of standing water and reflecting the willows beyond, their leafless arches reaching as low into the inundated field as they reached high into rainless sky; to the swollen streams that banked the watercress beds below the church; to the shallow ford out of the village that broadened ambitiously every autumn and shrank to dust every summer?

All these local miracles were accomplished without her. And as a consequence of not having lived in the village long – barely five months – she could also remind herself that they had got along very well without her before she ever knew of them. She was a newcomer and so was not to be held responsible for the process of the morning. And, as her husband was absent, she must keep it that way. Otherwise she might find herself wishing he were there, that her bed was occupied, or while making breakfast be tempted to share her meal with a passer-by. She must guard her privacy this morning of all mornings. She would take her cue from the sounds she could hear from beyond the dark curtain. The post-deluge operation being completed about the house had the quality of a clear-up after a riotous party the night before. In the face of this essential activity any socialising, impromptu village fetes or Christmas-card coffee mornings would be impossible. Could they not see the state of the house? The private poetry of the house's recovery from the rain would excuse her keeping to her home. The delay between the rain's falling in the night and the sound of the pipes around the eaves still spluttering to accommodate it was her alibi. And she would enjoy it, until the last, considered drops of water from the roof and garden had fallen, and the heavy shrub leaves had leant down silently to deposit the water on the gravel drive, as gently as any mother laying her baby on her bed.

In time she got up, put on her dressing gown and took the stairs like an instruction. Below it was dark, like going into the hold of a ship; at least all was dry below decks. She passed by the recessed window with the shelf of ornaments and went down.

The low ceiling of their cottage living room was always something of a reproach. The more modern kitchen beyond – an extension from the eighties – was relatively bright and efficient, but this, the main room of the house, was from the seventeenth century. The walls were thick and the windows small, as if someone had tunnelled out of the house years ago in search of daylight. These granted a view of a distant square of gravel or tree trunk according to where you stood in the room; never sky. Having moved there in the summer, the nod of a flower or swoop of a blackbird across the tiny aperture had done enough to make them feel it didn't matter; they thought the summer would impregnate the house with light and warmth. It hadn't. And now it was winter.

She always, instinctively now, felt behind the door frame

at the bottom of the stairs as she came down, to find the light switch. And more often than not she took her hand away, as if it had been burnt. She didn't want to admit the room was dark. She told herself that it must be allowed to be of its period. What were they to do? Install halogen spotlights above the fireplace? Scatter psychedelic cushions on the sofa like strategically placed cones around motorway roadworks, to make navigation around their living room safer? This was the image Tom had offered her, and she had laughed. Now, whenever she thought it was dark, she tried to think of Tom's joke and think it didn't matter. But he still swore quietly to himself when he sat over his case notes in the evening and dragged the standard lamp across the room like a school-teacher pulling a naughty pupil by the ear.

This morning she flicked the switch. This morning she would be modern, and not from the seventeenth century. It was the first morning ever that she had woken up in the house without Tom.

When they had lived in London it seemed to Catharine that he was always going away. But in all the five months since they had moved there he had never once done so. Had he organised it this way, to spare her the solitude? Had he been fearful of abandoning her to the low-ceilinged shadows of their tomb-like living room? Or had time begun to slow its progress in the cottage at the end of the lane, beneath the tall trees, such that each day became magnified, and one life, her life, had become elastic, seeing in those five months an entire lifetime of habit and ease, such that she was surprised, pleasurably outraged, even, that she should suddenly be left alone for a night?

Not that she had not known what to do with the evening

and night alone. She had cooked her supper, watched television and gone to bed early. The day of his departure had been ordinary. It was this, the waking to the house alone, that seemed remarkable. She stood still and looked down the barrel of the first window near the stairs and saw some gravel and a sliver of pine. She held it for a second. Behold the unique, still vision; Nature in microcosm, two-dimensional. The atom of a landscape. The broad expanse of Nature reduced to an artistic miniature. She wondered for a second at this paradigm of the solitary, unmarried vantage point. It was uniquely hers. Her husband was in Birmingham.

Crossing the room, she regretted having turned the lights on. How could she have been so foolish? She knew full well the price to be paid. There, to her right, against the wall, she now could not help but see, like a guest at a party to whom she was anxious to avoid talking, was her piano. Like a hostess who uses the oven and the suggested threat of burnt sausage rolls to excuse herself, she put her head down and strode purposefully towards the kitchen. She made it clear she could not stop. There must be no doubt about that. Except that this morning there was no small talk to be had elsewhere, no encounters with Tom to come between her and her now solitary guest. She would make her tea and, well-mannered girl that she was, find herself standing in the doorway, accommodating the upright presence in the corner. It was, after all, her responsibility.

When her mother had given her and Tom paintings of her family, or pieces of furniture that had family history, these things quickly became *theirs*. She would never have referred to the painting of her aunts Mabel and Flora, as 'her painting'. Just as, had they children, the children would have been *theirs*. But the piano was hers. Tom called it hers. Catharine's piano.

Yes, she'd make her tea – she was an epic, committed tea drinker – but she would be deluded, she knew, if she tried to kid herself with a sense of autonomy by wavering over using honey or sugar to sweeten it. Freedom of choice was useless if you were not free of essential compunctions. As she flicked on the kettle she knew that it was only a matter of minutes before she would be looking at the blacker than black demonic machine whose darkness no electric light could penetrate. Hers from childhood. She would wander to it, incapable of wavering from the route, denied by an unseen force the luxury of twenty minutes in the armchair beside it reading the *Style* section from the Sunday papers; suddenly an unthinkable indulgence. Instead, she would sit, tentatively, on the stool, between the two fake gilt candelabra that framed the music holder like an altar, and she would go numb, cast for the umpteenth time as the officiator at a religious ritual she felt wholly unqualified to preside over. Even the golden imprint CHAPPELL on the lid had, as a child, suggested to her an ill-spelt appeal to religious values beyond her ken. As a teenager she had come to envy those girls whose houses had a satisfyingly agnostic or at least unchristian STEINWAY or, even more daringly, a racy YAMAHA. These girls, she was sure, were safe from the feeling of self-imposed vocation.

Because this piano never went to Birmingham or Basingstoke. From college it had followed her, like a jilted boyfriend who claimed she had made professions of love she could now no longer remember, and had taken up residence wherever its mistress did. And at first she was thrilled. At an

6

age when you were defined by having nothing, she had this great vessel, this emblem of homeliness and art. Home was where you put your piano. She felt so grateful to her mother and father for giving her this thing, this object that was such an effortless bearer of hopes and fears. She ignored the fact – a fact they did little to disguise – that they wanted the piano out of their living room because it took up so much space and seemed, almost wantonly, to refuse to 'go' with any of the furnishings or decoration they put around it. So it followed Catharine and was witness to first flats and first houses, love, marriage and relocation. And, just as for her parents, it never 'went' with the IKEA of her early days, the Conran of her thirties or the tentatively chosen antiques Tom and she bought for the cottage at the end of the lane.

Her houses remained eclectic, and the one constant was her piano; never beautiful, always suggestive of beauty.

Notwithstanding one problem: Catharine wasn't very good at the piano.

For a period of some weeks when she was fifteen she had been subject to a terrible anxiety which had been brewing for nearly a year. She became convinced that she would never love anything or anyone as much as she loved music. Somewhere between Schumann's Piano Concerto and the Vivaldi Gloria, she felt such an ecstatic identification with what she heard that she feared something was about to be uncovered in her; something more disquieting than it was pleasurable. An implication, barely articulated, that she might be destined to find abstract beauty more satisfying than any associated with flesh and blood. She thought perhaps it had spoilt her, this ecstasy, and made her good for nothing. Would she ever feel towards a man, for example, anything approaching what she felt in the darkness of her room, the curtains drawn and the record player at full volume? Would love ever carve out a place in her heart of such magnificent, inner architecture as the nineteenth-century sonata form brought to its apotheosis in the Brahms piano concertos, or reflect such longings as Schubert *lieder*?

It all might have been different had she been any good herself. But she wasn't. Sometimes she felt she was the victim of some cruel trick. As if she might suffer from a disability or something akin to a speech impediment. For however clearly she imagined in her head the music that she loved, when she sat at the piano and tried to reproduce it she failed. Failed miserably. Between the instinct and the fact something terrible happened. A neural failure of transmission. It caused her actual, physical pain. The notes she heard come to feeble life at her fingers' ends were such poor relatives of the bright, dream-world inhabitants of her imagination, like celebrities long admired ratting on their nearest and dearest in a tabloid exposé. Sometimes she would try to kid herself, and look at the notes on the page and convince herself that they were pretty but not *that* pretty, and that she was investing them with too much profundity, and that a homely rendering of the music would be more honest. But she'd always go back to some great practitioner on the record player and hear the greatness all over again, and hate herself. It was she, Catharine, who was the homely talent, she who was surplus to requirements. So Catharine began her womanly life subject to a great, unrequited love affair. And though she despised fatalism, how could she not wonder if her failure in music would not at some stage be mirrored by a failure in life, in love?

Now she wished her father had not casually pointed out the stash of ageing LPs beside the drinks cabinet, and wondered out loud if she might find them interesting. Or had not dropped into the conversation over supper one night that his concert-going friend from work had called in sick that morning, leaving a spare ticket for Gala Classics at their local theatre. She had gone, not trying to please him, but so the ticket wouldn't be wasted. She was ten years old. She liked to help, Catharine. It had been an unwitting master-stroke on her father's part, the suggestion rather than the command. She went to the concert, she listened to the records. It was all perfect. Within two weeks she loved music more than her father had ever done. Except for the liberal paradox that, because she had been left to make the decisions for herself, she had no one to blame that it now caused her such misery. It had been no arranged marriage. It had been love.

The phase when she wondered if music was going to leave her good for nothing passed. Then, a few months later, just short of her sixteenth birthday, a boy began to take the same bus she took to school. He was a sixth-former, and at the grammar, a different school from hers. She'd never seen him before. He said things to the driver when he bought his ticket that made the driver laugh, though the boy barely smiled himself; he was keeping the world at arm's length; he ignored the younger boys' horseplay and scrutinised the advertising hoardings they'd slapped up by Woolworths with patrician disdain; even the lingerie ones in whose wake the younger boys whooped and wrestled like bear cubs.

When she went home now and the music played in the

darkness – Brahms's B Flat Piano Concerto was the piece of the moment – and she heard the long horn melody drawing the opening piano solo out of the depths, it was the cool, diffident manner of the boy on the bus that was now indistinguishable from what she heard. Her abstract panic of six months ago was replaced by something far more arresting: the idea that love and music, rather than fighting over the soul of a little teenage Faust, might actually join forces; that one might keep the other company, heightening both. Every morning she saw him, every evening she played the same piece. The whole world, the everyday objects of her suburban home, had become porous, soaking up the twin solutions of desire and music. She could not take the stairs to her room with her plate of Marmite on toast at five o'clock without feeling in the banister and in the construction of the staircase the assembly of the world, her body in relation to it, the ache of his presence on the return journey from school or her angst that he had stayed late; every operation of her muscles made her a fulcrum, about which she longed for the music to sway her closer and closer to her idea of him.

Then one lunch hour it had rained, and she had joined the more introspective pupils who claimed refugee status in the Music Room. She'd eaten her sandwiches and found herself staring at the long line of miniature scores that lined the walls. After Bach and Beethoven she guessed something was up. Something in her peripheral vision was messing with her. Sure enough she came quickly to the first of the Brahms concertos, the one in D minor. She knew if the first was there the second, the B Flat, could not be far away. But she daren't look. Too much. That it might be there was enough;

that the boy on the bus might one day look at her and she might find herself talking about herself to him. These conjectures were quite enough. She should arise and go and get the hell out of there rather than fuss around some extraordinary embodiment of what she had heard on her record player made text in front of her. Something that would involve a condensation of such density and profundity; a trauma of becoming. It was terrible; she wanted to cry. The inner, cathedral-like vastness of her feelings for the piece, the architecture of her youth – this was going to be held in a spider-like scrawl of notes and markings. It would be like death. It would be like a posthumous publication of her diary.

But she took it down, guessing which it was, without looking at the cover. The miracle outweighed the dread she felt. The unlikeliness of it. It was a fact she was going to have to assimilate. She couldn't deny it. And once she had accepted it as a fact she had no choice but to run with it. That she could take down the book from the shelf and rehydrate the desiccated symbols – that the reanimated organism would rise up and do her bidding, and do so with her heart and her lifeblood, had to be acknowledged. Never dead, only sleeping.

She didn't look at the cover. She trusted that it would be the volume next to the D minor. She opened the first pages. What would it look like, the part of her mind that was the storehouse chest of association, the wind around the bus stop, the cling of diesel in her throat and the cool change in her early-morning hand, the boy's pressed shirt and black blazer, another school's insignia and the promise of qualifications she had not yet taken? The first thing that struck her was that most of the opening page of music was empty. So many instruments lain out and nothing for them to play. What was that? Was all life made of vast acres of silence, of that which remained dumb while the included, the elected soloist made merry?

Then she noticed a single line of notes, recognised the word 'Corni' at the beginning of the line, and realised that, indeed, this was the gentle, sinuous horn melody that seemed to call the piano from out of sleep in the opening bars of the B flat concerto. Her eyes filled with tears and she became conscious of her limbs, heavy with dread. When this thin, single line began in the darkness of the room, she felt it was beginning her whole life, which though she be required to rehearse it again and again, she would never tire of, though she knew only too well the trials the music would put her through. At the end of the brief horn call, the piano began. Or, more accurately, as the whole notion of a concerto could not help but suggest – *she* began. The self beset by worldly forces, influences, treacheries and ambitions; sometimes no more than the accompanist, sometimes the isolated, virtuosic self.

The Music Room was emptying, the lunch hour was over. She had five minutes. She took the score over to the piano. The walk to the scaffold, for an unspecified capital crime, she knew so well. What choice did she have? How could she not do it? How could she not sit, and worry the spine of the little book till it held open? Not but remind herself, as she sat and settled herself, that the key was B flat and the horns were in F and if she wanted to play that line too she would have to transpose it in her head? She didn't *want* to do any of it. She looked at the piano part and automatically took in the terrain, the division of hands, the chords, the dynamic, dealing with this radioactive compound as if it had landed in what amounted to no more than her child's chemistry set. It wasn't even that hard, which in itself was a disappointment. She wanted, if truth be told, for it to be impossible. Why was she going to allow it to be up to her? Why should it be? Her responsibility. Already her hands were venturing down the keys to begin the upward figure. When did she will that? At what point did it become inevitable? The first note was so low in the register that she had to take a gamble that it was a B flat. She took comfort from the fact that was the key of the piece. Such classical absolutes were reassuring. She looked at the horn melody, played it in her head and ushered in her own self, her own conductor. Watched her own waking.

As soon as she began she wavered from the true line. Not all the notes were the composer's, but she had arranged her hands around the general chord of B flat as to prevent any discords. But she was hesitant and faltered as she reached the top notes. When she came to the end of the two bars she looked down at the white knuckles of her hands and saw the tension, the sinewy effort she had put into this shallow attempt to reproduce what she knew. Not that it mattered. It was still the most beautiful thing she had ever partaken of. That it was also the final confirmation of her irredeemably second-rate talent, her mediocrity and deficiency as an artist, was sad. It seemed rather brutal to have failed in this moment, at this confluence of so many different feelings: the thought of the boy on the bus, the memory of having listened to the piece only the night before, the fact that she was not even sixteen and therefore how was she supposed to know anything, especially how exactly you were meant to put all you knew of the world into two bars of piano sight reading. But she knew. She'd got the worst of it over. The rest of life wouldn't be too terrible. Of course it was doubly sad that she had equated the beauty of the piece with a certain moral hope for the world, and all she could do, she reminded herself, was not to take her failure at the piano *as* a moral failure. Yes, she had been passive about her appreciation of the music, and when called upon to be active she hadn't the talent. But that was no excuse to be passive in other areas of life. She would be strict with herself. She would never allow the indulgence of thinking that doing some good in the world was beyond her in the way that playing that piano concerto was beyond her. Even the thought that such a temptation might occur to her made her shudder.

She had closed the lid of the piano and placed the score back on the shelf. How foolish of them to leave such a thing lying around. Probably not in the history of all secondary schools had a pupil ever picked up the score of Brahms's B Flat Concerto and played it. It was foolish to even leave it on display like that. It could do damage.

She continued to listen to music, continued to take the bus. Then, when she started the sixth form herself, the boy was gone, and she listened more to *lieder*. The piano receded and the human voice, more forgiving, perhaps more imperfect, offered different consolations.

The kettle boiled and steam billowed at the kitchen window, blurring the inky collage of wet greens and grey sky, the faint glow of the gravel drive and the shabby winter borders. She was glad everything was in soft, stormy focus; it made her feel less on the spot. She took a mug and poured the hot water on her tea bag, sweetened it with brown sugar and felt the catch of the treacly miasma at the back of her throat. Time to let it cool and drink it before she went through to the imaginary party next door which, as hostess, she had unpardonably abandoned.

Catharine had long ago guessed that people found her attachment to tea to be evidence that she was impatient of pretension. That she was making a point. They found it a reproach. When they arrived to stay with friends or Tom's family she was offered all sorts of drinks: gin and tonics, elderflower cordials, Coke, home-made wines. As people got used to her the list got longer, as if they were trying lots of different keys in the lock. But she only ever asked for tea. And whoever they were visiting would look half exasperated and put on the kettle almost petulantly. Everybody had an opinion about tea. However much they might themselves crave it when they woke up or at four o'clock in the afternoon, they forgot those cravings and hated her for dumbing down their hospitality. Particularly the better-off ones who had perhaps just uncorked some special bottle they'd been keeping for their visitors only to have to ask 'Earl Grey or ordinary?' five minutes into the visit. Tea in the evening was for campers and mountaineers.

She knew they had extrapolated this one appetite of hers, pulled this one thread out of the tapestry of her character and were making her answerable to it. She even thought they swore less when she was present. A puritan. A puritan who disliked pretension. But who liked tea. So she would say, as brightly and unjudgementally as possible, 'Ordinary.' What was she to do, she asked herself, say, 'Double bourbon on the rocks,' just to dumbfound them? She loved tea. Was she to pretend she didn't? Was she to seek to justify herself, and say that the world would be a happier place if we all consumed tea rather than booze, heroin and religious dogma? That was, after all, what Tom liked to refer to as 'an incontrovertible fact'. It was his favourite expression. He said it quietly and he *was* a lawyer, but no one ever accused *him* of being a puritan. They asked her what she wanted and she told them. Only a glass of water could be cheaper and she always offered to make it herself. Was the very unpretentiousness of a cup of tea pretension when clung to as an appetite? A stubborn, superfluous honesty?

She knew she worried because it might be true. 'Puritan' was an old-fashioned word, and the thing of which she thought she might be guilty was much more elusive than that blanket term. It was something to do with strictness. Not of the disciplinary kind, but of the sort that went with consistency, straightness, integrity. It was clear she demanded things of herself, and her demanding of them was sufficiently on show for other people to feel implicated in the demand. She wasn't judgemental of others, but people could see that were Catharine to be, as it were, them, she would, as them, have demanded this and that of herself; and sometimes the people concerned thought that they weren't quite able to match the high expectations of their imaginary impersonator. So this immaculately modest woman found herself accused of the very thing she probably feared more than anything – self-righteousness.

Dark again, outside. A wave of new rain, like sand thrown against the kitchen window, made her look up. She had thought it was all over.

What was it Tobias had called her? The young nun. He was her first boyfriend at college. Towards the end they'd argued.

He had argued. She had listened to her crimes itemised in silence. A silence which had seemed to be held up as evidence of her guilt and which, after saying not a word, had seen her promoted from 'nun' to 'Mother Superior'. She did not understand this promotion. Tea had not even been mentioned. And besides, she could never have competed with Tobias's appetite for red wine. They had gone out for just over two years. He had some very good qualities, of which she had come to realise perhaps he himself was unaware. But his principal enthusiasms were wine and sex. She could only think that, despite her enjoyment of both these pleasures, it was her failure to keep up with either to the required level that earned her the accusation, after 'nun' and 'Mother Superior', of being 'frigid'. (As an example of what might be called her 'strictness' – suffice to say that all she could wonder, as this argument used to progress, was at the order of these accusations. 'Frigid', coming last, presumably implied that as a nun or Mother Superior you still had *some* opportunity to display your sexual enthusiasm.)

They split up, and Catharine realised that she had felt that Tobias' appreciation of her body had had no more to do with her than his nightly consumption of a bottle of wine had to do with the chateau that had bottled it.

Fortunately, she had Maria to dismantle the young man's judgements and wilder assertions. Something her best friend did with evident pleasure. After all, it meant Maria would have more of Catharine to herself. It was gratifying to hear such a stout defence made of what Catharine was all too ready to regard as her own shortcomings. Maria made it quite clear where the blame lay, revealing that she had never quite thought Tobias worthy of her friend.

What had puzzled Catharine most had been the fact that the qualities that she liked so much in Tobias seemed to be the opposite of the ones he seemed most eager to cultivate. His instinctive gentleness with strangers, for example, was constantly soured by his growing determination to swear as often and strongly as he could. His talent for impersonating people – politicians, tutors – was a real gift; why, at the end of a particularly funny riff, did he always have to sum up whoever he had been mimicking as a 'wanker'?

Maria was bracingly clear about it. 'Darling,' she said, 'we're surrounded by fucking puppies. They just need feeding, a good runaround, and a leg to hump.'

Maria Koshinsky was not an obvious candidate to be Catharine's best friend. No one, and with good reason, ever called *her* a puritan. Despite her exotic surname, she came from an impeccably suburban background, had gone to comprehensive school, had an uncle who was a vicar, chose to talk posh, took drugs and was the university's angry young woman. Before she even made it to Manchester she had graduated from being treated badly by unsuitable boys to treating suitable boys badly. As far as the academic ruling body was concerned and boys generally, hers was a scorched-earth policy. Only Catharine was spared. With her she was a different person. There was no territory over which they competed. Their friendship was the calm after the storm. And there were lots of storms.

Catharine watched, with a privileged, wondering detachment, the procession of boys through Maria's life. Her friend told her everything. Frequently in graphic detail. Sometimes Catharine wondered if the telling of the story of the latest seduction wasn't almost more pleasurable to Maria than the events it related. She almost hoped that it was, so that Catharine could feel reassured that she wasn't missing out. She didn't want a promiscuous life. But she wanted a full one.

No sooner had the latest boy been sent packing from Maria's bedsit – wondering what form his success or failure had taken in the fierce mixture of indulgence and irony on his temporary conquest's face – than Maria would hotfoot it to Catharine's room in the halls of residence and sit cross-legged on her bed and regale her with anatomical absurdities and risible chat-up lines. Weak with laughter, Catharine would ply her friend with toast and tea and do her best to be the perfect audience. She would be outraged where outrage was called for, pitying where pity was warranted. It was always confidential and, Catharine assured herself, never malicious. They were laughing at the process, she told herself, not individuals, and, after all, who would ever know? These first-night reviews, concocted immediately after the performance, were not for publication, but for her alone. Perhaps once or twice she worried that a young man had been lured back to Maria's room solely to provide copy for the later meeting. But on the whole she thought she and Maria were only too aware of what a trying cocktail of testosterone and hope for higher things motivated these tragically randy blokes. Catharine hoped there was redemption in their laughter somewhere. After all, Maria never promised more than she offered.

There were no correspondingly candid confessions from Catharine about *her* sex life. That was different. Tobias was on the scene for the majority of their time in Manchester and different rules applied. Maria might have liked to ask, but Catharine would never have spoken about it. She would just have said it was 'lovely'. And she knew that 'lovely' was no great endorsement of sexual performance generally. Maria reserved her special scorn for the 'tender fuck' school of love-making, which she always said was male window dressing, disguising lust with soft-focus foreplay and roses the next morning.

So Catharine listened to Maria's exploits and hoped that perhaps she also fulfilled the role of the friend who prevented her from going too far. She secretly feared that one day a Tender Fuck was going to be shown to have been a True Love and be found floating in the Manchester Ship Canal having drowned himself for Maria Koshinsky. But it never happened.

Occasionally she felt like a hypocrite. Catharine was obsessively even-handed. The idea of being given something denied to others haunted her. In that sense she remained grateful that she had not gone to a private school or Oxbridge. It would have paralysed her. And the great joy of being granted the friendship with Maria, and indulging in the latter's critique of the world, made her feel special. But she feared this. Who was she to be immune from the absurdity that Maria so mercilessly satirised? Catharine had a bold, funny friend, who did not require of her that she be bold and funny also. She was allowed to listen and laugh, while Maria went out and about. Should *she* be going out and about? Engaging more devastatingly with the world? She remembered the moment in the Music Room that lunchtime a few years before. She had tried to be responsible for the music and had failed. She hadn't wanted it to be up to her. Was this the same?

All of which was exacerbated by the last and most provocative piece of the jigsaw.

At the end of their first term, when she and Maria were not yet great friends, there had been a freshers' concert. The two young women had had several conversations and got on well enough, but though they were both studying foreign languages, they were studying different ones, and would not necessarily have become well acquainted. At the concert, however, they found themselves sitting together. Catharine was curiously nervous about the standard of music-making the night was going to offer. She wanted it to be high because she did not want to feel that she herself might have got up and played something. When she had been asked if she played an instrument, she had said no, and felt like Judas. But she was also nervous that the university was going to be full of concert pianists.

Sitting next to Maria, however, turned out to be the saving grace of the evening. The performers were so relentlessly earnest that Maria quickly began a low, running commentary in a variety of styles, ranging from catwalk notes on their attire, cod Radio Three analyses of their playing and thumbnail psychological portraits of their possible neuroses. Catharine wanted to laugh very badly and Maria was merciless and poker-faced as the tears streamed down the other girl's face. Someone had even turned round and tutted at the two young women. Then, chatting in the interval, Maria had gone off and not returned, leaving Catharine to take her place alone. Disappointed, she gave herself up to the last pieces of the evening, enduring the music as she herself had endured her own attempt at the Brahms concerto – substituting for the imperfect notes she heard the perfect ones she knew the composer had written. She cut and pasted the various lines of the string trio they played so that it once again resembled the piece Schubert had composed, and concentrated on the notes the pimply boy got right in the last movement of the 'Moonlight' Sonata, rather than those that blurred into a misguided impersonation of virtuosity. Without Maria's redeeming laughter Catharine was depressed rather than amused. She realised in her heart she did want other people to excel at that which she had always dreamt of excelling, though she herself had failed. But it was cold comfort.

Then, when the last piece was over and she thought she was to be released, the president of the music society appeared and announced there would be an extra, unscheduled contribution. And to Catharine's complete amazement Maria walked on with a pair of gold earrings and a violin tucked under her arm. At first she assumed her new friend was about to continue her extempory deconstruction of the night's efforts by some stand-up comedy, in which the violin was some kind of prop. Instead, Maria tossed her head to throw her dark curls out of the way, looked at the same pimply pianist as if they were about to elope and threw herself into a pyrotechnical gypsy dance by Sarasate.

Catharine was not competitive. The moment before, when she knew once and for all that she did want others to excel even at the cost of her own hopes, had finally proved this to her. But what she was sure about, even after a short acquaintance with her, was that music did not mean as much to Maria as it did to Catharine. And not just because Maria was a rebel, had spent her year off living in a squat, and had a reputation for colourful language even in languages not her own. But because even that evening they had talked enough about music for Maria to have betrayed a scornful distrust of the entire musical project. And when, in the following weeks, Catharine discovered that Maria never practised, this only confirmed her suspicions.

Here, then, was someone who could do what she was not even minded to bother much about. And this hurt Catharine. It was the sting in the tail. This girl had a ticket to the ball, but no interest in meeting Prince Charming.

There was no denying it – Catharine felt that music was a species of morality. That it was good. And so she felt an innate distrust of the idea that musical talent was just random. Of course there were elements of raw, naked facility. The prodigies. But generally she thought that artistic good gravitated towards moral good. They were the same words after all. True, she had refused after the Brahms debacle to see her failure at the piano as a template for moral failure. She knew there was good to be done in the world without recourse to artistic virtuosity. And she also knew, just from reading the back of record sleeves, that great musicianship hardly went hand in hand with impeccable morals. But that intellectual observation could not wholly placate her. The talented, she felt, she *knew*, could see to the heart of things; could allow the creation of something larger than themselves. Something that, for all the local selfishnesses of life, counted as generosity. The darkness of the bedroom, the music's depth, could be exploded, could bear the curtains being thrown open to admit the daylight and suffer no diminution of feeling. That which was made and first appreciated in darkness could, like night-time's child, graduate to a daylight maturity.

When Maria had her moment as the consummate gypsy, when she was the scene-stealing star of the concert, the fact that she was the naughtiest, most irreverent of students, challenged this faith in music. Or rather it redoubled Catharine's conviction that it was the musical process, not wedded to personality, that she must learn to celebrate. That it wasn't about her, Catharine. In deciding – if that is not too clinical a word for it – to become Maria's friend, it was with a distant hope that in swimming closer to this phenomenon, she would understand it better. She would learn if irreverence and talent went hand in hand, or if one, bizarrely, had sprung from the other.

Within a few weeks or months of knowing Maria, she had forgotten this debate had ever taken place in her head. Their mutual affection was such that they felt they had known each other all their short lives.

Catharine finished her tea and put the still warm cup in the sink. As she gave up this comfort she realised just how cold the house was. The central heating was programmed to co-incide with Tom's breakfast and the railway timetable to London. This wandering about the house in her dressing gown was strictly extracurricular. Out of hours. She only had herself to blame. And she had her peace to make next door.

She went through. There, in perpetual, mahogany mourning, was the piano. The dull morning light rested on the keys, themselves so uniform in their never-changing rank and file; always present, always correct.

She pulled her silk dressing gown tighter round her throat. It was cold enough for her to regret her own metaphor of the piano as party guest. Perhaps she should just have done and go upstairs to dress. But Catharine's strictness extended to a kind of thoroughness even as far as the private metaphors of her inner life were concerned. She'd started so she had to finish.

Approaching the piano, she felt like a girl. It was male, she felt, this muscle-bound hulk of polished wood and ivory. It was a fleeting sensation, but enough, with only a layer of cotton and a layer of silk between it and her body, for her to feel what a feminine house she was in now Tom was gone. No arm had sought and found her in the night. It was hers alone. Her body was her own. Even if there were nothing to be done with it but warm it with tea and feel the cold flags beneath her bare feet.

Normally they got up together, she and Tom; she liked to dress with him and join the world alongside him. For him to have left the house with her still in her nightdress would have shamed her. Though she was equally sure that he wouldn't have minded. She knew there were other women who went back to bed when their husbands left in the morning. She would never do that. There was never any doubt in her mind that she had as equal a job to do in the world as her husband, and that it would not wait. She got up to do it, bright and conscious. The fact that she didn't know what it was wasn't the point. Soon, she was sure, it would be to have a baby. But even before the idea of that had entered her life, she had always got up with this sense of abstract vocation.

When she reached the piano, she pulled the stool out from where it seemed to cower beneath the keys. The legs scraped the floor like the screech of an old woman and Catharine jumped at the first discord of the day. Then she carefully insinuated herself, as if she were a late arrival at a wedding, squeezing between pew and congregation, into her place. She didn't want to risk the awful sound of the stool on the flags again, so she made do with what space she had.

In place, as someone who must be secured before a journey – a child, or infirm person – she tested with her elbows and knees the limit of her freedom and looked down at the keys. As ever, they surprised her with their abundance. So many to make friends with all at once.

The sight of them, and the reminder that she always had to make to herself that this savage battalion of black and white shapes was not for decoration, but each the bearer of an individual sound, made, as if by a reciprocal conspiracy with the quietness around her, the house more quiet still. Like a wave drawn down the shingle of a beach in preparation for the next, so sound had quit the house, waiting for her coming. The awful truth weighing on her that no note would speak without instruction, none sound without her guiding will.

Now, before consciousness had completely spoilt the landscape of sleep, or memory snagged her with what she had or had not achieved, she could just kid herself that she was talented. It was perfectly possible that now would be the moment when she would do something definitive, even if only to play a simple piece immaculately. And because this was still theoretically possible, she could also indulge in the luxury, the deliciousness of holding off, of not playing at all. The moment in the Music Room years before might never have happened. And her love for music, and the piano's mechanical genius might still come together – so what if her love were merely abstract and the genius of the piano one of mere passive mechanics? She could at least imagine a happy marriage between the two.

But it could not last. She must lift her stiff, morning fingers, and place them on the unyielding architecture of the keys; she must remember the ivory hardness, the snags and pitfalls, the smallness of each note's target, the irrational geography of black and white; and the slipperiness of their patina when sweat came with self-consciousness. There she was again, the magician's daughter, caught a spell short in the magical kingdom, at the gates of the treasure house, cursed with the knowledge of what each casket contained, powerless to exercise the sorcery that would unlock them.

She shifted on her seat. Her body felt, where it touched the fabric of her nightdress and dressing gown, landlocked. Like a woman abandoned by her lover, she thought. She had never been abandoned and never glamorised any of her boyfriends with the term lover. Maria called them that; not Catharine. But now she cast herself as an imaginary figure thrown over by love. It fitted her mood just now. The sense of ecstasy just beyond her reach. It was only a metaphor, and surely she was entitled to a metaphor on her own at nine thirty in the morning in her freezing sitting room. But she had no lover.

Because instead she had the piano – the metaphor she tired of. It was the piano that was her lover. Why, she asked herself, succumbing to the image, did she not ditch this dysfunctional *amour* that brought no discernible joy to either party? The touch of the keys was as lifeless to her, as depressing as the joyless kiss of the middle-aged couple who no longer love each other, who turn to kiss too reluctantly or, having kissed, turn away too fast, who embrace for form, or to send the right signals to in-laws or children.

To counter all of this, half impatiently, she played a C major chord with both hands, and the room was suddenly full of the unnaturally bright sound of simple harmony, like magnesium in water, a brightness not of the world of experience, but elemental, impossible. One of nature's building blocks on show, only to be encountered under laboratory conditions.

If only she could make do with that. Where had the tyranny come from that deemed that greatness, that meaning resided in mixtures, in the complex compounds of Western art? The cult of the nuances of personality. If only one could make do with perfect chords, wind chimes, church bells and birdsong. What new ascetic order could she join so as to unlearn all she had succumbed to? It might be ascetic to some; to her it would be bliss. The C major chord, the bell-like resonance in the depths of the piano – it was so of the world. Nothing to do with her. What peace. Where had they taken her, all those great journeys she made in the darkness of her bedroom when she listened to the great symphonies and concertos of the nineteenth century? Weren't they just about her? She didn't want it to be about her.

'I'm tired,' she suddenly said and looked down at her hands as if they were someone else's. Her fingers were fanned out as if waiting to be manicured; inelegant. The piano still held the ultra-fine resonance of the chord she had played, fizzing in the machinery like a bee caught in the depths of an empty hive. When she looked up to see the sheet of music in front of her she felt doubly exhausted. It was so complicated. Even though she knew what it all meant, even though she could translate it into sounds after a fashion, she hated the complexity of the notation. My God, my God, why had she spent so much love on this incredibly difficult regime? She should have been out celebrating. What, she wasn't sure.

She closed the book of Chopin and placed it on the top of the piano. She wouldn't be a victim of it today. Today of all days. It was her party, after all. She would be a good hostess and regard the Chappell as nothing more than a piece of furniture. Nice to have a piano in the house. The wood is mahogany. Old, too. Just don't open the lid.

She sighed. She could see her breath it was so cold. She really ought to get dressed. She oughtn't to loiter in the living room with her bare feet on the flagstones or on the shiny, chill sustaining pedal that creaked as she played. Who should she keep entertained? Tom was no good, he was in Birmingham. Another tea in the kitchen? Stragglers on the stairs on the way to her wardrobe? She'd wait to be claimed. Those who needed you most came to claim you, eventually. She sighed again and wondered how many times you had to sigh till your breath came out cold.

Tom was in Birmingham. It sounded like 'in purgatory'; as if it were a state of being; as if things could be deduced from it. Stupid, she thought. I can deduce nothing from this statement. Why did he not tell me more? Ordinarily he went to London, to his offices near Charing Cross. He cycled the two miles to the local station, and made the fifty-five-minute train journey. He did it every day. He specialised in human rights cases. Immigration, asylum; Home Office protocol. He often didn't wear a suit, which surprised Catharine. He said it wasn't always necessary.

But yesterday morning he had gone to Euston. She wondered if it was a shock to his system to go to a different mainline station. She felt an undeniable twinge of vicarious excitement at the thought of him going off-piste in that way. Small but unmistakable. That was what you felt when you were married.

Even the tiniest experience the other person was having was translatable to one's own expectations, to then thwart or excite. She often wondered what it must be like to be Tom. His being in a different place today gave her the chance to see him freshly in her mind. Imagining what he would make of Birmingham and Birmingham of him. He seemed larger than a city to her. Odd for him to be pitted against an entire city. Not literally, but just in terms of scale. He, the centre of her life, was lost in a sea of souls. Did he feel diminished? Would it be up to her, on his return that evening, to make him feel significant again? On the whole he was independent; never clingy. But Birmingham? Well.

When they had first met, towards the end of their twenties, she had seen a photograph on his parents' sideboard, of him on what looked like a mountain peak. They had been together for a few months. Under questioning he had revealed that while at university he had been a keen mountaineer. His mother, hearing the word 'keen', had scoffed, as if to say that 'keen' hardly did it justice. Tom rarely enthused about things, so Catharine was able to deduce that this hobby had been fairly all-consuming. She asked him about it and he told her some of his adventures. He didn't make it sound exciting. He downplayed any danger he might have been in, and was adamant that people only got hurt when they either took risks they needn't have or were badly prepared. To Catharine's ears it sounded as if he had always been so well prepared that there might have been very little excitement left. Certainly the photographs of him on the various summits showed a younger Tom looking blandly at the camera, with no trace of gung-ho triumphalism. 'I could be anywhere,' his face seemed to say. She asked him why he had done it. It 'seemed like fun at the time'. Did he want to do it again? 'No.'

If she, Catharine, had been a mountaineer, she thought, she would have taken risks, though she hated heights and dangers generally. But if she had been Tom, which she wasn't, she would have been more radical. She'd felt that, looking at the photographs of his final-year summer in Nepal. She also didn't know why he didn't want to ever talk about it. It galled her far more than his not talking about his past girl-friends, about whom, of course, she would never have dreamed of quizzing him.

The only legacy of his mountaineering was the selection of cagoules and waterproof trousers in the downstairs cupboard. She and Tom had walked in their first years together. They'd gone to Wales and the Pennines, and she had made no fuss when he had bought for her these psychedelic acces-sories made by the same Swiss company that made his. And his had at least been faded – if ever such things can be said to be faded when still visible ten thousand feet up a moun-tain – by alpine sun and snow. Hers were in their first flush. She had put them on and wondered why he had not laughed. She had tried to think how glad she would be when caught in their first blizzard.

What was it? She was not vain. But she had been inwardly dismayed by these acquisitions. Amazed by them, by their strangeness. They were expensive, too, these Swiss accessories. He was an intelligent man, capable of a subtle and shrewd irony, and yet he had bought these things with a retail ease that fascinated her. She could still remember his Day-Glo face, lit from beneath by the reflective power of his cagoule; hers must look the same, as if they sat around the same emergency beacon. She could see the tiny hairs of his beard, like black handwriting that had had a highlighter pen go over it. His young face and young body had, as a student, been in the hands of this safety measure. It made her want to cry. To see his masculinity at the mercy of such functionality; he was never oafish, always intelligent, confident never arrogant. But he zipped up his waterproofs as if he were loading a gun.

She never forgot this conjunction, though she was unsure exactly what it meant. It hadn't reduced him in her eyes. Catharine was never swayed by externals. But it had made her fearful for him. *Something* must make him afraid, for him to be so careful in his choice of outdoor wear. She wouldn't fall out of love with her husband because she had seen him in sensible clothing. But his otherness, like the otherness of music from the written symbols on the page, was a challenge. Perhaps she suddenly wondered if Tom, like music itself, was in a process of translation once you engaged with it; and perhaps, like music, you were to a greater or lesser degree responsible for the outcome once you took it on.

She wondered, for example, if she was to some extent the reason for his continued concentration on human rights. It seemed to her that for their first few years together, she had not really known what his work was. And when she did begin to take an interest, and discovered it was in human rights legislation, was pleased. But she could not now ask, 'Why are you interested in that?' It seemed natural for Tom to do something which had at its heart fundamental decency. Yet it was not the best-paid work, and he had once, literally, had his eye on the summit. Had she dulled his ambition? She didn't want to be rich. But perhaps he didn't want to be doing good works. She wouldn't have blamed him if he hadn't.

She certainly had no doubt that he was good at it. Tom had a manner that emanated fairness. He could be stubborn in a way that looked at first like a deep-rooted conservatism, but which, if pushed, gradually asserted itself as the most heroic tenacity; a kind of militant decency. His pursuit of Catharine had been determined, and he had never been more attractive to her than in his dismissal of her objections that she was going on holiday with Maria to Greece and could not meet him for dinner next Wednesday. She had gone, not to Greece but SW3, and he had proposed. He had wanted the weekend to ask his father what he should do. Maria had gone to Greece with a man instead and returned with another, bearing no hard feelings. Catharine had never regretted a day of her marriage. That was nine years ago.

They were good at being silent together. They had a mutual contempt for most television, but made holiday with prime-time nonsense when the mood took them. They hardly ever argued: she found it ugly, and he admitted that he hated turning into a lawyer – which is what he was sure he would do if they did argue – at home.

When they met Catharine had been working for the British Council. For a while she kept the job, the plan being that she would work till she had a baby. Then they would sell up their small flat and move out of London. As it was she had given up the job and found the cottage at the end of the lane, fifty-five minutes from Charing Cross, all while still trying to have a baby.

It didn't come naturally to Catharine to agonise over conceiving a child. She kept a strict eye on herself, policing her attitude for evidence of any sense of entitlement. She felt herself to be a lucky woman and to have quite enough to be grateful for. To expect that a child would just arrive was tantamount to bringing a curse down on her head. She and Tom agreed that to become over sensitive or to see each month as evidence of some kind of failure would only make conceiving more difficult. But a year, then two, then three, passed. In the New Year, it was decided, they would seek help and undergo the first set of tests to establish what, if anything, was the problem.

When Tom was there she didn't find it so bleak. The early mornings, watching him get ready, seemed full of hope. Especially if they had both woken early and had sex. And in the evenings, too, when the time of his arrival got closer, especially if they had not had sex that morning but might that evening, she felt the anticipation pleasurably.

But in the day, alone, she was prone to depression. She would catch herself throwing reproachful looks at the piano, as if it were that which was preventing her from having a child. She ought to take an axe to it, sooner rather than later. The very act of violence against the smug inanimacy of the instrument would release in her a flood of hormones, guaranteeing conception. Drama was required. But anger was alien to her; violence, too.

She knew what she should have done. Moving house ought to have been embraced as a rite of passage; a break from the past. She should have politicised herself somehow, eschewing the powerless role she had felt thrown into by the need to excel in the liberal arts, and she should have raged with new womanhood against the cabal of nineteenth-century great men who held her imagination captive. But she knew it was an act, for she had no emancipatory fire; she had no worldly grievance. Not really. Her grief, such as it was, had been over her mediocre talent. There was no one to blame. So the delivery men carried in the Chappell and tuned it to her hopes and fears. And still no child came.

It was worse, too, in the country. Going to buy milk in London, it was easy to think there were quite enough human beings to go round. One extra, for all it might be the bearer of love, might one day seem neither here nor there. In the country there were flowers and brooks and sunshine that required a witness, and since she felt it was the child, in herself, Catharine, that enjoyed these things, she could not help but feel that more children were required. To be witnesses. To refresh the world.

As each month passed she bore her period with increasing fatalism. She felt herself become as heavy and intractable as the piano itself. Like it, she did nothing, bore nothing. And just as the piano waited for the application of a magical talent to exercise itself upon it, so Catharine felt in her body the same dumb pause, the same uselessness of furniture unless redeemed by the magic of something which was actually far more common than musical talent – a baby.

Some of this she felt able to articulate to Tom. Though not the stuff about the piano stopping her from being able to conceive. He wouldn't think she was mad, but she might begin to suspect herself – what we say to others being sometimes no more than testimony we ourselves will take down and use in evidence against ourselves, however innocent we remain in other people's eyes. Mainly she just wanted him there. She began to dread Sunday nights like a schoolgirl for whom Monday brings the bully in the playground. And this was a new feeling for her, the need to cling to his presence. She was neither a clinging friend nor lover; never had been. Tobias had, on occasion, been reduced to begging her for more explicit demands on him. But she was measured. Not lacking in passion, but she baulked at even the hint of emotional manipulation; the thought that she might be parading emotion to increase her hold over someone appalled her. Made her ashamed. But now, with Tom, the ache she felt in her body – for a child, for him, for the imminence of the Monday-morning abandonment – made her cling to him in the night while they slept, and cling still harder when they made love in the early, winter dark.

Once he was gone, she gave herself up to patience. That came naturally to her, at least. She would rather listen to the rain dripping from the eaves than wallow in self-pity. She had Maria's cheerful profanities to listen to on the phone and an occasional pizza with her in London after one of her concerts. She had the house to organise and many boxes still to unpack. She would wait. Even the thought of IVF she felt as an importunate affront; she didn't want her desire for a child articulated by that abbreviation into desperation. Sometimes she wondered if she was sufficiently aware that she was mortal, for however unhappy she was she didn't want to hurry things. Perhaps a baby would come in thirty years, perhaps fifty. But it would come.

A month after they had moved in the vicar called. His presence at her front door had made her want to laugh. Not cruelly, but because it was such an antiquated custom, the visit to a newcomer; she had not supposed such things ever happened in the twenty-first century. Instantly she wondered if he would have called had she been a Muslim. If he would have done, would he still have knocked had he known she would be fully veiled? If he had known her husband was not there? If she had been a lesbian? A gypsy? A council tenant? She wanted to know the criteria. Maria would have asked these questions. In fact, had Tom been there, he would have probably asked them, or at least thought them. But he had been at work. And though she wanted to know the answers she was glad she was alone. For all her curiosity she always took what was offered in the spirit with which it was offered. She knew how to receive, Catharine; that rare art.

She showed him into the kitchen and put on the kettle. He was thin and wore cords and a checked farmer's shirt; he was losing his hair. He was Tom and Catharine's age but behaved as if he were much younger, deferring to Catharine's married status and talking of visiting 'householders' when they first moved to the area. He reminded her of Tobias's younger brother, who, when she had gone to stay with his family, looked at her as if she were a form of advanced study which one day might be his.

He complained that he was a team vicar of three large and disparate parishes and that there were gaps both in attendance and upkeep of the churches. He must have seen something in Catharine's face to suggest sympathy because he talked as if he hadn't had anyone to talk to for some time.

And Catharine did feel sorry for him. She knew as well as anyone what it was to be left without an audience for the exercise of that which one loved, whether it was Brahms or the Judaeo-Christian God. An empty church was an empty church. His almost permanent frown was of someone who, having gone through the valley of the shadow of death, has come through the other side determined to do good, but having the opportunity denied him at every turn. He even drank her tea as if he hadn't had the opportunity to say thank you for anything for several weeks. While she poured, he talked. Secular village chat to begin with, then increasingly reverting to the subject of the Church and its role, or lack of it, in the village.

With her natural keenness to understand, she placed herself in the vicar's position. She nodded and prompted. She floated the notion of secular compromises in a twenty-first-century world – a theme he took up with sorrowful gusto; she hinted at the role the church had had in the village where she herself had grown up, and, being of a similar generation, his voiced tightened with recognition, as if he might be not a million miles from tears. She poured more tea, and felt as frustrated as he with the General Synod and Parish Council in equal measure; and as forgiving as he was towards both.

She could not help but compare experiences with him. He was passionate and he was disappointed. As she had been. But whereas for her – if she extended the metaphor of her great passion, music – the disappointment had been total and final in the scene in the Music Room – a Damascene *un*conversion, if you like – for the vicar it had been a long, disorientating process of thwarted charity and good works.

Brahms could become someone else's business. But you were stuck with God. Used and abused for marrying the unbelievers, the Authorised Version of the Bible hijacked for beautiful phrases; for burying the same, with the consolation of the Book of Common Prayer. Rhetoric for repentance. It just wasn't right.

She had put the kettle on again and fresh tea leaves in the pot.

The memory of this meeting was to return to her on this present, winter day, later that morning. She was to remember how sorry she had felt for him that August morning, talking to him. A deep, enduring pity. A pity she realised that she might not have felt so purely had she been a Christian herself. Catharine had no faith. But the absence of any made her, if you like, a more pleasingly hollow vessel in which the crisis of another might echo. She was the perfect listener because she was not implicated in the conversation. There was no competition. Watching him carefully she could even see that for him her absence of faith was working a magic over their conversation, though he was unaware of it. In speaking the way he spoke she could see plainly that he sought a dispassionate observer, not a fellow complainer.

It was this pity, though, that caused Catharine some alarm. Pity, she thought, came from a position of confidence. You pitied that which was unfortunate. Usually, though not always, that lack of fortune highlighting your own good fortune. You pitied that which you would, if you could, remedy. So why did she pity this man, whose troubles she could in no way remedy, unless to offer him the solace that, after all, there was no God? She pitied him because he was afflicted. Wasn't this insufferably superior of her? Who was she to listen to a man's crisis of vocation when she herself had none? Sympathy she could offer, but not empathy.

Catharine was pathologically honest, keen to the tiniest flicker of motives disguised or feigned. So now, as the moment passed when she could with any ease confess her godless state, she felt her face flush with her crime. He had begun to say 'we' when speaking of faith, and 'us' about Christian hopes and fears.

And, of course, also holding her off from the confession was the very pity that she questioned her right to feel. To admit she was a secular soul offering tea and sympathy to a man who had given his life to do good only further diluted the Church's role in the village. The very thing he was lamenting. She might be the last straw.

She felt like a woman who has agreed to meet a friendly man whose marriage is in trouble, only to be told over a glass of wine that the reason the marriage is in trouble is that the man has fallen in love with her. And since they're there, in town, drinking wine, why don't they find a hotel. And she goes just because she feels so bad about the effect she's had on his marriage, and the man has managed to make her feel that her attractions made his love inevitable. She is responsible. So they fuck, and it all ends horribly. Except Catharine hadn't been responsible for the vicar's crisis. Or had she? Wasn't her lack of faith the thing that turned him into a peripatetic part-timer in each parish? If the churches had been full there would have been no problem.

It was difficult, the vicar had said, to find people prepared to offer the time and commitment to the upkeep of the fabric of the church. The word fabric had appealed to Catharine. It made her think of the Bayeux Tapestry. It was a rough but noble word, used by people who worked in the means rather than the ends of production. It seemed to have no vanity in it. And it placed the church in the very centre of her idea of the village to which she and Tom had moved. She thought of the actual substance of the church, barely a mile away. It was faced with flint, each stone cut open, showing the smooth rain-cloud-grey flint streaked with white, like strands of sheep's wool caught on dark barbed wire; the liquid disclosure of what was once molten, like cut fruits. That this was part of the *fabric* softened it in Catharine's eyes, joined it to the country-side, somehow, and highlighted that it might be built from the very flints the plough upturned in the field that rose behind the watercress beds behind the tower; 'fabric' seemed imme-morial. Necessary.

Would Catharine herself care to contribute to the upkeep of the fabric of the church? Now? she had thought. Now, in the twenty-first century? She would have to ask her husband.

But if the vicar called again and got Tom, Tom would smile and explain with Queen's Counsel exactitude that he and his wife were both atheists. This was an incontrovertible fact. Catharine would be called to the front door and made to repeat, under oath, that this was, beyond reasonable doubt, true. And then the seduction of the vicar this summer morning would, in retrospect, be complete. He would cast a lingering look at her with wounded eyes and wander back to tend the fabric alone.

Of course, said Catharine, what was she thinking? It was the twenty-first century, she did not need to ask her husband. She would do what she could. With pleasure.

This answer seemed no more than he expected, and the vicar had finished his tea, frowned and mumbled something about 'priorities'. They would discuss it on Sunday, he said, standing up. Sunday? she had repeated, frowning, her turn now to feel as if she were the victim of a liaison out of her control. The vicar had only smiled back and pulled out a little sheaf of church leaflets with the times of their respective services, one from each of his team of parishes. Catharine wanted to burst into tears. Because of the misunderstanding, yes. But she also thought perhaps because she had no faith.

It was time to act.

Flowers. She loved flowers in church. She had a vague memory that the job of arranging them was something her mother had done. Long after funerals and weddings she would be able to remember the altars; sometimes she suspected herself of remembering the arrangements better than the fates of the deceased, the bride's dress or her future happiness. The fulsome green, the firework-like explosions of asters and chrysanthemums, the fat peonies lolling beside the choir, the whole arching excess, the very profligacy of it against the severe stone thrilled her; as if the building itself were unbelief and only the flowers true faith – the profanity of the flowers had, to her, their own 'thou shalt'.

She could do that. Fearful of the accusation of hypocrisy, she could arrange flowers to serve the community and satisfy her agnostic desire all at once; if she were ever rumbled she could publicly confess to pure selfishness, knowing all the while that her mixed motives had always contained a real instinct to help. To place peonies beside the altar was surely not too subversive; no one need know the quality of the soul that placed them there. That she went there at midweek and breathed their perfume and handled their heavy heads would be her secret; the arranger would be virtually anonymous. No one would see her carry the oasis, leaden with water, to the brass bowls, nor see her hands ruffle the new petals, their colours as fresh and of the moment as the stained-glass backdrop was merely illuminated history. Yes, she must remember this from seeing her mother do it; there was no other explanation. The peonies had heavy heads, heavy almost as a child's.

It was very kind of her, but Mrs Mountjoy had done the flowers now for many years. The way the vicar said this was meant, Catharine realised, to let her know that this woman neither needed nor would tolerate a deputy.

Catharine surprised herself by a sudden feeling of irritation. Who was in charge in this parish? Was it right that the vicar should so plainly be at the mercy of this absurdly surnamed gorgon who claimed a monopoly of joy in the village? He had plainly looked at Catharine and looked away when he said her name. He was compromised, embarrassed, ashamed. She felt even more sorry for him, despite her panic over the misunderstanding about her faith.

But she knew her anger was also fed from another source. She had embarrassed herself by how much she wanted to arrange the flowers in church. Something in her wanted it as keenly and savagely as a child. No grafting of her motives onto the charitable strand of her appeal would adequately disguise it; she wanted it. And because she was honest, she held up that profane desire and made more of it, as a kind of penance, than really did her justice. Her generous impulses she ignored, and she decided to see her dream of those flowers

43

on the altar as a blasphemous reverie. Who did she think she was?

Catharine gave far more thought to her lack of faith than most devout people ever gave to its presence. It seemed to her a far more demanding garden, requiring constant tending, rearranging and controlling than the formal, low-maintenance orangeries and box-lined walkways of orthodox religions. But she liked it that way. It would keep her honest, she told herself. If she could have been said to believe anything, it was that to make any sense of your atheism or agnosticism, you had to manage it as carefully, as mindfully, as generously, as any faith. If *you* were to be the measure of things, not God, it was even more essential that you were a you worth measuring. You had that choice. Since no remission of sins was likely to be forthcoming, best not to sin.

So this moment at the kitchen table was uncharacteristic of her. She could only explain it to herself by thinking that she wanted to be welcome in the village, and had been wrong-footed by the vicar's visit: the offering of welcome from, well, a divine representative. She had forgotten her freelance status for a moment and been drawn into an argument about the closed shop. Because of her sudden desire to parade a few peonies on Sundays she had been careless. What was she, a child? It was easier in London. City life was private; here you must be diligent. You couldn't afford to be careless in the countryside.

The vicar went on to say that he would speak to Mrs Mountjoy about other, pressing chores to be done. He was sure that even if the flowers were taken care of, between the three of them they could come up with something. He would leave directions to Mrs Mountjoy's house so that, should Catharine wish to call in before Sunday, she could introduce herself and explain how eager she was to help out. He had cheered up since his depression at the first mention of this other woman; Catharine seemed to have a cheering effect on him. He told her the address like a doctor leaving a prescription and put his thin jacket back on. Other patients were plainly claiming his attention, and through a growing irritability with this breezy divinity, Catharine felt her own sense of being the victim of a promiscuous doorstepping; as if it was she now who had been seduced and abandoned in a quarter of an hour. All for not saying, 'Not today, thank you.'

Having seen the vicar out into the warm sunshine, she stood in the dusty shadows of her living room. She remembered the directions to Mrs Mountjoy's like the telephone number of a lover; private, implicatory information that could not be easily forgotten. She had sat down immediately at the piano and played through a Haydn piano sonata far too fast, careless of wrong notes.

That evening, for some reason, Catharine did not tell Tom about the vicar's visit. They always told each other the progress of their respective days. She had a cup of tea and he a glass of whisky; he told her with relieved informality the dreadful formality of his court cases; she told him her progress with the legion of boxes, half of which were still unpacked, that had followed them from London. She could not remember anything in their lives together that she been unable to tell him. Certainly nothing in any of the packing cases had the ability to shock. The closest she had ever come to censoring what she told him had been her initial hesitation, after about a year of trying for a baby, that she had her period and was not, that month, pregnant. And she had solved that awkwardness by telling him the moment he came through the door, and sometimes, when they might have been particularly hopeful, ringing him at his chambers. Once he had joked, to make her feel better, that she could always leave a message with the senior clerk. That night they had had two cups of tea and two whiskies.

By removing the suspense she felt she was removing the theatricality of disclosure. Catharine hated theatricality in herself, in spite of liking it in, for example, Maria. But she didn't want to be disempowered by it in the matter of the baby. She felt if she made too much of it, her disappointment would be commensurate with the fuss she made.

But she still couldn't tell Tom the vicar had called. Nor could she find in herself an adequate reason why she could not tell him. She was just paralysed. She didn't fear his ridicule, though she had no doubt that deep down he would have found her behaviour with the vicar ridiculous. But it still wouldn't, she knew, make him think any less of her. Tom's sense of their equality was absolute. He was without chauvinism, without condescension. She knew he would have laughed at the situation, not at her. But still she could not tell it.

Day by day she asked herself why this should be so. At times she thought that his respect for her was the problem – that she wasn't allowed, in either his or her eyes, to be guilty of a moment's female confusion. But who was being the chauvinist in that analysis? She was. Then she wondered if she was, at root, disappointed with herself, and that she was using not telling Tom as a way of denying this to herself. And so reasons spiralled out of control, none of them defusing the absurdity of the situation. It would have been easier if she had found the vicar attractive, and was simply required to admit to a moment's infatuation with him. One thing was certain – she envied Tom the quickness of wit which would have nipped the problem in the bud.

But she had not clarified her position with regard to religion. What about that? The logical perspective of her worrying over this was simple, and was the vanishing point of all such quandaries – she must have willed the misunderstanding. She was a free, intelligent agent in the world, and she had allowed the situation to develop with the vicar when she could at any point have stopped it. She wanted it. Just as she must want some aspect of this absurd subterfuge with her husband, concealing the fact that she had had a visit from a representative of the Church of England. Her passivity had been mischievous.

What did she want, then? To rough up this village she had moved to? To sow subtle dissent while her husband was at work, disenfranchising venerable Mrs Mountjoy from her good works in the parish? The attraction of the flowers in church was just the beginning of a sensual career of mixed motives – the atheist's inevitable terrorising of the faithful. And her unawareness at the time that this was her subtle agenda, was proof in itself that she was a child in this matter; a wilful, exacting child. The flowers had attracted her as a prepubescent girl shows an obsession with jewellery and make-up, prefiguring the promiscuity that will follow a handful of years later. And Catharine had been promiscuous in her cultivation of the misunderstandings between herself and the vicar. At any point she could have come clean.

How was she to bear this demotion in her husband's eyes to a sort of child-bride, a needy mischief-maker? She, who was regarded as so mature by family and friends.

Or was *this* analysis equally flawed? It was perfectly possible to regard it as reflective of her desire to see herself as having a latent, rebellious streak, whereas in fact she was irredeemably conformist. Maria might have done what she was accusing herself of having done. But Catharine? She might be dressing up a simple faux pas with self-accusatory bunk. Almost trying to make herself more interesting than she really was. Surely one was allowed to get a bit confused in a social situation without afterwards having to dismantle one's entire personality.

Whatever the truth, she didn't tell Tom. Her failure to understand her own motives and her frustration that she had been placed in what had suddenly become an uncomprehending universe reduced her, temporarily, to a kind of teenage funk. She wanted to run to her room, slam her door – something she had never done when she *had* been a teenager – and bury her head in the pillow.

On a more practical level, she had to make up her mind what to do about Mrs Mountjoy, who might well have been told about Catharine's charitable ambitions. Sunday loomed. What if the vicar made a call on his way back from church, to introduce himself to Tom and enquire if flu or a family tragedy had kept them from Communion that morning? Tom would be stood in the door with his dressing gown on, nursing a frothy coffee, and ask, with ruffled hair and a defence counsel's mild, interrogatory demeanour what, in the name of all things holy, the vicar meant by saying they had been expected at church. Then Catharine would attempt to come to the rescue, appearing at her husband's side, and have to explain that her husband (in the vicar's eyes a lawyer and therefore logical and therefore cruel) was not a Christian. But it would be useless because, in the vicar's eyes, Tom would be the man repressing his wife's faith, and Catharine would suddenly belong to the vicar in some creepy way, and her protests that no, she too was an atheist would be no more believed than an abused wife's denial to the police, in front of her husband, that the bruise above her eye had been made by the kitchen cupboard, not his fist.

On the first Sunday they were saved by a summons to Tom's mother's; the second by a trip to a garden centre. But on the Monday following Catharine decided she could trust to luck no longer, and as soon as Tom was safely on the eight thirty-five train, she threw a scarf round her neck and went out into the lane.

In her mind she had taken the imaginative journey to Mrs Mountjoy's house many times since she had been entrusted with the directions. Each time she felt the imaginative struggle not to come off second best. In all the visits she had felt she was not going of her own accord, but only as a functionary of the vicar's insistence. But now that she came to be actually walking there, living out the fantasy, she felt unexpectedly powerful. The prow of the moment, whilst we concentrate with such pleasure on the way it cuts into the water, ignoring the now insubstantial waves, is a far more arresting part of the journey than the journey's end, which when perceived as an end in itself seems insubstantial and pointless. So for Catharine this walk through the village felt radical and novel. She even felt that she might be able still to tell Tom this evening that the vicar had called two weeks ago, and guess what, she'd made friends with a woman in the village with a view to helping out in the church.

It was now the beginning of September. As she walked towards the centre of the village, the post office, pub and school, there was coming towards her, as on the tide, a flotilla of mothers and prams, each having delivered their children to the school for the first day of a new term. Some had younger, preschool children in tow, some had free arms and smiles, swearing with novel freedom, laughing with exaggerated pleasure, struggling to enjoy their liberation to the full. There were at least seven of them. The pavement couldn't accommodate all of them at once, so they wavered into the road like drunks; a couple of them seemed young enough to be the sisters of the toddlers, but Catharine knew in her heart that they were mothers too.

She crossed the road to pass by on the other side. Some of them watched her. Childless, like a witch, thought Catharine, putting herself in their place for a moment. She was conscious of her smart linen skirt and designer scarf, which, compared to the functional, housebound clothing of the mothers and desultory attempts at attractiveness, made her feel, for all her modesty and restraint, as if she were walking the village lane like a catwalk. A young woman said something and the others laughed and someone pushed her into the road; she rounded on the aggressor, pushed her back and they all laughed. Catharine thought they were laughing at her until the woman in the road caught sight of her, betraying the fact that Catharine had not been noticed before. The young woman was embarrassed and scowled a little. But the rest of the women just looked at Catharine dumbly and in seconds they had passed.

It seemed strange to Catharine to see this multiplicity of mothers. When she thought of having a child, a baby, the desire for it, the embryonic joy she sensed, was so *of* her, she wondered with amazement that it existed in collective form. Those women together seemed so confident, brazen, casual with their profound achievement. Unshattered by love. She feared she could not pass off such a thing. Those women, village women, alarmed her. She was meant to have things in common with them, and that was an imperative Catharine had always baulked at. She could never laugh as they laughed, or push people into the street, or scowl. And it wasn't merely a class thing. Women all together like that – with what for Catharine was the true north of affection, a single friend, obliterated from the dynamic, replaced by a gang – that horrified her. She wasn't streetwise enough for it. And that they had children too doubled the horror. Perhaps, thought Catharine, only half ironically, she *was* a witch.

For how long would she have to be constantly coming to terms with the fact that she wanted a baby? How many phantom self-accusations would she have to endure before she just melted into that one, heartfelt fact? She wanted what that gang of women all had; what everybody had something to say about, the commonest thing, and yet the thing that was, surely, irreducible to detail, to ambition, to vanity, to the pseudo omnipotence of the electronic age, above even the crude mechanics of sperm and egg; something to redeem her from the madness of peonies and chrysanthemums in church. A child.

She turned her head and smiled at the mothers, but it was too late. The leaves on the oaks above the lane had already turned a slight brown and one or two wheeled round her. She pressed on.

After the post office the road bent to the left, and to the right a little lane carried on down the slope, at whose base were watercress beds fed by a narrow stream. Hawthorn overhung the unmade road, through whose scruffy branches the stubble of wheat fields that rose up beyond could just be seen in their uniform yellow. At the foot of the slope, before the field began, there was a little bridge over the shallow water, and out over the liquid field, no longer used for cultivation, there were concrete walkways where once they harvested the watercress. To the left of this reservoir, just before the bridge, another path, better kept, wound round to the church and a little row of cottages that preempted it, at the first of which, the vicar had told her, Mrs Mountjoy lived.

Catharine remembered that she had gone as far as the church on the morning of the very first day she and Tom had spent in the house, though she had no memory of any cottages. She had walked to the post office for bread and milk while they waited for the removal van. She'd seen the sign 'To the Church' and allowed the slope to draw her down towards the shadow of the hawthorn. It had been an inconsequential moment of truancy. The stream that fed the watercress beds had been no more than a trickle and the gravel path to the church had been dry with drought. She had taken in the church with a tourist's objective appraisal that now, only six weeks later, seemed patrician compared with her adolescent, September, misgivings. Faith had been other people's affair and the tower was mid-thirteenth century. Now she had ties.

She wished she could have ignored the sticky gravel path and crossed the bridge, climbing across the face of the field and gaining a view to see what autumn was beginning to do to the countryside. In July she had gone into the church, out of the savage daylight, and hoped, with a simplicity that now amazed her, that she and Tom would be happy in their new house. Now, in September, she wouldn't make it to the church. She must stop before that, at the cottage. It was Monday, and by an association with the days of the week she thought her presence in the church itself would be doubly unwelcome, given that it must recovering from its efforts of the day before. So she wandered up the path, her heart beating hard, and knocked at the door. A dog began instantly to bark. There was some scuffling, which Catharine took to be an unseemly altercation between dog and householder over the right to be first to the threshold; at least the protestations of the dog seemed to Catharine a kind of welcome. But they also gave a feeling that her arrival at the cottage was already being made much of, if only by Mrs Mountjoy's pet.

The door opened six inches and the woman who guarded the church flowers contract as if she had the keeping of the Holy Grail peeked out, frowning, the front buffer of her sculpted, dyed auburn hair pressing against the door frame like some percussive insulation against the hardness of the wood. She bounced back.

Yes? she'd said. She had a dog lead in one hand and was obviously about to leave the house. The dog was dancing and making little staccato barks, against which, like a string melody over insolent woodwind, Catharine explained her reasons for being there. She mentioned the vicar and she mentioned the flowers in church, simply to get that subject out of the way once and for all. Mrs Mountjoy frowned at Catharine and then smiled at the dog, the lead still dangling above the Jack Russell's head as both treat and punishment. Then she took a step back and opened a little cupboard under the cottage stairs and, with the help of a booted foot, guided the dog inside and shut the door. There was silence, and Catharine guessed that the dog knew that only perfect quiet would secure its release.

Now there was silence she felt able to look at Mrs Mountjoy properly. She wore a Barbour jacket and no make-up. The rather high-pitched voice, which Catharine had thought was meant to carry over the yapping of the terrier, did not subside; it seemed designed to carry. She had scrutinised Catharine very hard when she first arrived and now did not look at her at all, giving the younger woman the feeling that nothing she could now say, even after three minutes, would alter the impression she had first given on entering the house. Mrs Mountjoy didn't seem put out at having her walk interrupted; at least no more than that everything seemed something of a ordeal to her; all action, even taking her gloves off, being reflective of the futility of all action against life's trials. Her movements gave one the impression that she regarded her personal strengths as the only possible solution to difficulties, and that she would be merciless in her prosecution of other people's weaknesses.

She reminded Catharine of a caricature of a headmistress, but of a solid type who might moonlight as rugby coach on Tuesday afternoons.

The woman made the assumption, which was not in itself unreasonable, that Catharine had actively petitioned the vicar for voluntary work. She even went so far as to make sure that Catharine was aware that any work she did would be strictly unpaid. This was exasperating, and if it had not begged the question 'What on earth was she doing there, then?' she would have told Mrs Mountjoy that she had no desire for any work at all, save arranging an odd peony or two.

They moved through to the kitchen, which was painted yellow, and stood opposite each other over the kitchen table. It was a small room and an Aga was pouring heat out. Catharine unwrapped her scarf from round her neck and put the fashionable thing on the table. Mrs Mountjoy stayed wrapped up. She, in turn, put the dog lead on the table.

Now she started talking. It started very like a headmistress, establishing boundaries and reminding of rules, as at school assembly, and gradually changed into a kind of confessional. She spoke exactly as if Catharine had called for the very purpose of hearing her life story, and had put off walking her dog so as to fulfil her obligation.

Mrs Mountjoy – first names apparently not a biographical necessity – had grown up in an immense house whose picture was on the mantelpiece above the Aga. In parentheses, as it were, she added that it had been a school, not an aristocratic home, but she left Catharine in no doubt that Mrs Mountjoy herself liked to regard it as the latter. Her parents had run the school, then the father had died and the mother had hit the bottle, and the ten-year-old only child had been thrown out of Eden to go to Croydon instead and live with an aunt. The aunt had been brutal and the teenage girl had developed an attraction for the stage, secretly applied to the Central School of Speech and Drama and obtained the offer of a place. The aunt had refused to allow such a thing, and in protest the girl had promptly married a garage owner, Terry Mountjoy. The aunt died, rough Terry did well, became Terence Mountjoy of Mountjoy Motors of Croydon; now nationwide. After ten years, to the couple's surprise, a baby came, a little girl, and Terry bolted, sending odd cheques and taking the daughter on expensive holidays. The daughter was at boarding school, having left the day before to begin her second year of sixth form.

Catharine found this narrative a kind of relief. To have life taken out of her hands had its attraction. It flowed around her like water around an inconsequential obstacle. She had only to offer the customary interjections, 'I see', 'Ah', 'Of course', and, without even engaging in the sense of what she was being told, a life obtained before her. The woman seemed sufficiently driven by her own voice for Catharine to believe that the story would have come out pretty much the same whoever she was telling it to. Perhaps she dwelt on the fall of the family's fortunes and the turrets of the school a little more than she might have done if she had been talking to one of the women who had been walking through the village lane a few minutes before; perhaps there was a little social pressure to be respectable, but essentially the linear narrative took care of itself.

Slowly the woman's words began to become a tune, merely, and Catharine's attention, released by this morphing into a kind of kitchen music, began to wander. She noticed that beneath the collar of the Barbour jacket Mrs Mountjoy wore a silk scarf covered in nautical mottoes: anchors and flags. It was blue and gold and didn't go at all with the rest of what she wore. Catharine couldn't help thinking what a mistake it was. Most of all she saw the older woman's hands, which were thick and had short, bulkily feminine fingers, on one of which was a similarly chunky ring ranged around with diamonds like the European flag. If they had been real diamonds, Catharine thought, she wouldn't be living in this little cottage. As the hands gestured and gripped themselves, both being conducted by and leading the musical rise and fall of Mrs Mountjoy's biography, Catharine thought: What are we when we are reducible to prose, to those hands twisting and gesturing; rings imitating riches; peonies imitating faith?

But however much she might tell herself the narrative would exist without her, that she changed nothing in the older woman's life by calling on her, she knew, of course, that you could not make of yourself a cipher so easily. Mrs Mountjoy asked a sudden question and the hands went still. Catharine asked for it to be repeated. It was about her husband. And she realised that no, she had the woman's life in her hands for the duration of the visit. That was what visits were. Hadn't the vicar done exactly that to her two weeks before? Self-annihilation could not come so readily. To punctuate the woman's monologue, albeit with inconsequential sounds, was to punctuate and publicise the woman's life; though her life, spelt out in fifteen minutes, might seem slight justice to the effort and emotion that had gone into the living of it; without that fifteen minutes it was nothing; now was now.

It struck Catharine that what eventually would bring her back to this truth was offered by the woman herself, without knowing she offered it – the scarf, the distant, softest scrape of the terrier's foot on the cupboard door, as it tried the limits of its incarceration. These details bound Catharine to the moment and so to the woman's history. As with adultery, the betrayal is not in the generalised infidelity but in the individuality of the person newly loved at the expense of the old. It is a detail of their manner, of their gracefulness, or lack of it; or the devastating memory of a single word that betrays, and whose origin we are left to pursue whatever the cost, because we can't help the call to arms that has as its imperative the celebration of another's otherness; it is not the casualness that wounds the moment, but the specific. And in the appreciation of another's life such as Catharine had a moment of, in Mrs Mountjoy's kitchen, she was face to face with this same paradox – she would remember not the turrets of the school the woman evidently regarded as her lost childhood, but the ill-suited scarf and the terrier's impatience. Making the moment representative of the woman's whole life; its apotheosis.

Unlike the adulterous analogy, of course, it was a chaste observation, and therefore the effect was not devastating, for the moment that had been offered to her was not required to live on; it was not a life which, as it is for the adulterer, must be possessed and for which he or she might have to sacrifice their family, even their sanity. If anything, for Catharine, she was able to derive some comfort from the observation, for in the telling detail of the person's otherness, which did not need to be claimed or possessed, she was to be reminded that our death is still only *our* death.

That though we create somebody else's life by the social intercourse of our listening, of being there, we do not destroy one by our demise. That while we might see the day of our extinction as being a general one – the world, at least for us, dying with us – our capacity for seeing another consciousness flower before us by virtue of simply having watched and listened, is to give us a glimpse of the solace parents no doubt seek in the thought that they may, God willing, die before their children; a wish, the granting of which makes of their own death something not only not to be feared, but welcome.

Mrs Mountjoy stopped speaking, leant forward and picked up the dog lead, and Catharine realised it was her cue to leave. In a couple of curt sentences, she was told that the flowers in church were taken care of, but that enquiries would be made and some alternative employment would be found. They shook hands and Catharine went out into the daylight again. Behind her she heard the sound of the released Jack Russell flinging itself against the front door. She walked home. Only hours later did she remember she had promised herself a walk through the watercress beds and up the wheat field beyond after her interview with Mrs Mountjoy. But it was too late.

Now that she had met the woman she stopped worrying about not having told Tom about the vicar. It seemed inconsequential. Now it was December and she did not think of it. If she had she would have regarded her confusion over the matter as a symptom of the early days of moving in, to be forgiven and forgotten as no more of a mistake than to have considered placing a sideboard *there*, rather than in its present, obviously correct position, *here*.

'Hello?' said Catharine.

'It's me,' said Maria.

'Hello, Masha.'

'What's the matter?'

'Nothing.'

'You sound a million miles away. You sound odd. What's the matter?'

'I'm on my own.'

'Did you think I might be Tom?'

'No. Hello.'

'Hello, love.'

'I listened last night.'

'What? You didn't.'

'I told you I would.'

'I thought you were joking.'

'I liked it.'

'Did Tom like it? Hardly, I should think.'

'He wasn't here.'

'Shame. Did you like it?'

'Yes.'

'But you don't like Bruckner.'

'No.'

'But great listener that you are you could pierce to the heart of the second violins and hear your Masha sawing away for thirty bob.'

'Yes.'

'You hate Bruckner.'

'Yes. Yes, I do. I rang you after.'

'There's no reception in the fucking Albert Hall. It's a dungeon.'

'At home.'

'Wasn't home till late.'

'I liked the Mozart too.'

'He's good, that kid. Wanker. Sexy, too.'

'I couldn't tell on the radio.'

'That's why you have me, darling. I'm your roving reporter. Your eyes on the ground.'

'Raving reporter.'

'Where's Tom?'

'I just couldn't work out what that cadenza was. Why didn't he play the Mozart one?'

'Pretentious, wasn't it?'

'Why didn't he? He wrote his own, did he?'

'The privilege of stardom. Wankerdom.'

'Tom's in Birmingham.'

'What?'

'Birmingham.'

'It's now. The time is now!'

'What do you mean?'

'The time you said he was going away. It's here already. I thought it was ages. The New Year.'

'No. It's now. Today.'

'That's why you were able to listen to me last night.'

'I would have listened anyway.'

'Yeah, right.'

'Masha . . .'

'All right. I bet Tom *loves* Bruckner.'

'You don't know that he doesn't.'

'No. I only know that he doesn't like me.'

'He likes Mozart.'

'I could have come and stayed.'

'We went through all that. Don't you remember? You had the concert.'

'I could have had you all to myself.'

'We'll do another pizza.'

'When?'

'Whenever you say.'

'I've loads on.'

'You see, you're the busy one.'

'And you're the one living in Outer Mongolia.'

'I nearly rang you later, too.'

'I was late back.'

'Really later.'

'What time?'

'Late. Really late. Half midnight.'

'Are you joking? It must have been two in the morning when the Bruckner finished.'

'Silly.'

'Why didn't you?'

'I don't know. I thought I might be interrupting you.'

'Doing what? Shagging?'

'Is Mark away?'

'No. He was around.'

'Last night?'

'Yes. No, you're quite right, a shagging scenario was a possibility, but in this case, no. He left shagless.'

'Poor Mark.'

'Poor Mark? Poor me.'

Pause.

'Masha . . . are you still there?'

'Yes.'

'Now *you* sound odd.'

'Ah, so you admit you were sounding strange when you answered the phone.'

'What's wrong? Is it Mark? I thought you were nonchalant about him.'

'I am. He's a cunt.'

'Maria.'

'What? If it takes a woman's word to condemn a man, more power to our elbow, I say. That's right, laugh.'

'Is it that bad?'

'I'll tell you when I see you.'

'Why not now?'

'Too hard on the phone.'

'That sounds serious.'

'Not too serious.'

'Serious-ish.'

Another pause.

'Masha?'

'Serious? What's serious? I don't want to talk about me, I want to talk about you. How is your solitude? Is it delicious or are you missing your husband? All those acres of unoccupied duvet. I hope you're making the most of it. I hope listening to me on the radio isn't the high spot.'

'High enough.'

'That sounds like an admission of defeat.'

'Defeat? Of what?'

'Of your profound life.'

63

'I wasn't aware I had a particularly profound life.'

'What, compared to your shallow friend out fucking and fiddling? It's epic.'

'I assure you it's not.'

'Listen to you. "Assure me." Well. So a little solitude hasn't made you envy me my life?'

'No.'

'Pity.'

'Oh, I don't mean it nastily. It just wouldn't suit me. And I don't know where you got the idea I had a profound life from. It makes me sound very serious.'

'What? You're the most serious person I ever met.'

'I don't think that's even remotely a compliment.'

'I love you, it doesn't need to be a compliment. It can just be a fact.'

'It's such a relief to talk to you. I wish I'd phoned you last night, but it was so late.'

'So what if you'd woken me up?'

'You might have been cross.'

'When was I ever cross with you?'

'I don't know. I think a bit of me has always been scared you might be cross with me.'

'Never in twenty years have I ever been cross with you.'

'You were cross when I got married.'

'My nose put out, yes. Protective, yes. Outraged at the cheek of any man to take you from me – murderously so. But cross? Cross with my friend? Never. Will be if you get divorced. Excuse me, but how did we get on to divorce as a subject for discussion?'

'I don't know. You started it.'

'Not true, actually. How is the dear Tom?'

'Don't ask unless you mean it.'

'Of course I mean it. I want to know if he's coping without having had me baiting him for a while.'

'He's immune to your taunts.'

'Lawyers' front. The balls haven't dropped that I couldn't put back, given a glass of wine and half an hour with the jury.'

'What are you talking about?'

'Nothing. I'm keeping you entertained. The main feature hasn't started yet.'

'Tom's fine.'

'Oh, we're still on that, are we?'

'You asked.'

'I suppose I did.'

'It's raining here. It rained in the night.'

'Pissing down here. Why won't you tell me what the matter is?'

'You wouldn't tell me either. You said not on the telephone.'

'No, Catharine.'

'Don't say my name.'

'Well, I'm not calling you what Tom calls you. You know I won't do that.'

'Yes.'

'What's wrong with Catharine?'

'Never liked it.'

'Look, why don't I come and see you?'

'Pardon?'

'Come and see you.'

'No.'

'What?'

'I'm good for nothing. Tom's back tonight.'

'Not till late, yes? Birmingham. You can drink sixteen cups of tea and tell me all about it. And, anyway, I want to talk to you.'

'I know, you said. About Mark?'

'Amongst other things. What were you doing when I rang?'

'Well, I wasn't mid-shag.'

'Perish the thought.'

'What does that mean?'

'I don't know, darling. I'll see you around four.'

'There are traffic lights on the way into the village.'

'What?'

'Traffic lights. Be careful.'

'See you.'

'Four. Bye.'

So Maria was coming.

Catharine could hear now that they were practising the bells in the church, and a pigeon was mewing its closeted lament from the branches of the trees above the house. Suddenly the silence of the house was broken, both by these village sounds and by the thought of a real guest, to go with the phantom ones who had peopled her imaginary breakfast party. Now she must get dressed or be committed to a lunatic asylum by lunchtime; put on shoes or slippers or lose her toes to frostbite. It must be for the best to be shamed out of such a hopeless reverie by a real person; wasn't all of history that? People imposing themselves?

She had thought it might be Tom, yes. It wasn't such a foolish thought. They hadn't planned to speak till he was on the train home in the early evening. If at all. But he loved her, didn't he? And love might burst its banks once in a blue moon and draw an unsolicited phone call out of the ether. She wasn't utterly barmy to think that. Give up that hope and you might as well give it all up. Might as well divorce and dismay Maria.

Had she been disappointed that it hadn't been him but her friend? She had to know. She was in the mood for casting stones into the well to see how far they fell and what sound, if any, would echo in the depths.

She was impatient. *Had she been disappointed?* Between the sound of her great friend's voice and her consciousness organising itself to say 'Hello . . .': was there gratitude or dismay? As she now concentrated her mind on this tiny moment, this narrow window of daylight – like those windows cut in castle walls, wide enough to shoot an arrow through but too thin through which to be shot – this moment seemed to open out on an unknown landscape, in which other people or she herself might operate with the blitheness of historical figures, whose adulteries and general misdemeanours are so far distant from our present morality, that they seem absolved from any moral judgement at all.

And she seemed to glimpse her attitude; the one that had briefly braved itself against the daylight, like a photographic image in the darkroom, developed but not yet fixed, brought out too soon, showing a ghostly visage, and then obliterated by the general light, turning the paper black. So, in this interstice, she saw the Catharine who pre-dated Maria; who perhaps pre-dated all attachment. And it hadn't wanted to engage with her great friend. It had wanted oblivion. Something in her had shuddered at the otherness of the woman with whom she was about to speak. And Catharine feared that it would have been true even if it had been Tom on the phone. A skulking, guilty thing, fearful of being observed, of being subject to the foreign language and currency of another person's territory. You *colonised*, it seemed to Catharine, when you met other people. You set up a tiny government on foreign soil and eventually you made freedom fighters of the people you were there ostensibly to civilise. We should all keep apart.

But inevitably you succumbed. Once the moment was over, she was delighted to hear Maria's voice. She loved her. After the awful moment it was easy, like the relief of a wave that reaches its highest point on the land, is held there for an instant, endured, and then, the tipping point passed, pulls back down the shingle; succumbing to the greater force, which is to return, rather than pursuing the first impulse, which had been to throw itself on the face of the land. At the tipping point you know yourself; and the rake of the water back down the slope afterwards tells you it is the self from which there is no escape.

What was Maria now? It hadn't been easy, Catharine thought, to maintain their friendship. When one woman marries and the other remains resolutely single, it is bound to mean awkwardness. It was difficult for Catharine to have the spectre of an objective judgement on her life so close at hand. Maria had seen everything; she had known Tobias. She had a privileged position – knowing Catharine as well as herself and yet not having to *be* Catharine. She could pass the kind of judgement the public cast on a film when they think an actor they are especially fond of has been poor – rejigging in their minds aspects of their performance to make it more like the one they gave in their last film, little realising that the truth inherent in someone's work — either in life or art — is not founded on the cosmetic detail of an interpretation, but the result of everything about that person — their past, their present happiness or unhappiness — and the reason for an artistic failure is never one single factor or detail overlooked. It takes as much effort to write a bad book or give a bad performance as it takes to write a good one; and the same with life. If Catharine failed with Tom, Catharine at least wanted Maria to see that she had given everything. She wanted her to appreciate the wholeness with which she approached the role of wife.

But that, of course, was precisely what Maria would find hard. And she had admitted as much. Even in the phone call just now she had admitted it. Catharine had to accept her reluctant acceptance of her marriage. 'As long as you're happy,' Maria said whenever they spoke of Tom. And she *was* happy. But since we are — as Catharine had realised so clearly when she visited Mrs Mountjoy and listened to her history — each other's soul's biographers, whenever she told Maria *her* history, it was rendered in her friend's hearing not a wholly happy one. She had to bear this disparity. Catharine thought she was happy; Maria's idea of happiness was such she couldn't believe her friend. Not completely.

At first this was felt as a great shame by Catharine. In the early days of her relationship with Tom she had fantasised about shared dinner parties and rented holiday cottages together. But the very first meeting of best friend and boyfriend had been a disaster. Tom, by some unconscious word association, had thought Maria might be of Italian descent and had booked a table at La Bella Signora trattoria in

Clapham. He and Catharine had been together for two months. As is almost inevitable in such circumstances, each party had only the limited biographical sketch that Catharine had provided as a foundation on which to get acquainted. Both Tom and Maria clung to the least flattering detail of the other. Tom decided Maria was a promiscuous diva and Maria that Tom was a hearty, mountaineering pedant come to bore them to death. Catharine watched helplessly as Carmen met Edmund Hillary. She was amazed that two people about whom she cared so much could care so little for each other.

Maria treated men as a separate species. And the fact that she had captured so many of them, observed them at close hand and then released them back into the wild, made her no closer to accepting a shared destiny with them than a butterfly collector wonders if one day he will sprout wings and flutter away. This attitude, coupled with Maria's misgivings about Tom, had a curious effect on Catharine. As the years passed she began to find it weirdly attractive. Instead of pining for a union of friend and husband, she began to see their differences as a bracing alternative; to see the fact of Tom being so unloved meant a greater, thrilling contrast for her own, continued love for him. She felt it was telling her what love really was. That the art of living lay in enduring the multiple narratives that it threw up and recognising that the way of love and marriage was just one way; the fact that perhaps it wasn't an absolute was reassuring; she had a choice; and her choice was to be with Tom.

Yes, that first meal had been a disaster. The following morning Tom turned lawyer in his dealings with Catharine. Standing in the living room of his new girlfriend's flat he had carefully presented the case against Maria. Never had he been

so affronted by anyone, so needlessly prejudged, and worse —
by a shallow, flighty fool of a woman. He had been there in
good faith, she had been there to find fault; he had tried his
best, she was a —

Catharine had had to stop him there. She had no desire to
see Tom behave in a way that might make it more difficult to
accept him as her life partner. Tom saw the look on her face,
and saw that she was saving him from himself. He went very
quiet. Then Catharine, disarming him still further by great,
unnecessary candour, described her relations with Tobias; said
Tom was entitled to be curious about past boyfriends but not
disapproving about her friends. It was all done very quietly
and gently. But both of them were aware of the obviousness
of Tom's response, and both were shamed by it. Catharine
had pitied his cagoules and mountaineering paraphernalia;
now she felt no pity. Tom saw this, spent three days drinking
with old friends convinced that Catharine was too good for
him, and then proposed. In nine years of marriage they had
never once argued over Maria. He raised an odd eyebrow,
but that was all.

What, then, did she feel when she heard Maria's voice? The
past? It is one thing, in later life, still to be friends with someone
who has been present when the great events of one's youth
happened; another to have been present during a time defined
more by what has *not* happened. Such was the case with
Catharine. She had not been ambitious. Music, her love, had
been a failure. No professional vocation had offered itself.
Maria had done all these things, not Catharine. All that

Catharine had to show for this time was Maria herself; friendship was required to stand for all these things, defining the voids in Catharine's life as those spaces on artists' canvases are defined – the so-called negative spaces – where it is the void around the object that defines its true shape, the blue horizon caught between Venus's breast and Mars's arm; the ragged olive grove in the Holy Land that congregates around the dove descending to His forehead.

Perhaps it was also that Catharine did, now, have an ambition; a vocation, too. She wanted a baby. The void, the negative spaces, might be filled any day now. So a piece of her wanted to say to Maria, 'You can't come here, I've work to do.'

But she had no work to do.

There was always an accusation hanging over these thoughts about Maria. And that was that Catharine was in a form of competition with her friend. She had never *felt* competitive about anything. It simply never occurred to Catharine to set herself against what other people did or what they had. When she couldn't play the piano very well she was sorry, that was all. Deeply sorry. And when she met Maria and saw Maria dress up as a gypsy and be remarkable, she marvelled at her friend. It was always a relief to see Maria. She had the quality almost of an artistic creation. She was a character like those figures who crop up in novels which the writer has written with particular, anecdotal energy, investing in his patchwork creation a vibrancy that makes them instantly recognisable, either through some idiosyncrasies of speech or attitude, maintaining a through line which makes us glad when they reappear after an absence, not least because they seem to have a life of their own, releasing us from the burden of having to remember who they are, or reimagining what they might be like. Taking the responsibility of who they are out of our hands. And, also, perhaps, by the same virtue, who we are.

That was it. Catharine had had to be responsible for the music she tried to play, and hadn't the technical expertise to fulfil that responsibility. Maria took care of all of that. Their friendship was out of both of their hands, and all the more pleasurable for it.

But now, in the cottage at the end of the lane, now that Maria phoned from London, with a life still full of men and music, and with the ambiguous pause before she said, 'Hello,' to Maria on the phone, Catharine asked herself – was she in competition? Was she envious?

It was true that sometimes she felt like an older sister to Maria. When the latter was particularly petulant or childish, she told her off gently. Maria seemed to expect it. But where did Catharine get older-sister status from? An older sister got it from being older; it was natural authority. Did Catharine think she had a kind of natural authority over Maria? By definition *competing* with her? It was true that it had got more difficult to take Maria's wilder exploits. Once upon a time it had been awkward undergraduates the two young women laughed over; now Maria was more likely to ring at midnight with tales of married men, seeking sympathy that they would not leave their wives, or outrage that they would. It was hard to keep up, and more sobering, too. She knew Maria wasn't malicious; she knew that Maria must feel a lack of self-esteem somewhere along the way; she knew it all. But she didn't want to be drawn in to having to place her life alongside that of her friend's and pass judgement on it. She just wanted to put it down to them being different.

Perhaps more and more different. When they met in town, as they did about once a month, and they met for a pizza, it took Catharine longer and longer to decide what she wanted. Maria ordered instantly, sometimes in the process of being shown to their table. She had appetite – appetite she knew about, that she obeyed like a friend she knew by now she must indulge. Catharine – at least in the limited confines of the pizzeria – envied that. It made things simpler. Not least because in Catharine's inability to choose from the menu she gave off the signal that she was fussy and hard to please; that, in fact, it must be she who was the real bohemian because she appeared to care so much about what she chose; an exacting appetite being less acceptable than a rampant one. The truth was that she simply found it harder and harder to make a decision about anything. Even the way Maria ate whatever it was she had chosen told Catharine that for her friend life was getting simpler. At least as far as pizzas were concerned. She told herself that the reason she couldn't choose from the menu was that she had fetishised choice because her life was closing in, in the cottage at the end of the lane. About other things she had no choice.

In some respects it was as if Catharine wasn't ready for life yet. The mixture of perfectionism, strictness, tea-drinking and thwarted vocation had led her almost to accept that this life was just a rough draft. An essay to be rewritten, with new confidence and on new, tested principles, at a later date. If she held off, from music, from London, from choosing which pizza she wanted, it was with the disinterestedness of the impartial observer, the scientist. She would be the placebo whose life, unaffected by radical developments and ambition, would allow the effects of those forces to be measured and evaluated. She would balance Maria's engagement.

She *thought* this, but in practice it felt like superiority. How could it not? At the end of one of Maria's confessional tirades about men, Maria always sought Catharine's absolution. And always got it. But it was becoming harder and harder to accept the line that 'all men are wankers'. More and more Catharine wanted to mount a defence against this wholesale condemnation. But she only knew Tom. Tobias had been a strange mixture of accusation and adoration, sometimes simultaneously. But Catharine's instinct, her conviction, even, was that all relations were 'fifty–fifty' in terms of blame to be attached. It was her mantra. But she never said to Maria that it must be just as much Maria's fault as the wankers'. She just forgave her.

So Catharine decided that her love for Maria must be a slightly superior one, and that, horribly, love and superiority must sometimes go hand in hand. She was like a parent to her, her love founded on protectiveness and indulgence, like that of a mother to their child. And this was dismaying.

'Who do I think I am?' she said in the freezing air of her living room, the cold now settling in her bones. The words died in the soundless chill. And as she said it she knew she had wanted to say, 'Who the fuck do I think I am?' but had not wanted to swear. What a crowning, private absurdity to censor herself in her solitude. What superiority, she thought; loathsome, puritanical woman, at the end of her country lane, wringing her ageing, childless, failed pianist's hands.

She must get dressed. What would Tom have said, to see her standing, still in her nightdress, in the freezing air? It would do her no good to gather the folds of the dressing gown round her, as if to deny that it was insufficient to keep her warm. She must get dressed. Now.

She looked at the clock. Five past ten. What would Tom say? Gone ten and not yet dressed. What was she, some kind of delinquent? He would never have said that. But he might have raised an eyebrow. What would Tom's mother have said? Were she still alive. Would she have raised an eyebrow as she had when the couple had moved into their first flat together, six months in advance of their marriage? Or would she have supported Catharine in her nightied state and demanded of her son that Tom be understanding? Would they both criticise or both not care? Did it matter? None of it mattered. Tom's mother was dead. A horrible death.

Aside from these judgements, whether of the living or the dead, what if, more pressingly, this standing around in a nightdress was a slippery slope? Tom had gone for but a day. What if the next time he were to go further afield? Newcastle, say, or Aberdeen? What if he stayed away a week? Would she cease to brush her teeth? Her hair? Would her degeneration continue in a linear fashion till she ate with her mouth open and didn't wash at all? Eventually she would forget to pay the bills. Her electricity would be cut off; water too. She would wear four jumpers and make tea from water boiled on a tripod over the fire. Who would fetch and cut her wood? She would need a constant supply of logs. What else could she do but go out into the fields herself and forage for firewood in the naked hedgerows; it would be she who explored the hollow haunts of foxes and rabbits, tracing their worn paths in search of sustenance; she who would climb the meadow beyond the church like a peasant woman, before the fading embers of a winter evening, bending and collecting, stretching her back beyond the water meadows above the church's dark tower and the sinister tracery of branches against the open sky. Christmas would have come and gone, but she would gather kindling and hold it to her breast as if the bundle were a child; only this thought would keep her warm. Tom would be long gone.

'Catch, put your slippers on.'

That's all he would have said, probably. It was unfair of her to think he would have been critical of her bare feet. He wasn't a stickler. It would just have been, 'Catch, you'll freeze.'

That was what he called her. Catch. Not Kate or Cathy. But Catch. Maria hated it and would not call her it, though Catharine called her Masha. No one called her it but Tom. Catharine had no memory of where it came from. It wasn't very feminine, but it was quirky and different, and she would rather have felt those things than have a cute girl's name. When Maria occasionally called her Catharine it was nice and serious; a relief. Catch was playful, dry, ironic. Maria had been called names like Moo and Mimi by boyfriends; she always mimed two fingers down her throat when she confessed to this, but never, so far as Catharine knew, told them not to.

She must get dressed. She would make one more cup of tea and then take the stairs. Her cold limbs set off, amazed, it seemed to her, that they would do as her warm mind bid them. She was mobile, this repository of thought and feeling, and able to subsist in more than one room. Extraordinary. Catch could allow herself another cup of tea, where Catharine must climb the stairs dutifully.

In the kitchen the kettle had cooled considerably since the first cup. She flicked the switch. The lights dimmed briefly as the current diverted. She was going to take a cup of tea back to bed with her. The kettle breathed its asthmatic sigh. Catch would take a cup back to bed and look, dry and ironic, at her retro manners and be a suburban housewife, allowed to do such things.

No, as a nickname it wasn't feminine, but Tom had said she was the most feminine woman he had ever known. What? No, not Maria. Paradoxically, paradoxically, mind, Maria was not deeply feminine in *that* sense, because in spite of the long dark hair and jugular lipstick, that wasn't what femininity was strictly about. Not to Tom. What it was, he didn't say. Except that Catharine was it.

Was Tom all masculine? Catharine didn't know what an extreme of gender entailed, apart from being an obvious stereotype. He'd played hockey at school. Played it very well. That cross-gender game suggested a kind of quaint confidence. Not macho. A prickly jumper worn for warmth. Hockey, mountains and a law degree. Decency. A man.

The kettle reached its crisis and went quiet.

Unscrutinised by Tom, in his absence she scrutinised him back. Perhaps so she needn't scrutinise herself. Was that a kind of revenge? Or an inevitable reaction to waking alone in the house for the first time?

She warmed the pot. Steam came up from the dark hollow, fecund and inner; it wreathed her in a faint flush of condensation; the ambient air was cold. She threw in the loose tea, gritty and dry, caught a bit between her fingernails, shook her hand and poured the hot water in globs and splashes inside;

the dryness of the leaves slaked, she covered the contents with the lid and waited.

He was a little dour, sometimes. His grandfather had been Scottish. He was understated. It drove Maria demented. As it must anyone given to overstatement as much as she was. Sometimes Catharine wondered if it worked, being a lawyer, and being so economical with your expressive powers. She worried for his restraint. That at some vital moment he might fail to galvanise the jury. That they might mistake his calm for defeatism.

On the other hand, perhaps he was excellent. Perhaps he had a persona in court unlike anything she had ever seen at home. How was she to know? Perhaps as well as the domestic Tom there was a firebrand lawyer who, given the liberty of the courtroom, let rip. All the more so in that he was able to express the very things he could not express at home. It's always the quiet ones, they say. Going quietly mad in the low-ceilinged cottage, a Georgian courtroom would be just the thing. She knew he wasn't without passion, without rage. She'd seen him when the pilot light on the boiler went out; she'd seen him raise his eyes to heaven. Think about it. He might, in court, raise his whole arm; might bring it down thunderingly on the bench before him and dare, dare the Home Office to obfuscate further; dare them to convict.

She thought she would be cross if there were this other Tom. Was she meant to do without this alter ego? Was it not for her consumption? Not in front of the children. They had no children.

She must commit a crime and then he could defend her. She must do something herself to conjure the Cicero in him and cause him to weigh their love in the balance. To champion her. Fight for her love. Do you, Catch, solemnly swear ... ? She wanted him to fight her corner. But he was in Birmingham fighting other people's corners. Where was his passion? Yes, she brought out his passion in bed; she knew he wanted her. But there might be more to articulate. Perhaps the full articulation of a child needed more than just their bodies interlocked; something of the courtroom was lacking, perhaps. The whole truth and nothing but the truth. A baby. He left his real potency in court. He was spent by the time he returned on the five past six. And she would be left gathering firewood and falling on the parish. Tragic. Tragic.

For the time being she would have to begin her deprived existence by taking her tea back to bed with her. Like a lover. What else was she to do with only this shadow of a husband? She, Catharine, was plainly a sideshow, an adjunct to the main event, his righteous court life. She was nothing. A woman to be made love to out of pity; to slake her child thirst. Shallowness, members of the jury. Shallowness from which my sperm has baulked at fertilising. I leave you to decide ...

The tea had stewed. The pot seemed as heavy as the tea was dark; its mahogany looked as potent as whisky, but she poured a cup and added milk this time. Perhaps the strength would, like a dram of something, make her shudder and forget the morning self who was about to climb the stairs. Her downstairs self was about to die; to be obliterated. The early-morning foray into thought and recollection was just a first draft of the day; to be looked at after lunch and repented of. Only the phone call with Maria had yielded anything. A meeting. Ironic then that it was the phone call that seemed least real to her; least *of her*. But then conversations were partly and inevitably out of one's hands, weren't they? It took two people. The morning self is dead; long live the morning self. Acres of incompleteness, unresolved friendship; the mysterious motives of others; the marvellous sound of the rainwater dropping from the eaves; an excess of detail going nowhere. Could you call it a life? If not, what else was it? Thinking of the piano and the boy on the bus – that she recognised as life. Just not hers. The Chappell still brooded like a coffin in the corner. That wasn't life, no. More like the other thing.

She headed for the stairs as towards a fairground ride she might, if she wavered, be too frightened to take.

Halfway up, where the stair turned, there was the little whitewashed alcove set into the thick wall, with a window looking out on the gravel drive. However many times she passed this little recess, it always managed to surprise her. It was the house's secret spot; something that the otherwise obvious domesticity of the house was keeping to itself.

Always it arrested her, for she knew that, as far as territorial claims were concerned, this was Catharine's corner. From the very first moments of their household careers, this little shelf had been earmarked as hers. Which made it all the more strange that she should be surprised by it each time she passed it. She wondered sometimes if she was being altogether candid with herself – was she ashamed that she should have a spot that was just hers? The daylight behind the white wall lit the alcove so neatly and conveniently. She had no memory of having done anything so proprietorial as claim a piece of the house just for herself. Perhaps it had no more been selectively christened hers than simply having a removal man place a box marked 'Catharine's things' on the shelf and forgetting about it. Perhaps he had been on his way upstairs and forgotten to come back down to collect it. All Catharine could allegedly remember now, members of the jury, was that within a few days of moving in several ornaments had found themselves ranged on the little white, immaculate shelf. Tom had never mentioned them.

Odd. Odd that he should never mention them. If *she* baulked at this little self-shrine, what would *he* make of it? Having completely failed to mention it, perhaps he was embarrassed. Ashamed. Objects from her past. Fetishes. A piece of the house kept for her ridiculous feminine indulgence. Where no man could tread. Ugh.

But why should he ignore it? If he had issues with it, then confront her. That was what he did, wasn't it, in court, being paid handsomely – confronting people with incontrovertible evidence of their selfishness and general illegality? These paltry objects were evidence of her sometime existence in the world, and, excuse her for pointing it out, but was not her existence in the world meant to be of some importance to him? Correct her if she was wrong. He had been irritable about Maria's apparent hold over his wife-to-be's past in the debacle of the Clapham Italian – could he not accept – even be interested in – the presence of three – *three*, M'lud – remnants of her life before she was married? For Christ's sake. They meant nothing to her. Nothing. Three shabby *objets d'art*.

One was a little box given to her by her father after a family holiday near Clermont-Ferrand. Of course this meant a great deal to her, but she had never doubted her father's love for her, never needed material gifts as reassurance. She was given it when she was a teenager. She supposed now that it had been meant for jewellery. It was curiously light, papier-mâché, perhaps, and had an abstract design on the lid. It remained in her life because to have thrown it away would have been brutal. She was never sentimental. She could not now remember what, if anything, it contained.

On either side of this box, like the thieves flanking the Cross, were two figures. One was a Chinese man in porcelain, glazed, with a pack on his back and a face tilted questioningly. Like the piano it had migrated mysteriously from her parents to Catharine; from family to marriage. Looking at it now it meant nothing to her – she had no memory of it being given her. It was not beautiful and might have been either extremely valuable or extremely cheap. The pinched face and smiling eyes could have been stereotypical orientalism or Dynastic mastery. It was certainly inscrutable. It annoyed Catharine for its knowingness and ugliness, as if it were pulling a face at her constantly. But each time she climbed the stairs she looked at it, drawn to her own response. The fact that it was her past, and that it was fixed, revolted her. As if she might still find an adolescent fury at suburban complacency which she hadn't had at fifteen, but could still be brewing in her. The fixedness, like a still life. The oriental face from home, the family; so local; school having been this and no other; her talents so, and not other; eyes blue, eyes brown; loved, unloved. The childless house. It was fixed.

The second figure, more forgiving, but even more painfully still, was a little alabaster ballerina given to Catharine by an unpleasant aunt when she was twelve. It was her oldest possession, but even for this she had little affection. When she saw it she saw the toy of a child. A portion of the upturned face was missing, chipped off years ago, but the rest of the figure still arched with a tragi-comic effort to please, its arms lifted together above its half-face, the worn dye on the light blue tutu fading first from a girl's touch, now from the daylight in the whitewashed alcove.

She saw the figures, and felt a kind of instruction as to what her attitude to them should be. She was clearly meant to extrapolate the present self back to the small hands that had held these childhood objects. Meant to see this present moment as the high-tide mark of the swelling sea of her life, which, bitter or exultant, was, at least, now. And in its nowness, triumphant. If only because she had made it this far. In that sense self was given meaning purely by virtue of what had gone before. It was a thread, the end of which she held in her now grown-up hands and said, 'I am here.' But Catharine resented this instruction. The little theatre of the alcove seemed to her sanctimonious and contemptible. It was dead.

Because the past, it seemed to her, was useless. She couldn't be creative with those layers of time, and see her life as having a magic depth, like those exquisite shades of skin that the old masters achieved in their portraits by the painstaking application of successive films of paint. She couldn't make of her life a satisfactory story. Certainly not one that just had to be told. Years brought new attitudes and new insights, that was all; the old ones weren't interesting. And to find them so seemed to her narcissistic.

But she also feared that her failure to do this, her failure to be creative with her sense of self, was at the heart of her mediocrity as an artist; as a musician. This must be why she had failed. Her instinct looked out, to appreciate, to love. But she didn't want it to be about her. So no alchemy obtained between her and the world. You had to be Maria, crying, 'Not good enough!' picking up her bow and trying again. You had to dispense with what was second-rate, whether it was boys or music. And you had to think you were interesting enough to believe that what you had left at the end of the struggle was worth it. Maria wasn't a soloist; she played in the back row of the second violins. But Catharine knew she still thought it was worth the work.

No, Catharine accepted the givens of life. She loved Tom, so Tom became a given. Without bitterness or ambition, she was just happy. She never needed to question it; she wasn't a lifestyle junkie; she didn't seek an aesthetic life any more than she would have bought a CD because she liked the cover. She bought the best recordings. She wasn't a snob. If she saw a CD with an ugly cover she was tempted to buy it to *prove* that she wasn't a snob. In that sense she was almost against *decoration*. She wanted the truth to be within. She wanted her mind to accept every detail of her life: the petrol smell of the bus, the dust in her throat, as well as the dark eyes of the boy in his newly pressed, equally dark blazer.

So what if you were mediocre? This little constellation of objects in the alcove had finally confirmed it to her. If she were a real challenger of life, a true original, she would have plundered these objects for their meaning; she would have engaged with the resonance of the past, retrieved the microscopic associations that memory yielded and worked out a life in the present on new principles. All right, it was too late now to play a piano concerto; too late to practise. But she knew from her apathy that it had always been too late. It was never going to happen. What was she to cry 'Not good enough' at, now? Tom? Her marriage? Not having a baby? Yes, probably. But that was different. They practised that, but it never came right.

It was all right for Tom. He could stand in court, and when the givens of life threatened to yield an outcome unjust or unfavourable, he could cry, 'Objection!' He had a structure, a set of rules that he could work within. And if the judge cried, 'Overruled', you still slept easily at night. At least you'd shouted. There was even that expression that smelt of the courtroom of life: you had to *Do yourself justice*. Guilty or innocent wasn't the point.

Chiller and chiller she stared at the savage triumvirate. Box, Chinaman and dancer. All inscrutable, in fact. All physical presence, all the sense of 'out there' was inscrutable, come to think of it. What extra quality could make it scrutable except proof of the operation of divine will? She shivered. She must get dressed.

Divine will? This morning there was only *her* will. What was she to do? She was desperate. Suddenly she knew. It was obvious. She must get dressed and internalise. She was insane to continue with this blind faith of looking out at the world with such acceptance. She should not look out at objects, at the givens. She should box up this little cast of characters, and if not actually put them out for the rubbish she should forget them. She, not the objects of her past, was what was important. Her mind must be the theatre, the courtroom, the alcove, and she herself the defence and prosecution, the prime mover. Internalise, internalise. In the absence of a child, her thoughts would be like dream children, peopling her lonely, vocationless life. There was politics, there was feminism, there was charity more pressing than the flowers in church. And the strength for all of this would come from within. It wasn't too late. She would have her day in court. She must begin as soon as possible.

Only thoughts were real. She stared. And the little ballerina – or more truthfully, the little object of dye and broken alabaster – she supposed stared back. But not only was the forced expression one of faked interest, but to believe of the statue that it meant anything was absurd. It was not real. It was a simple revelation, but it warmed her within, as if the sudden focus on her own mind might fuel the coming day. As if she might *think* something extraordinary.

She went on up the stairs, as if running with her revelation to another place; perhaps with a natural curiosity to know whether the truth she had uncovered would subsist on *terra nova*, as the Pilgrim Fathers might have stared at the wide prairies of the New World and wondered, with a tiny, agnostic crisis, whether the truths they had brought with them would find an easy berth among the cactuses and canyons of the Wild West.

She took her tea to bed, held the mug in supplicatory hands, and drew first duvet, then knees, up to her chest and looked out from her white cotton outpost at the cold bedroom. The hardness of her knees against her breasts induced in her body a sense of vital, foetal security, as if they must now lock there to keep her safe; perhaps even till summer came. She sensed a sweetness in her forehead that suggested one or two tears might easily come to clear the air of emotion. The window brightened as a gap of cloud allowed the sun through and the warm grain of the chest of drawers winked like a lighthouse.

Tom's things were in there. Hidden. He left little evidence of himself in the room. He left no wake. Catch was different. She left a trail of things: clothes, letters; they fell from her like leaves. She raked them up every now and then. She wasn't slovenly; it was just that Tom was tidy; he left little to implicate him.

On top of the chest of drawers was a clothes brush. It had been Tom's father's; the son never used it. And there was a bottle of aftershave someone from his chambers had given him last Christmas. Nearly a year had gone, now, and the little vial remained stoppered up. Catharine wondered who might have given him such a thing. She was sure he had never told her. Presumably it couldn't have come from a woman. Far too intimate. Unless leaving it there so ostentatiously were a double bluff, to avert suspicion. Yet odd for a man to have given it, too. To give something connected with male allure. It was a mystery. Whatever its provenance it had never been used. It just wasn't Tom; she knew that. It was in a misty, ground-glass bottle with a silver funnel and had HOMME in bold, block letters on the side. The absurd, masculine chic was foreign to Catharine, like a joke she did not get. She knew that she would never have married – probably never have even talked to – a man who put such stuff on his face. Piano concertos didn't come into it. It was just not her life; not for her.

Why should Tom have never tried it? Someone had given it him, however misguidedly. It was a gift. Brusque of her husband to leave the thing wholly untested. Someone else had set in motion the process of gift-giving, which had, as its last act, its denouement, the application of the product – utterly absurd to stop short of that. Why should he stop short? Embarrassment? Self-consciousness? Cowardice? What, Tom? Conqueror of Mont Blanc in his gap year? Her True Love?

It was a fact, incontrovertibly true, that it was possible she might have found the smell of it attractive. She might, in fact, have found it irresistible. He had plainly not considered her in the snub he gave this gift. It was, after all, designed to make a man attractive. Teams of French people no doubt assembled in Parisian suburbs to concoct new and devastating scents, of which this might be their career best. Why hadn't he tried it? Was he so sure of the nature of his wife's libido as to preclude unilaterally HOMME from their lovemaking? She might have conceived in the fecund haze of Left Bank masculinity. It might have been the incremental detail missing from their union, the little touch of HOMME to make a man wholly man. But no, he was so sure. So sure it was unnecessary. My God, my God, how we take one another for granted in this life; how we leave acres of the unknown, the great untrodden pastures of experience unvisited either on our own or on others' behalf; we leave our dreams on the shelves marked HOMME and FEMME.

All unknown. But what she did know was that beneath, in the drawers, were the underpants and handkerchieves; the Armani boxers he wore when he was being smart, and the terrible ones they had bought in a French supermarket when they were on holiday, which he wore when the washing got behind. Over his choice of underwear she knew his mind intimately. Here she was, guardian of useless secrets. The tabloids, the television – intimate secrets made the world go round. They sold papers and made people famous. Here, in marriage's estate, such copy was cheap.

What a privilege it ought to be to live beside another. To look, with the same curiosity as we watch the workings of a pride of lions, or the career of a termite colony, at the peculiar otherness of another person. To see the given which we accept is life, moulded as if by another hand. To see the prosaic sock drawer subject to the guiding choices of another set of hopes and fears. Wasn't this art enough? What the hell did she want? Didn't marriage have that precise quality that defined great art – the eternal encapsulated in the parochial; the poetry in the prosaic?

She didn't need to internalise the drama of her life, to live within her own head; she needed no inner alcove on the stairs because marriage was precisely that theatre of demands, claims and counterclaims. Here was the true drama of inconsequentialities, played out in camera, before the invited audience of their younger selves, mountaineer and pianist. *Marriage* was the alcove, lit by rainy light. Still life. And it ought to be good.

She *must* get dressed.

It wasn't a still life if one of the objects in the picture got up and went to Birmingham. If you got up and went to the Midlands you had effectively died. Yes, it was clear now, looking at the chest of drawers, that it was nothing but the effects of the dead. The aftershave would never now be tried. He had died before taking the chance. And the socks within were laid out so as to make the job of boxing up the deceased's possession easier for the survivors. The childless widow. They say that is when the hearts breaks – not looking at the unresponsive face of the dead, but at the post-mortem disarray of the objects they leave behind them.

He had always dressed it up as doing his bit on the domestic front. 'Leave it to me, washerwoman,' he liked to say, before taking the basket out of her hands and putting his things away. He was able to call her washerwoman because actually he did a lot in the house. He liked to tease her with a chauvinistic alter ego. She teased him gently with his neatness. She was grateful for it really. But now she knew it was just a preparation for death. A putting of things in order. Subtle of him. If the train left the rails that evening and he were killed she would have little to do. And the neatness might still leave her unmoved, there being not enough personality in a well-ordered sock drawer. A dirty one on the bathroom floor might cause her to break down. She'd find something to cause her to lose her mind. She couldn't even smell the HOMME and be reminded of him. Best just to assume he was long gone and that he would be sorely missed. Had he ever existed, though? He had been gone so long. She wouldn't remarry.

She threw back the duvet, dousing herself in cold air. She'd tear her knees from her chest and dry what tears came. Wake up, Catch. Wake up, washerwoman. He's dead the man you loved. He never lived.

She took the white nightdress in the fingers of either hand and lifted it over her head. Why should *she* be shrouded when her skin was so warm? *She* was alive. Someone had to live longer. She stretched. Her knuckles grazed the low ceiling. Her breath came in clouds. The nightdress crumpled at her feet like an ineffectual opponent. She stepped away from it.

Of course, of course. There is only nakedness. Every morning, if only fleetingly, there is the same reminder. You might have married another, you might have worn perfume; and if you wait, naked, another life might come to you. Not only a different erotic career, but an actual calling. Our body's calling. This is what she felt, every time she stood naked in the room. That with no clothes she would begin life over again. It wouldn't be a rehearsal this time.

Now she caught sight of herself in the mirror. There she was. There am I, she thought mechanically. Winter white; dark pubic hair. Tobias had asked her once to shave it off. She had not wanted to. Some of it. No, she had not wanted to. Did she not want to do anything novel? he had keened, allegedly ashamed of his desire for novelty. Why, she had said, were *her* wants called conservative and *his* adventurous? What could be adventurous about doing what you did not want to do? It wasn't as if she didn't want sex. You *say* that, Tobias had muttered, loud enough for her to hear.

She had never quite come to terms with the effect she had on Tobias. Or at least on the effect he constantly told her she had on him. Her body meant little to her, she thought, compared to what it seemed to mean to him. He had eulogised areas of it she was but dimly aware of – the backs of her knees, the base of her shoulder blades; he might have been a trainee medic he seemed so thorough. For someone as naturally unprovocative as Catharine it was strange to see him so provoked and be able to do nothing, except the obvious, to stop it. And for a while she found the most visible sign of this alleged provocation – his erection – dismaying. Something that happened because of her, but had nothing to do with her. Catharine sensed that Maria regarded the erect penises of her lovers as joint property – something that, like a bottle of wine, was taken jointly to bed and with which fun was to be had. Much as she enjoyed the effect it had once inside her, for Catharine, in the cold, student bedsit air, exposed, it seemed like the wrong prop in an amateur dramatic production, not fit for purpose. So she pulled Tobias to her and got on with it. She had loved his closeness. Why had he always wanted to be considering her from a distance, watching her? Chill out, chill out, he had always said, before *passing* out.

Naked before the mirror, this morning, she lifted her hair and tied it roughly up; the cold kissed her nape.

She dressed.

Downstairs the phone was ringing, like an alarm going off.

Standing, dressed, in the freezing living room. The phone was on the windowsill opposite the piano. She found it and took it to the centre of the room to talk. She was dressed in a woollen, tartan skirt and a soft jumper her friend Maria had given her years before. No make-up; no jewellery. Still no shoes. As she answered the phone she stalked a pair of slippers by the sofa till she faced the right way to slip her feet inside.

'Catharine?'

'Yes.'

'Valerie.'

'I'm so sorry. Who?'

'Valerie.'

'I'm afraid you might have a wrong number, but you know my name, so it seems unlikely. But I don't think I know a Valerie.'

'Valerie Mountjoy, Catharine.'

'Oh. I'm . . . oh, I'm sorry. I don't think you ever told me your Christian name. Your first name. How are you?'

'I thought you would have known it. Never mind. I'm fine thank you. Now, are you busy today?'

'Fairly. Do you need help with the flowers?'

'The flowers?'

'In church.'

'I wonder if you'd be so kind as to do something for me.'

'Of course.'

'I've been speaking to David.'

'David?'

'Dear me, you don't know anyone, do you? Our vicar.'

'Oh, yes. I know David.'

'I have my daughter staying with me at the moment. Have you met my daughter?'

'No.'

'She's staying with me at the moment, and I've been speaking to David, and frankly I'm beside myself.'

'Oh dear.'

'You studied history of art at university, I believe.'

'No.'

'What?'

'I studied modern languages.'

'What? That's not what David told me. David, our vicar. He's spoken to you. He told me you studied history of art at university. Manchester University.'

'I studied modern languages at Manchester University.'

'I'm beside myself.'

'Valerie. What's the matter?'

'I want you to speak to her. My daughter. She has come home for the week and she's saying she wants to study history of art at university. She's in the sixth form now, you understand. History of art. Her father will have provoked her. And

I know she is partly saying it to provoke me. I know it. Can you imagine? I just thought that if you had studied it, and David swore blind that you had, you could have had a word with her.'

'To dissuade her?'

'Of course to dissuade her.'

'But if I'd studied it, I might think it was a good thing to study.'

'In this economic climate? Are you mad? Anyway, you didn't study it, so it's irrelevant. Don't paint me as a philistine, Catharine, thank you very much. You know that's not what I'm saying, perfectly well. Presumably you knew people at your university that studied it?'

'Umm . . .'

'Of course you did.'

'I can see that job opportunities in that area might be limited.'

'Thank you, that's all I was saying. Look, you were a student. If you remember, that was a luxury that passed me by. You haven't children, Catharine. You don't know how difficult it is to say the right thing to a teenager. I can't advise her. Anything I say is wrong. Would you be a dear and just come over and talk to her and give her an idea of her options? It would only be half an hour of your time. You'd be doing a good deed.'

'Of course. But it's a long time since I was a student myself.'

'I'm sure these things don't really change.'

'Sure. I'm just warning you I'm no expert.'

'You think I am? It's her father. He knows the effect this will be having on me. He knows perfectly bloody well. This is his way of reminding me who pays the school fees.'

'What time would suit you?'

'Now. I think I heard her stirring. I'll put the kettle on. I'll expect you. You know where I live. Goodbye.'

Extremely annoying and extremely desirable, this peremptory summons. It was flattering and rude to be taken so for granted. It was as she imagined doctors feel when the appeal comes through from the theatre manager – 'Is there a doctor in the house?' A sense that there was no end to the real vocations; you were always answerable. The woman's arrogance and self-centredness were inflammatory but made Catharine's trip to the lane by the church all the more essential. Here was a girl who had had to endure Valerie Mountjoy as her mother, and who had, out of the wilderness years of rural teendom and the institutional vulgarity of boarding school, hatched a redeeming dream to study the fine arts. It showed some pluck. And in the face of the objections of small-minded philistinism and the Church of England, Catharine was on hand to cry, 'Objection!' herself. Sooner than she could have imagined, her moment in court had come.

It was a time in life – the teenage years – with which she felt a particular affinity. She had lived slightly in the shadow of the intensity of her own, and she remembered the seriousness with which one took oneself, the crippling self-consciousness, so vividly, that the thought of another girl enduring it made her heart beat fast with compassion and pity. There had been art galleries for Catch, too. Before she was Catch. Trips to the Tate with school. Once, daringly, alone. Handsome Burne-Jones knights and the impossible glamour of Rossetti women. The Walkman years of feeling you were in a film with a perfect soundtrack of your own devising. Painting, almost more than music, because it was out there on the wall rather than in her own head, was daringly sensuous.

So Catharine knew it all. And this morning, during which she felt she knew precisely nothing, was suddenly a preliminary to the devastating truth that she must get off her hands – that she knew all too well what it was to be young, and that she who had no youth, no child to nurture, could at least respond to the heartfelt cry from a young woman who might be the reincarnation of her own girlish self. When she met Maria she would be able, for once, to look her in the eye and think that she had done something creative of her own – she had made the imaginative leap into the mind of a seventeen-year-old, and she had attempted a rescue. She was useful. Suddenly the rainy day was blooming at the windows. Polished by the rain. Clean.

Miss Mountjoy. It seemed, with the prefix Miss, as eighteenth-century Jane Austen as the Mrs was twentieth-century suburbia, and created in Catharine a delicious tension. Suddenly she was like a second chance; she gave Catharine the opportunity to look back over the morning and regard the thoughts, the stasis of her relationship with the piano, with the house, as the natural staging posts of consciousness that would see her fully wake now under the dutiful call to this girl's defence. Each indecisive moment, each failure to get dressed was a battle stripe, to be worn proudly, as evidence that true callings came with the administration of charity, not introspection, and that the virtue of her cause was all the greater in that it had come from a soul-searched morning. She could forgive the hesitation when the execution was pure. Miss Mountjoy was not only a second chance at the morning – she was talismanic youth; she was a second chance at life. Already Catharine loved her.

She knew perfectly well that she must be careful. To go to the young in the guise of adviser or counsellor was to court disdain and ridicule. To step towards them was to invite a step back. And even if you did a great job you would never be thanked for it. Not directly. All you could do was be there, be yourself, be honest, be compassionate, and credit the young person with individuality. Then leave. If you were lucky the teenage psyche would take from the meeting what it required; probably without even knowing it. Some imperceptible movement towards self-knowledge and a greater trust in the world and in their right to impose upon it – that was the most you could hope for; and the results might not show themselves for a long time. They were savage years, the teens, however much they might be gilded by memory in middle age.

But Catch didn't hesitate. When she thought of what the Mountjoy girl must have to contend with coming home at weekends and holidays – church with the mother and careers advice from Vicar David – she shuddered. What was their problem? They ought to have been glad she wasn't snorting cocaine and getting tattooed. Surely a young woman of limited means was permitted to go to university and study art history without some Hardyesque villager mumbling over his cider, 'That there Mountjoy girl's got ideas above 'er station.' Wasn't she? She didn't have to conform to type and find a decent chap to marry. It's the twenty-first century, for Christ's sake. Economic conditions notwithstanding. The days of elite universities catering for dilettante subjects on the one hand and polytechnics for the grateful underclass on the other were over.

Now there was a gorgeous raft of unpretentious new universities offering a guilt-free liberal education. Capitalism sorted you out a job at the end of it. What did it matter if your thesis on Caravaggio left you managing museum internet sites or designing old master mouse mats? You still got your term in Florence. Your secret soul held hands with beauty for a while. And the Mountjoy *mère* and Reverend David weren't going to stop it.

Catharine went to the cupboard under the stairs and took out her raincoat. It was a long scruffy thing she'd bought in a charity shop in York a year before she met Tom. A period in which she had tried the limits of eccentricity, and on a whim had decided to buy clothes only from charity shops. This was her only acquisition. But whenever she put it on she remembered the sense of self-invention and freedom in an unknown city; the tolling of the Minster bell; the assumption of a costume. It was like a magician's coat she thought, privately. Tom said, 'Come on, Catch, you scruff,' whenever she put it on, and she tripped after him, imaginary book of spells in hand. Going to see the Mountjoy girl in it gave her confidence; her instinct told her that to be too conventional was not what the girl would need.

Gathering the collar round her throat she stepped out into the weather; the front door slammed behind her, dismissing domesticity. A spot or two of rain pricked her cheek and she was glad – it made the donning of the magic raincoat more than just the vanity of an aspiring magician. It was necessary, or else she would get wet.

Above her, the tall, naked boughs swayed like drunken dancers; broken branches that had come down in the night lay in the potholed lane. She set off. Though she had put on wellingtons, she still dodged the puddles conscientiously. Catharine felt the pull of an outdoor life; she thought of allotments and playing fields – places where you must still be outdoors, even in bad weather. She loved the absence of choice.

Turning left, she skirted the pavementless verge; then, after a hundred yards, the road dropped and a raised path took the pedestrian on a walk above the traffic till it rejoined the road and dropped down to the post office. On this path, aloof from the traffic, were the few smart houses in the village, one of which, a tidy Georgian house, was owned by Graham, Catharine's only other acquaintance in the village, a retired army officer. There was no sign of him this morning, and in a few minutes she found herself in front of the Mountjoy cottage, in sight of the battlements and the carved, warlike saints of the church.

The mother opened the door with a very particular expression already in place. It signalled worry; it warned the caller that behind her, in the depths of the house, was that about which one should be extremely concerned; something which needed immediate treatment. It said, 'The outdoor world from which you come is all very well, but I have that within which is threatening the very heart and hearth of life.' So she would have met the gas man come to see an exploded boiler, or a pest-control agent to see to a trapped rat. So she greeted Catharine, come to minister to a child bent on art history as her wrecking ball to middle-class aspirations.

'It's terribly good of you to come, Catharine, dear.'

Having virtually genuflected before this display of neigh-bourly solidarity, Valerie now stepped back to admit her visitor.

It was a disarmingly gentle welcome, and Catharine had a momentary misgiving.

'I'm not entirely sure I can be of any help,' she said.

'Someone to listen, my dear. Yes? To listen. It's all any of us can do for the young, isn't it?'

'And not to be too harsh.'

Mrs Mountjoy grimaced at the obviousness of this remark and looked at Catharine with distrust. As if she already doubted the wisdom of having come to her for help.

'I've never been harsh,' said the mother, turning from her guest and marching to the kitchen. 'Not as harsh as mine were to me.'

'Your aunt?'

'I had a place at the Central School of Speech and Drama. Did I tell you that?'

'Yes.'

'I had talent, but she wouldn't let me go. I begged her. Begged and wept till she thought she had a lunatic on her hands. But it was no good. She was intractable.'

'Yes.'

'Quite intransigent.'

'But if that was the case . . .' She risked taking a seat without being offered one 'then,' went on Catharine, 'if you wanted something so badly and your aunt stood in your way, why is it that you object to . . . to . . . what is your daughter's name? I don't think you told me.'

'Angelica.'

'To Angelica following her star.'

'Her star?'

'It's an expression.'

'It's a nonsensical expression. Coffee?'

'Tea, please. If you have it.'

'Of course I have it.' Valerie placed the kettle on the Aga, then went into the hall. 'Angelica! There's someone here to see you.'

There was silence upstairs.

'You didn't tell her I was coming?'

'No. You just popped in, all right? Just popped in. People do call on one another in this village. We got to talking about university. Do you have a problem with that? Do you want to help?'

'Of course. But if you want me to be of any help, you're going to have to tell me a little bit more about your daughter. It seems odd to me that you thought I did art history myself and yet want me to dissuade *her* from doing it. I mean, I might be offended.'

'Are you?'

'Offended? No, but . . .'

'Well, then. You know what I'm talking about. I know what you think of me. That I'm some sort of village battleaxe who doesn't understand her daughter. Well, if you want to see it like that then that's your affair. Nothing to do with me. Her father left when she was two. I did it all on my own. Do you understand? On my own. Wouldn't pay maintenance. Had to get the courts onto him, though he was riding about in a new car every other week. Wanted nothing to do with her. I was on my own. No one to be a father to her, no one to be a man. David's tried to give her the odd word of wisdom, but I ask you. He's hardly the man to be a father to her. He's a bloody waste of space, if truth be told. A good enough vicar, but a waste of space. Then suddenly she's thirteen and her father wants to pay for her to go to a smart boarding school. What was I to do? I wanted what was best for her. I wasn't going to stand in her way if she wanted to go. Not out of spite. Or pride. She said she wanted it so she went. Look, if you don't want to help, Catharine, we'll say no more about it. No hard feelings, all right? But your husband's at work, you've no children of your own . . . I mean, what have you got to do with your day? Forgive me. I'm at the end of my tether. Milk? Sugar? As it comes?'

'Yes. Thank you.'

'Which?!'

'As it comes. But I still don't understand. If she's gone to a good school . . . a good arts degree can be a route to many lucrative jobs. What's your objection to Angelica studying history of art?'

'My objection is that she's a bloody fool! Ah, here she is.'

In the doorway was a seventeen-year-old girl. She had a pale face and prominent cheekbones, but her mouth seemed to rest above little support from her chin. Her eyes, similarly, protruded slightly; her hair, which was greasy and dark, was pulled back tightly off her face by an elastic band and the forehead showed the stipple of blackheads, and to the side, there was the subterranean activity of acne, like a cold front's approach on a weather map. She wore a white T-shirt that nevertheless was not as white as she; a faded logo on the front was too washed out to be read. The minute she entered the room she looked down at the floor, as if she and it were equally trodden upon.

This sight had a strange effect on the mother. She went instantly to work, arranging chairs, biscuits on a plate for Catharine, tea towels primped and refolded and ranged along the Aga rail. It was as if she was maintaining her sanity in the face of this apparition which, if she had stopped and stared at it, would have driven her mad.

'Catharine, Angelica, Angelica, Catharine,' she said, like a hurried catechism.

'Hello, Angelica,' said Catharine, hearing her own soothing voice and being aware of the great difference between her affected gentleness and the repugnance she felt; and as soon as she was aware of that difference all her repugnance turned to pity.

The girl just drifted, as if pulled along by invisible threads, her legs on castors, to the sink, where she took a mug from the draining beard, washed it half-heartedly, and put a tea bag in it.

'Surely you can say hello,' the mother said, barely disguising the shriek in her voice.

'All right?' said Angelica.

Catharine found it strange to be looking at this girl who had no notion that it was on her account she was here. It gave the meeting the quality of a psychological evaluation; Catch couldn't help feeling that if she blew a whistle some men might come and lead Angelica to a van outside and then to a safe house where she could do no harm. And she knew she felt that because she guessed that that was exactly what Valerie Mountjoy wanted to happen. Her pity for the teenager deepened.

'I don't think we've been introduced, have we, Angelica?' said Catch. 'Your mum was the first person I met when I moved to the village. Oh, about five months ago, now. I'd been a bit rubbish making friends, but your mum made me a cup of tea. I was looking to do the flowers in church, but I reckon she's guarding the monopoly on that. Thought I'd come back and have another go. Are you in the sixth form, now?'

'Yeah.'

'That's right. Your mum said you were going over choices about university courses.'

'Yeah. I'm gonna do art history.'

'I did languages.'

'David told me you did history of art,' said Valerie. 'He swore blind.'

'Well, he was wrong. But I knew people who did the course. And I used to go to some of their lectures. Funnily enough.'

'Tell her what it entails,' said the mother. 'Tell her!'

'Well, I could tell you a bit about it. Valerie, why don't you leave us to it for a while? What do you say, Angelica? Will you talk to me? I know you've only just got up, but I'd love a cup of tea and a biscuit. I don't bite. When I applied to university I would have loved someone just to talk to me about it, but no one ever did. They all seem to think you know what you're doing.'

'Oh, she knows what she's doing, all right,' said the mother.

'I'm sure she does,' said Catharine. 'What do you say?'

She looked brightly at the girl.

'Whatever,' said Angelica, but not unfriendlily.

'It's all right, Valerie,' said Catharine. 'Go on. Your lovely Jack Russell must need a run.'

'Are you sure?' said Valerie.

'Absolutely. Go on. I've got these biscuits. I've got all I could possibly need.'

But Valerie was wavering, as if she had set something in motion she now wished she could undo.

'I could pop to the post office and pick up my newspaper,' she said, half-heartedly.

Then, just as she had sprung into action on Angelica's entrance, some sort of shock went through her again, and she was all activity, finding the dog lead, putting on her coat; as if busyness could eradicate the horror of her daughter's morning apathy. Soon she was gone.

Angelica was still at the kitchen sink, her arms pressed straight down on the draining board as if they were preventing her from collapsing. Now the mother was absent, Catharine felt with a shock the closeness of this other person, and realised that the imaginative leap into the mind of this teenager, which she had felt so sure she could accomplish, was impossible. Or, rather, she could do it – to see Angelica was to know exactly all her misery, all her prickly self-consciousness – but she could not sympathise with it. To have played the part, as it were, would have required the destruction of one's own self to a traumatic degree. All that life had offered in terms of adult solace would have had to be torn up, allowing the horrible nakedness of inexperience to assert its primacy. That was what teenagerdom was, it seemed to Catch. It was beyond her. It was false and middle class and vain to think you could do it. You had to be an adult. In the end there was no choice. Empathy got you nowhere. She could see the source of the hysterical self-control Valerie Mountjoy had to exert to prevent her assaulting her own child. Angelica's unresponsive back, with the shoulder blades showing through the T-shirt sharp and model-like; the skin that was bad, but with a cleansing regime need not have been *that* bad.

Catharine struggled to be conscious, to keep her head.

Was not this exactly the kind of hopeless response that adults always had, and which she been wise enough to guard herself against when she was on her way here? She had said to herself that she wasn't here to take any personal satisfaction away with her. That she was here to help the thankless. If you baulked, you showed up the fact that you were as lost in your middle age as they were in their teens; that could not be so. She would not allow it. Youth deserved counsel. Ignore the unwashed face, the blackheads, the pallid, vacant listlessness. Every child, in truth, was an ugly duckling. Every one.

'Angelica,' she said, to break the silence.

'What's this about then?'

'What's what?'

'You, calling in. To have a chat. You really a friend of my mum's?'

'I told you.'

'Yeah, right.'

'Why is that so hard to believe?'

'She's never mentioned you before. And I've never seen you before. So what's it all about?'

'I don't really know.'

'Eh?'

'I said I don't really know.'

'Hmm. Do you know David?'

'Yes. The vicar.'

'You a friend of his?'

'I've met him. I wouldn't say I was a friend.'

The girl had turned now, and had her back to the kitchen side, like a boxer against the ropes, waiting to see what Catharine could throw at her.

'What did she tell you?'

'Only that you wanted to study art history.'

'What a fucking crime.'

'Absolutely. I was a bit surprised myself that she was so adamantly opposed to it. I think because I went to university she just thought it might be a good idea to talk it over. It's not so crazy, Angelica. I don't know you, do I? You really don't have to talk to me if you don't want to.'

'Normally she gets me to talk to David.'

'Right.'

'What's wrong with that?'

'Nothing. It was you who seemed to suggest there was something wrong with that.'

'He's a prick.'

'Right. I'm never too sure about vicars myself.'

'Don't you believe in God?'

'Umm, no,' said Catharine, frowning.

'Did she tell you I tried to kill myself last term?'

'No. Did you?'

'Yes.'

'What did you do?'

'Pills. And vodka.'

'Why did you try to kill yourself?'

'Because I wanted to die. Is there another reason?'

'There are lots of reasons people try to do that. Sometimes they want to die. Sometimes they just don't want to live. Sometimes . . .'

'Expert, aren't you? You ever tried it?'

'No.'

'Thought of trying again this morning.'

'Did you?'

'Yes. In fact, you don't even know I haven't already taken them, do you? I might have taken a whole couple of bottles and come down here for some tea to keep them down.'

'You might.'

'And here's you going on about the fact there's no God. What would Mum say about that?'

'I don't know. When she gets back we'll have to ask her. If you're still alive, that is.'

'Funny, aren't you?'

'Why do you want to do history of art?'

'What's it to you? Why do *you* care?'

'I don't, especially. I told you. You don't have to talk to me.'

'If I had taken the pills and only had a few minutes left to live, I could try and convert you to God. Come to think of it, it might be the greatest moment of my life. And you'd have to believe me, because I was dying. If I said I saw the Kingdom of Heaven waiting to receive me, you'd have to believe me.'

'Why would I have to?'

'Does Mum know you don't believe in God?'

'No, I don't suppose she does.'

'"Don't suppose." You're posh, aren't you?'

'Not really.'

'They're all posh at my school.'

'Come on. Why do you want to do history of art? It's the rest of your life, Angelica. It's interesting. You're an interesting girl who is about to make a choice that will determine all sorts of things about the way your life will go. It's got to be worth a chat over a cup of tea, hasn't it? Why do you want to do it?'

'I don't *want* to do it. I'm *going* to do it. And you're not going to stop me.'

'I don't want to stop you. Though, presumably, your mother could refuse to pay your fees.'

Angelica smiled.

'I see,' said Catharine. 'Your father is offering to pay.'

'Learning fast, aren't you?'

'And he is particularly keen because he knows how much it is going to annoy your mother.'

'He won't stand in my way.'

There was silence.

'It's not worth it,' said Catharine.

'What's not?'

'Choosing a subject of study just to annoy your mother. This choice is about you, not them. It will still be about your life when both of them are dead and buried. If you really want to rebel, choose something you really want to do. You. You know?'

'How do you know I don't want to do it?'

'I don't. But it's my guess that you don't want it that much. And doing a subject like that, if you don't really love it . . . well, it's a bit of a waste of time. I think you'd be bored. Really bored. Some things just aren't worth doing unless you want them more than anything. Have you ever been to an art gallery?'

'Lots of times.'

'Angelica? Really?'

'What? You think art galleries are just for posh people like you?'

'Far from it. Have you ever been?'

'They don't let me go *anywhere*.'

'Let me tell you something. I wanted to be a musician. I listened to music all the time. It's what I loved. But I wasn't good enough. I tried to tell myself the only reason I wasn't good enough was because I was too lazy. But the fact is I just wasn't good enough. It's taken me years to admit that to myself.'

'Don't get the connection.'

'What I mean to say is that loving something isn't enough. You have to be good at it to succeed. But if you don't even love it – what chance have you got of being happy? You think there's nothing out there that you really want to do. Well, I bet there is. You think it's all out of your hands, and all you can think of is annoying your mum. Well, I say again, it's not worth it. Break with the past and find something you want to do. You won't regret it.'

There was a long pause.

'You like pictures, do you?' said Angelica.

'Pardon?'

'Paintings. You go to art galleries and stuff?'

'Yes. Sometimes.'

'What do you like about them?'

'I like paintings. I like all the arts.'

'Why?'

'Goodness, that's a big question.'

'You're the one who reckons you know all about it.'

Catharine suddenly felt the spotlight on her, in a way that the careers rhetoric had inured her to. Though she was talking to a teenager, she suddenly felt on the spot; as if Angelica might have been an undercover arts correspondent. She suddenly had to answer for her own sensibility.

'Angelica, I don't know anything about anything. I like to look at pictures, yes. Which means . . . well, let's see . . . that I must like to look at things . . . intently. I admire the skill of someone who has put life out there, for all to see. If you look at a Rembrandt portrait, for example, you can see all sorts of life – the inner life, the social life, the artistic life – all mixed up, with all its contradictions, in just one face. For example. Lots of life is about contradictions,' she added thoughtfully.

'Sounds like a right fucking gas.'

Angelica was looking at Catharine triumphantly. Catch laughed.

'Well, there you are. History of art probably isn't for you.'

'Ha bloody ha.'

'What's the matter?'

'I don't know. I just get pissed off when people start sounding clever.'

'Why?' said Catharine.

'Because it sounds like showing off.'

'Really? And swearing and trying it on with grown-ups and winding people up about something as stupid as what degree you're going to take isn't showing off? Excuse me, Angelica, but you can fuck off too.'

'Wow.'

'I came to try and help you. But I can walk out of here without a backward glance. Trust me. Thanks for the tea.'

'Can't you take a joke?'

'Probably not. I'm famous for my lack of a sense of humour.'

Her own seriousness surprised Catharine; she was amazed she could dismiss this girl who an hour before she had been sure she wanted to rescue. She felt a slight heaviness about her limbs and a novel, but somehow familiar jerkiness to her movements; then she realised that in her dismissal of the girl and the flushed emotion that went with it, half angry and half unexpressed, she was being just like her own mother. Her body had been hijacked.

'You don't have to go,' said Angelica, drawing her lower jaw down in a sort of gormless appeal to nothing in particular; the gargoyle face designed to dismiss the gargoyle manners.

But Catharine had screwed up her face, too, and was looking at the rain, which had started again outside.

'What you're saying,' said Angelica slowly, 'is . . .'

'I'm not saying anything. You have to find your own way, all right? Look . . . what do you like to do? Come on. What? Do you have any hobbies?'

The girl shrugged up her shoulders till they were like a scarf round her neck, and then let them go with exaggerated despair.

'What?' persisted Catharine.

'Draw.'

'What?'

'Draw pictures.'

'Seriously. Tell me, for example. What are you best at, at school? What is your best subject?'

'Art.'

Catch looked at her. It was nearly too much. She wanted to lean over and cuff the recalcitrant, greasy-headed girl. But before she could have done, with the first display of motivation since she had entered it, the girl left the room. It was arresting, this sudden movement, and Catharine sensed something was up. Not only did she begin to wonder if she had completely misrepresented the girl to herself, but she felt the stirring of hope, of a romantic excitement about what Angelica might be about to show her. This girl did have some fire — enough, at least, to go upstairs and do something as brave as show Catharine her drawings; unless she had merely gone upstairs to swallow another bottle of sleeping pills. There was a rumpus in the distance; the girl was rifling and fetching, claiming something from the detritus of her life.

It occurred to Catharine that the inherent philistinism of Angelica's background might be responsible for two possible outcomes, the second of which she had overlooked. The first, obvious one, was that she was unappreciated by Valerie Mountjoy, and given scant cultural signposts with which to navigate through an elitist education. But the second, more radical one, was that she was, in fact, gifted, and had a spark of something real enough not to be eradicated by parental negligence.

There was a stumbling trickle of teenage steps down the stairs — something between falling and dancing — and Angelica appeared with a portfolio. She was brisk and quick in clearing a space between the tea and biscuits on the table; deft at unclipping the leather front with her stubby fingers, their nails bitten to the quick. Catharine's heart beat faster. She didn't expect much; just a flash of commitment, of engagement was the most she hoped for; a talent that might be worth working on and encouraging. Something feminine, something graceful; something to show for the term's work besides a suicide attempt. The hands worked confidently, all the apathy dissolved; it was an extraordinary transformation. Catharine felt completely humbled by the young woman, as if she had been shown who was really the boss.

Angelica opened the portfolio and carefully detached three drawings from the pile and laid each one out on the pine table.

She laid them there with the same incongruous care the roughest girl from the roughest quarter of town might lay her baby down, softening all.

What it is to have this, Catharine said to herself, this manner with the world that comes with expression – the sketchbooks and the flower arranging, the piano practice and the jigsaws; the fact that the world is not quite full enough of things but mankind must go tampering and adding. She succumbed to this thought; it felt like wisdom. She felt infinitely forgiving of people when she saw how they saved their best for an attempt to render the world. She knew that whatever Angelica had done was the best of her. The care with which she held the edges of the luxurious artist's paper, just a corner between her fingers, showed that this was so. As if she did not wish to relinquish it wholly. How wrong she had been to judge the girl; to be harsh.

She looked at the first drawing.

But she was confounded a second time. As her hope had risen when the girl prepared the viewing, so it sank now, irretrievably. The first picture – a still-life exercise – was a conflation of every technique Angelica had been taught, laboured over here to terrible effect. The subject – a wine bottle, newspaper and car keys – had begun as a minute, detailed study, with fine shading and a microscopic attention to detail; but when it became clear that she had misjudged the headline of the paper so that the last letters would have to be twice as narrow as the first, she gave up on the literal presentation and with some heavy smudging veered into impressionistic smog. Then she had reworked the entire picture as if this had been her intention all along, so over the minute shading were heavy black lines outlining the forms, all having been added last in an attempt to give the thing coherence. The second picture, a nude, lacked everything a picture could lack apart from obviousness. The third she did not look at.

'Angelica,' said Catharine.

'Yes. What do you think?'

'Did you really enjoy doing these? Honestly?'

'I don't give a fuck if you don't like them.'

'I didn't say I didn't like them. I'm asking you if you enjoyed doing them. You're right not to care whether I like them or not. Do *you*?'

'What?'

'Like them.'

The girl shrugged her shoulders.

'They made me do them.'

'What?'

'The teachers.'

'But you ran upstairs to get them as if you were proud of them.'

'I did them, didn't I?'

'Yes. And you have been very diligent in applying what they've taught you. But . . .'

At this point Catharine suddenly had a great misgiving that she should be there at all. Why was she carrying on with Angelica, applying her own judgements to the poor girl's efforts? Surely it was suspect. The mother had asked her over, but Catharine was under no obligation to knock the daughter into some kind of art-school shape. She was just making another hoop for the girl to jump through.

She sighed.

'You know what, Angelica? I think school's tough. And I

reckon you have a pretty tough time of it. As I say, try and find out what you really like doing. That's all I can say. Don't try to please people too much; don't try and fuck them off too much. Just find your own way.'

'By breaking with the past.'

'Sometimes. But, you see, you like to cultivate a reputation for being a rebel, as someone who doesn't even want to live, but . . . I would say looking at these pictures the problem is that you actually want to please. Don't you? Look at all this shading and then these flowing lines, just like you've been taught. You want to please people by showing that you've learnt your lessons. They've got you all wrong, haven't they?'

The girl was staring at her, very still; only her face's almost unnatural stillness betrayed the fact that emotion was perhaps worrying the surface of the pale skin, unseen.

'How do I break with the past?' she said again.

'Oh, I shouldn't have used that expression. All I mean is that needing to please is hard, especially when it seems that the only way you can please them is by not trying to kill yourself, or not doing a history of art degree. You need something positive to do rather than just pleasing negatively, don't you? Do you understand?'

'I think so.'

'I think that will come. Something that is just you. Just for you. We all need some respite from being in our own heads too much.'

'How do *you* do it?'

'Me?'

The question was unexpected. Catharine had trusted to the egoism of youth that she herself would go unchallenged. The sense of sudden equality between youth and age was alarming. Something in her wanted to say, 'Cheeky . . .' But she was appalled at this instinct; she wanted to believe that middle age had no great, special purchase on being young; she hated the pride of experience and the condescension of adults; she knew that teenage experience was unique. So she wanted to be honest; and she also, herself, wanted to know how she, Catharine, did it. How *did* she survive?

She frowned and tried to look kindly at Angelica, whose bottom lip now lolled open, waiting for Catharine to speak.

'I'm just a boring middle-aged woman, Angelica. You can't learn anything from me. All I can tell you and I'm being quite honest with you, is that I, too, when I was your age, liked to look at pictures.'

'What sort of pictures?'

'Oh, all sorts. You see, the great thing about art galleries is that when you go from painting to painting, gallery to gallery, you realise how completely personal the different artists' ways of looking at the world are. There are pictures of great battles on canvases twenty feet across and tiny studies of everyday objects eight inches wide. Everybody finds their way, dear Angelica. Everybody.'

'Where did you go? What galleries?'

'London, mostly. But I went to the Louvre, in Paris, once. Huge place. All the pictures are different, and what's more, so are all the people looking at them. It's a celebration of difference.'

'I thought you were supposed to be telling me not to study it.'

'I don't think you really do want to study it, do you? You'll find something.'

The gulf between her and Angelica was, by now, making Catharine dizzy. She could hear the platitudes she was saying, could hear the slightly sing-song tone, and was powerless to stop herself. What was worse was that she meant everything she was saying. But the inability to bridge that gulf, and the sight of the wet, lolling bottom lip of the girl was making her feel faint.

Angelica looked down at the drawings on the table.

'I knew they weren't any good, really.'

'Trying is everything.'

'I knew it.'

And she took the still life and tore it neatly in half.

'Oh no,' said Catharine softly.

Then the same with the other two.

'That's better,' said Angelica. 'Breaking with the past,' she said, with finality. On the table were the shreds, like white shards.

Catharine tried to smile. Some justice had been done – it was incontrovertible. It was a relief to see the dreadful drawings disposed of; the pretension and obedience of the things destroyed. Catharine didn't want that to be true, but it was. But at the same time she desperately wanted the things to be whole again, and wished the act undone. She suddenly hated herself for her critical eye, and wanted to swear that she would live all the days of her life with poor paintings on her walls and the inartistic in her heart. Anything not to have to see the act of destruction. But it was too late.

'Would you recommend, like, any particular painters to start with?' said Angelica.

'Start with?'

'Yeah. Ones that you liked when you were my age.'

'I could.'

'I'd be really interested.'

'OK.'

'I'm off tomorrow, but I get back just before Christmas. Then I go to my dad's on Boxing Day.'

There was a pause. The young woman seemed fulsome now, almost social, now the drawings had been dispensed with.

'Will you come here again?' she said.

'If you would like me to. I'm only up the road. You could come to tea. I used to like the Pre-Raphaelites. And, as I said, Rembrandt. I don't know much about it, though, I warn you. I know more about music, and not much about that.'

'I don't care.'

'Well . . .'

There was a pause, suddenly lacking in tension, that seemed to leave both parties nonplussed.

'Where's your mum, do you think?'

'She'll have popped into David's and be wittering on. She can't bear him, but she's in there most days.'

'I should go.'

Angelica's lower lip closed briefly in acceptance and Catharine stood. She put on her coat.

'I like your coat,' said Angelica.

Catharine frowned. As if she was worried that the girl liked it. She was nervous of the thing's magical qualities, now. Then she saw herself, hostessless, to the door and let herself out, struggling, even when she was outside and walking the path back to the post office and the main road, for a suitable final remark to make to Angelica.

In the high trees that lined the path the rooks swung, as if swayed by bell ropes in the uncertain wind.

The whole meeting seemed farcical to her now. I mean, what a thing to be asked to do. Counsel a teenager on what she should do with her life. A girl you'd never met, and would doubtless never meet again, unless it be to see her years later and remember this day and your inability to put into words how the years will go by so quickly. By which time they will, indeed, have gone by so quickly.

It was clear the girl should, under no circumstances, study art history, and that Valerie Mountjoy, whatever her faults, had been right to be wary. Angelica's father obviously egged on his uncertain daughter, and she was a pawn in an emotional game between him and the mother she probably only half understood. Nevertheless it had been heartbreaking to see the girl unpack her drawings like a bank robber laying out sheaves of fifty-pound notes.

What was this artistic endeavour, this creative folly that gave pleasure to no one, not even the girl who painstakingly adhered to what she was taught and produced nothing of the slightest worth? It enraged Catharine. She hated the assumed importance of it. Why the hell did schools go about dallying with the creative arts, when they produced nothing but mediocrity and gave the children concerned just enough awareness of what they were about to realise that they *were* mediocre. Absurd, liberal vanity. Suddenly Catharine loathed all the arts with a vehemence that amazed her. Loathed the insistence that everybody have a go; that 'self-expression' was good for you; that everybody could do it. Everyone sing, everyone draw, everyone cook. Loathsome lie. Not only could they not, but once everyone tried their arm the results were so dismaying they made you doubt the point of masterpieces. After all, a drawing by Michelangelo and a drawing by Angelica were not essentially different. Only the little right-wing dictator in our heads called taste told us which was genius and which could go the way of critical genocide. That tyrant that told us what to love but not why we cared what we loved. Encourage all, and ultimately you must condemn all.

But what were the repercussions of this, then? What, Catch – could you question the legitimacy of something if just one instance of it failed? Could you ditch art wholesale because Angelica couldn't draw a newspaper, bottle and car keys? Marriage wasn't completely discredited every time someone got divorced, was it? Or was it? It was. We're all in this just to aspire to be the exception in a series of flawed archetypes. We all fall short of art – even if it's only our attempt to draw Mickey Mouse for our grandchildren – but we have Michelangelo to console us. OK, so what did you do with marriage? The same? Visit the Hendersons at number thirty-eight just to appreciate the elan, the deft juxtaposition of irony and affection, the sublimated passion, the chiaroscuro of wit and intensity in their breakfast badinage; my God, that's marriage, that's greatness. Genius.

The siren call had nearly got her. She'd wanted those drawings to be good. She'd heard Angelica rummaging upstairs as if she were going through the detritus of Catharine's heart, seeking out that part of teenage vision that still subsisted in her. Catch had sought a little artistic gem in that cottage. She was ready to celebrate an uncelebrated girl. Why? Because she herself, Catharine, felt uncelebrated? Because the pale, greasy-haired girl was going to realise the older woman's hopes?

Ah yes, of course. It was parenting, wasn't it? That was

what you did with children. That was how it worked. You coun-
selled the young not to make the same mistakes as you made
so that they could, actually, be like you. That crazy paradox.
You didn't absolutely care about their separateness, you just
pinned your hopes on them. Their failures, like the artist's
failure, we take personally. It's an affront. In this case Catharine
had seen both fail simultaneously – the child/artist not being
up to it. If she were to become a mother she would just be a
critic; that's all mothers were. So much the better that sperm
and egg had not conjoined beneath the eaves of their cottage
bedroom as she slumbered in Tom's affectionate embrace. Oh
well. Good to know the news now. She couldn't help children.
She was living a rehearsal still. Still only a girl. A strict head
girl, but a girl nevertheless. A girl-child, a failure of maturity,
an unrealised aspiration made thirty-something flesh. She had
nothing to offer this girl but platitudes and received wisdom
and the thought of her own unexpressed life. She, Catharine,
was worse than Valerie Mountjoy would ever be.

And above all—

'Good morning!'

She stopped on the path. She had passed the post office
deep in thought and was on the high footpath, a hundred yards
from home. The voice had come from nowhere.

'Are you blind, woman?'

The voice came from behind the yew hedge.

'Up here.'

She looked up. On a stepladder, looking down at her, was
Graham.

'I'm thinking of becoming a highwayman,' he said.

'Well, you'd make a very good one. You scared the living
daylights out of me.'

'Weren't you looking thoughtful.'

'What on earth are you doing?'

'What the fuck do you think I'm doing, woman? I'm trimming the hedge.'

'In December?'

'It's an evergreen. Yew. It doesn't care. Don't kick the trimmings into the street or I'll have to sweep them up.'

'It's all biodegradable.'

'I don't give a fuck about that. I just don't want a mess.'

'Graham, you'll freeze. It's December.'

'I've got red blood in these veins.'

'Red blood and whisky.'

'Cheeky cow. How are you?'

'Are you going to stay up there? I'm getting a crick in my neck.'

'I'll come down.'

The man descended. He was dressed in a tweed jacket and had a red spotted handkerchief showing in the top pocket. He had bushy eyebrows and healthy skin, a carefully shaved face and his thick white hair combed back off his forehead; pale blue eyes and a brisk manner. He was in his late sixties.

'Well,' he said, coming through his garden gate and mock-confronting her on the path. 'What have you got to look so serious about?'

'Oh, I'm all right. Well . . .'

'What?'

'I'm cross with myself, to tell you the truth.'

'About what?'

'About too much to put in a few words. Don't mind me.'

'Oh, but I do. I do. Come on, woman, come in for coffee.'

'No, I can't. Really.'

'Why not? It's not Valerie Mountjoy, is it?'

'How do you know?'

'Saw you going that way earlier. Saw her going up to the vicarage twenty minutes later, looking determined. Determined woman, Valerie Mountjoy.'

'Have you been up there all morning?'

'Most of it.'

'Why didn't you shout down when you saw me pass?'

'Preferred to watch you, unseen.'

'Perhaps you *are* a highwayman.'

'Perhaps I am.'

'I still think you might have said good morning.'

'Spying is more fun. What else I am to do with my time?'

'Oh no, not self-pity.'

'It's all I've got. And my memories.'

'Oh Christ.'

'Come in for coffee.'

'No.'

'I'm lonely.'

'You're not lonely. You have two ex-wives and five children.'

'Ungrateful beggars all.'

'You can't complain.'

'I sleep alone.'

'A hefty army pension, a beautiful house and good health.'

'I sleep alone.'

'So you sleep alone. You're not even a widower. You left your wives, as I recall, Graham.'

'True.'

'Do you regret it?'

'Not for a second.'

'Well, there you are.'

'I think you may have a point. I think it's not so much that I'm lonely, but that I'm randy.'

'There could be some truth in that.'

'There could be. Look at you, trying not to be shocked.'

'It always takes far more than people think to shock me,' said Catharine.

'I don't doubt that for a second.'

'Go and get yourself a new wife if it means that much to you. I don't think you'd find it difficult.'

'But leaving her would look so bad.'

'How do you know you'd leave her?'

'I just do.'

'You might die before you got the chance.'

'I'm indestructible. No, I'd leave her, and my bastard children would look at me disapprovingly – the young are so ball-breakingly judgemental, don't you find? And they'd get all jumpy that I was going to do them out of their inheritance. Which, by the by, is far larger than they imagine. No, I'd leave her in weeks.'

'Why?'

'I never enjoy talking to women.'

'You seem to do all right with me.'

'Oh, you don't count.'

'Is that meant to be a compliment?'

'It can be whatever you fucking like. I like talking to you. When I look back over my marriages I just remember the silences. Just praying the thing would end or they'd die. You know? Holding your breath in the hope that they'll die.'

'Charming.'

'I thought about doing away with the first one. I mean, only technically. The ins and outs. 'Course I didn't have it in me.

Bloody difficult, even if you've been in the army, you know, actually to kill someone. Requires a suspension of your moral faculties.'

'You don't say.'

He laughed.

'These yews,' he went on, 'are nearly two hundred years old. Did you know that? Planted during the Regency. You're all right, anyway. You married a true gentleman.'

'You've barely met him.'

'I can tell. Your sort wouldn't marry a cad.'

'Aren't you a gentleman?'

'My dear, I've been called a few things in my time but gentleman is not one of them. An officer, yes. No gentleman.'

'Graham, I have to go.'

'Why?'

'I . . . I don't know.'

'You have no reason. It's obvious. What's the matter? The rain's holding off. Isn't it nice to stand in the lane and talk about murdering our spouses and the cruelty of our offspring? Except you don't have any of those, do you? Don't abandon me. What else is there to do with one's time?'

'I don't know.'

'Precisely. You're my muse. Don't abandon me to my hedge clippings. Even dirty old men have feelings.'

'Oh, Graham, you're not *old*.'

The retired army officer's cool blue eyes creased slightly and he laughed to himself.

'What did the Mountjoy want?' he said finally.

'She wanted me to talk to her daughter.'

'Crumbs. Not the mad girl? I didn't know she was back. And you agreed?'

'Why shouldn't I? And what do you mean, "the mad girl"?'

'That was unkind. Accurate, but unkind. Everybody's been co-opted into giving that girl a talking-to at some stage. It used to be David till Valerie bollocked him one too many times. He wanted her to see a shrink. The daughter that is, not the mother, though two for the price of one wouldn't have been a bad idea. He mentioned social services to Valerie and Valerie got a bit jumpy about what people would say. I ask you. They can't say anything worse about the girl than they're saying already. The girl's school can't handle her, but they'll only talk to the father. He pays the bills.'

'Have you talked to her?'

'What? Valerie knows better than to ask me. I'd put the bitch over my knee and knock it out her. The daughter that is, not the mother. Though on consideration . . . Seriously, though, Valerie Mountyjoy may not be my cup of tea in some departments, but if you'd seen what that girl has done to all and sundry, you'd agree with me. She's a vicious minx.'

'She tried to kill herself last term.'

'Well, second time lucky.'

'Graham!'

'Oh, don't be shocked, for Christ's sake. She's a menace. What's the matter, worried about what you said to her?'

'Yes.'

'Why, what was it?'

'Oh, nothing.'

'If you'd come to me I would have marked your card. You can't win with her, so don't give yourself a hard time. What was the pretence of the visit? How did Valerie dress it up?'

'Angelica wants to do history of art at university.'

Graham laughed.

'That's a good one. What makes you qualified to talk that one through?'

'Valerie Mountjoy thought that's what I'd done. But I did languages.'

'My dear, you get more and more interesting every day.'

'Stop looking at me like that, Graham.'

'Sorry. The father will have put her up to that one. Valerie hates arty-farty stuff.'

'Angelica admitted as much.'

'No harm done, then. What the hell if she does study art? Keeps her out of mischief.'

'That's what I thought.'

Graham looked at Catharine for a while without saying anything.

'What?' said Catch.

'I was just considering what a boon you are to our little village. Soon I think we will all be wondering how we ever got along without you. Never had the likes of you around. You'd better watch out, my dear.'

'For what?'

'Oh, you know. Clever, attractive woman. Intellectual.'

'What, you mean people might think I'm a snob?'

'No. A snob is someone who thinks they are superior. You might be taken for something worse. Someone who *is* actually superior.'

'What rubbish.'

'If anyone gives you a hard time, you come to me, you understand?'

This offer made Catharine look down at the path. She

wanted to say that she hated every day that she lived; hated the empty days without a baby, without her husband; that she hated the winter and the lane that led to her house with the khaki puddles and sharp flint stones; she hated the early sunsets and lamplight at supper; and right now, most of all, she hated the flirtatious banter that she found unavoidable with the one person she regarded as a friend in the village, such that she must go home now feeling vaguely ashamed, as if she had been the perpetrator of a minor infidelity.

'Graham, I have to go.'

'Goodbye, sweet lady.'

She looked up to say goodbye.

'Good God, girl, you're not crying? What is it?'

But Catharine just shook her head and smiled.

'Don't ask,' she said.

Graham looked at her affectionately and saluted her with parade-ground formality. She laughed again, gave the man a little wave and set off back to her house.

Once she had turned off the main road and was walking along the little lane that led beneath the tall trees to her house she felt safe. She was pleased the potholes and stones made the route treacherous to traffic; glad the trees camouflaged the fact that there was a house there at all.

So, as she had walked the route to church an hour ago, Graham had watched her pass beneath. Without saying hello. She wasn't sure whether she was altogether pleased about that. It didn't seem quite right. It made her uncomfortable. But something about it was pleasurable, too. To be observed by an unseen observer; to have been placed in time and space by a third party, beyond the compass of her own consciousness.

She had come to know Graham by chance. Walking back from the post office it was inevitable, their routes being the same, that they would find themselves walking in parallel. His manners were such that he would never ignore someone, particularly a woman. A nod, even a half, self-parodying bow. They moved on from pleasantries to his joshing her that he had waited for her, his 'highlight of the week'. She'd stopped once or twice for coffee; she had introduced Tom, as they passed.

She liked him. Used to being self-deprecating, he provoked her to defend herself, and that involved, in some part, being provocative back; showing off, even. She was far more risqué with Graham than she would ever have been with Tom. She knew Graham consciously tried to shock her, and she was determined to be unshockable.

And all of this came with a very large dose of flattery. That was undeniable. This morning it occurred to Catharine that that wasn't quite right. He had seen her pass and said nothing; when they met he flattered her. All the 'my dears' and calling her his muse. Yet he had watched her coolly as she passed. The old-school comedy of manners was all very well, but the truth was that she had no control over his appreciation of her; she couldn't modify the role he cast her in. And though, in spite of herself, she liked it, it also made her impatient.

Because she was a serious woman. She knew that about herself. At root, she was made of serious material. Sometimes, she thought, too serious. But there was no escaping it. And Graham didn't, or wouldn't, see that. All the flamboyant flattery, the flirtation. Perhaps that was the problem with old-school manners – they didn't, in the end, allow for seriousness. You weren't really *my dear girl*, because being *dear*, to be pedantic, was to be loved; to be loved and known seriously. Yet using the word was meant to be a shorthand that still invoked the form if not the content of affection. So it was dishonest.

So why did she like it?

She was determined to be fair. She knew she provoked him. And she knew she loved him saluting her and making much of her. He had the gift of making her feel as if all the world ought to be regulated in accordance with that which was Catharine. That was it. When he called her his muse, and said that the village was lucky to have her, he was offering a picture of her as a universal principle which the universe ought to be grateful for. If there was any justice, Catch would be a grand fact about the world. Self-deprecating or not, Catharine loved that, secretly, in her heart. Just as an idea. Where everybody would be as wary as her, as thoughtful, as strict. She couldn't voice it as her ambition, for that would be to disqualify herself from the aspiration. But she could warm to someone else doing it for her.

Ostentation in her family had been unheard of; and he was of her parents' generation. But in his flattery of her she warmed to the baroque in his manner. He was being an artist with his perception of her: giving her roles, giving her lines, almost, that she should say. That he had sat in his crow's nest above the yew hedge and watched her pass cast him as her social creator; her social life in the village was subject to his eye and his analysis.

So why did he not appreciate her seriousness? Chauvinism? Well, that was what male artists did, wasn't it? The man-artist.

Confident, manipulative, always casting women in roles purely reflective of the male imagination – devised to throw light on women's capacity to delight or dismay. She was meant to be flattered, and she was, whilst wanting also to shout, 'But that's not the whole truth!' But she didn't pick a fight with him because that wasn't her style. She hated to be rude. She had no choice but to take unreconstructed pleasure from his unre-constructed flattery. What else was she to do? Say 'We don't do things like that any more, Graham. This is the twenty-first century'?

But what if he was right to ignore her seriousness? What if *she* ought to ignore it? He might be all too aware that it did her no good. Just as he was sensitive to the damage Angelica had visited upon her mother. Graham had wanted to beat that out of her. Did he want to do the same to her? To make her a more worthy wearer of the magician's raincoat?

As she let herself into the house and went through to the kitchen, flicked on the kettle and stared into space, she compared the house she was in with the one she had left. There was a notable absence of Angelica, who had effortlessly filled the Mountjoy cottage with her self-consciousness and restless nihilism. Easy for Catharine to come and go.

What if Angelica had been her daughter? Not so easy then. How had Catharine dared to judge the mother? She would have done no better. She would have done worse. What, suffer that insolence and ingratitude and loathing? When good manners had accrued in her life an importance commensur-ate with religious observation? And for her failure as a mother to be effectively published abroad by offences in the village, and suicide attempts at school. *Suicide?* To see your child attempt to destroy herself. To see your love for your child rendered utterly useless to protect her from self-harm.

She would have gone mad. Tom would have to deal with her. Catch would take herself to bed and put on her night-dress and Tom would sit their child down and reason with her. Cross-examine her. That was what he was good at. He would secure the correct conviction and establish that, although the blame had to be shared, they did all love one another. They would take her out of school and educate her at home. They would be a family again. But the girl would shout *fuck you*.

Catharine would never be able to bear the failure. She, who had become inured to her own creative failures, would not be able to bear the greatest creation, a child, being unhappy. Useless art was a failure of personal ambition; to fail as a mother was to fail the universe.

Never, never have children. She must be prevented. Thank God it has not happened yet, she thought. We have been spared.

Graham was right. Beat the ungrateful little bitch's backside. Could she not see that the adults were suffering, too? What was the point of this teenage obscenity? For that was what it was. Selfish, self-obsessed black hole, sucking everything in, so dense that not even light could escape its gravity. She wanted to go back and wring the girl's neck. The fact that Angelica wanted to provoke people with such a petulant, middle-class wind-up, *what degree you were going to do*, was doubly enraging. It didn't even have the legitimacy of a vivid *cri de coeur*.

What ungenerous thoughts. Repellent. It's just fear. Wholly understandable. To imagine a child that is not yours being yours is bound to be alarming. In practice it's not like that.

You have grown used to their existence. You grow up with your child, and every shock is laced with love and understanding. You never disown them. Valerie had said it. 'She knows exactly what she is doing.' And Valerie did too. So nothing is that shocking. Besides, it's all terrifying. It's terrifying if they're unhappy and try to kill themselves. It's terrifying if they are as good as gold and happy as the day is long and killed by a joyrider. That's the covenant. There's no escape. I want children more than anything in the world and alongside any great desire is terror. Terror if you get what you want; terror if you don't. If you want to escape from that particular conundrum the only course for you is suicide.

The one thing I will never do, Catch had always said to herself. The one thing. Suicide. Too obsessively even-handed for that. She could never be that certain. Too ostentatious. That was it. To draw that amount of attention to yourself was not her style, aside from what she regarded as the unpardonable selfishness of the act.

But why was she so angry with Angelica? If it was fear for her own fractured confidence at her fitness to be a mother, wasn't the lesson to be learnt that having a child was, for Catharine, particularly provoking because having a child, also, was an ostentatious thing to do? Her womb would be ostentatious whether her psyche was or not. And in that sense, best to admit that another word, virtually synonymous in this case with the word ostentatious, is the word creative. She didn't lead a creative life, Maria did. But by God, if she had a baby she was being creative. And she was so hard-wired to judging creativity by standards of good and bad that she could not help but judge Angelica just as she judged Angelica's drawings. So she must give up judging either.

But if you did that, what power did you have? What did you have to show for the years of your life that were meant to yield a sound judgement? Catch believed that power rested with justice, and that only grown-ups really understood it. With age came power. She had innate faith in the United Nations, for example. As an idea. She had faith in the courts her husband worked in. Yes, she recycled, she voted – she wasn't deaf to the still, small voice of green living and dutifully divided the household waste at the point of its disposal into plastic, glass and green – but true power was elsewhere. It came with the maturity of perception and the maturing of institutions best able to serve the world. Adults.

Angelica upset this. In Angelica, and particularly in her attempted suicide, she saw the most powerful of all provocations – the readiness of someone to see life as disposable. The girl's potency lay in the fact that she regarded all action as impotent. Leaving only suicide. Her worth would be proved, if she were successful, by her sense of worthlessness; proved by the distraught mother and sorrowful school at her funeral. And if not suicide then her choice of degree. She would sacrifice three years of her life to annoy her mother. That's power. To sacrifice yourself. Just to annoy. Not to effect an immaculate revenge or right an invisible wrong. Just to annoy. Just to make them wring their hands, wonder where they went wrong and scream, 'But we love you!'

However much it might enrage, however much she might pity her, Catharine felt in awe of this. Because, albeit by different routes, this self-abnegation was at the heart, was the end point, of any examined, spiritual life. At least it seemed so to Catharine. Soldiers, at the moment of self-sacrifice for the sake of their comrades; religious martyrs setting their selves aside for God; even Catharine's abstract notion of a great artist making art *with* the self but not *of* the self. Angelica was driven to set the self aside, too – benefiting no one, it was true; creating nothing, only destroying – but asserting, at least, the impossibility of there being any point to accruing favour by clinging to self. Nothing to be gained by clinging to the local attraction of appetite. Breathing. Eating. All vanities.

Of course she knew it was different. The soldier, believer and artist all identified with some thing larger than themselves; Angelica, if she did identify with anything, must do so with some fairly epic lack of self-worth. It was tragic. She was the citizen of an occupied territory, deprived of rights, as she saw it, reduced to seeing the ultimate sacrifice as the only meaningful gesture, and taking as many bystanders with her as possible.

If she had been their daughter, would Tom have given her rights? It was his special field. Angelica was operating beyond the city walls, with guerrilla tactics. Would Tom have set up an interim administration? Brought democracy to family life? Brought her under his rule? 'You're not in court now, Dad. Fuck democracy!' How could he possibly have reasoned with her? How did anyone reason with that? You didn't reason with it. You just sent the troops in.

Tom would become enraged. It would fall to Catharine to defend her daughter as best she could. Exalting emotion above reason. She and Tom would polarise. That's what happened. Angelica would provoke Tom because he, as a father, would be infinitely provokable, being rational and objective and not easily emotional. A daughter would demand a response; she would want to crack the facade. And for heaven's sake why shouldn't she want to do that? You couldn't expect a sensitive girl to live alongside an emotional cripple of a father who only became himself in court and who, at home, had become a sulky zombie. No, it would be up to Catharine; up to the woman who once had been known as Catch to her husband, but no longer. Not since their daughter stuck her fingers down her throat when he called her it, and anyway he didn't now because he didn't love Catharine any more, at least not in that Catch-like way he had at the beginning of their beautiful but doomed love affair.

All up to Catharine. Up to the mother. Who the fuck else was it meant to be up to? Tom was out killing, or at least convicting, metaphorical bison and sabre-toothed tigers; Catharine was back in the cave. Tom had to have his time away, honing his bison-killing skills away from the demands of a mewling girl-child. It would be up to Catharine and the other bison-widows like Valerie to knock said girl-child into shape. And that was an abomination in its own right. She'd seen the posse of mothers in the lane months before; she could not be part of that. None of what she, Catharine, was good at would be brought to bear on the management of a trouble-some girl. Piano concertos were just useless as a starting point for bringing up children. You just mutated into suburban platitudes, and when they didn't work nagged the ineffectual vicar, like some watered-down complaint to God.

There was a knock at the door. She walked through to the hall and opened it. There, in the misty rain, was Valerie Mountjoy.

'Hello,' said Catharine.

'I think you know why I'm here.'

'Is everything all right?'

'I think you know why I'm here,' she said again.

'Umm . . . no.'

'I'm furious. I'm beside myself in fact.'

'What's happened? Do come out of the rain, Valerie.'

'Mrs Mountjoy.'

'Oh. Not . . . are you . . .' The older woman strode into the dark hall. 'Not . . .' continued Catharine, closing the door, 'angry with me. You are. I see that.'

'Come now, Catharine. Come now, young lady. Let's not play games with each other. We don't need to do that, do we? We're beyond that. I know I am.'

'Games? I can honestly say I have no idea why you might be angry with me. Well . . . unless it has something to do with Angelica.'

'Yes. So in fact you know precisely why I am angry, and with good reason. Don't pretend to be stupid.'

'Will you please—'

'Did you or did you not instruct my daughter to destroy her A-level art coursework? You did. The only exam she's got the faintest gift for, and you told her to tear it to shreds. What are you, a monster? I should be here with the police.'

'Oh dear.'

'Yes, Catharine. "Oh dear" just about covers it. I love the way you look surprised. What possible explanation can you give me for such a heartless act of vandalism? In fact, I don't know why I'm here. You should be arrested.'

'No, no, no. One second. Let's go through to the kitchen.'

In the shadows of the hall, all Catharine could see of the woman was a dark silhouette against the bright window; in outline Valerie Mountjoy seemed more threatening.

'I'm not staying here to talk to you.'

'You must. Because this is a misunderstanding.'

Still the woman would not move.

'Valerie,' said Catharine, almost shrilly, 'will you allow me to explain or are you going to just abuse me and leave? What possible reason can I have had for causing you or your daughter distress? Please go through and sit down and allow me to explain.'

'Cool, aren't you?'

'Not at all.'

Valerie looked at Catharine for a second, and sighed.

'I don't know,' she said, finally, almost to herself, as she were a disgruntled shopper contemplating taking her trade elsewhere. Then she set off to the kitchen, but still talking, so as to give no ground. 'You keep cool about it, but I don't think you realise the seriousness of the situation.'

'Valerie,' said Catharine, following.

'Mrs Mountjoy.'

'Have some tea.'

'Hmm.'

'Please. I will make a fresh pot, and I will explain. I do not know why you're so upset. That is, I do. But you cannot be upset with me. You rang me this morning and asked me to speak to your daughter. As a favour. I agreed. I was surprised you wished to entrust to me such a particular role, but I wanted to help.'

'You destroyed her art. Destroyed it. I mean, what sort of a woman are you? You're like a sort of terrorist. We have a terrorist in our village. You say you are an educated woman, with a feeling for the arts and you go to a young, impression-able girl and you tell her to tear her precious efforts to pieces. I phoned David and he was flabbergasted. Flabbergasted. It was her art. Two years of art, gone!'

Catharine couldn't help herself.

'Well, it's hardly a loss to the nation, Mrs Mountjoy.'

'What did you say?'

'Of course I appreciate its value as coursework. No, please don't interrupt. You've said quite enough. Now I want to explain. Firstly, I had no idea it was coursework, and secondly I did not tell her to destroy it. All right? Have you not had enough trouble with your daughter to imagine that she might not always be telling the truth? I'm sorry, but you cannot come in here accusing me of goodness knows what without establishing what actually happened.'

'Did you or did you not tell my daughter that she should break with the past?'

'It may have been an expression I used. One which at the time I—'

'Did you or did you not watch and witness her tear up her drawings?'

'I did.'

'Did you try to stop her?'

'No.'

Valerie Mountjoy nodded grimly.

'You know, Catharine,' she said, in a sudden sing-song certainty, 'it's almost funny. I asked you to come and talk to her and try and dissuade her from embarking on a ludicrous career choice, and to top it all she tells me that you'd said it was a glorious thing, painting and the arts and all. She's doubly certain, she says, that it's what she wants to do.'

'That's a mistake. I said that she would be bored. I said it wasn't worth doing if she was just doing it to wind you up. I defended you.'

'You told her which painters to study and you told her you had spent a magical time at the Louvre, Paris.'

'I never used the used the word magical.'

'She has already rung her father and he has agreed to pay for her to go, during the next holidays, to the Louvre, Paris, to see the magic for herself.'

'Valerie, stop. Stop. I spoke to Angelica like a grown-up. I told her a little bit of my experience as a young woman. I was sympathetic. I listened. I have to admit to being shocked when she tore her drawings. It came completely out of the blue. And, as I said just now, I told her that I thought she would be bored studying art history.'

'Never mind being bored. She'd be unemployed.'

'Well, you don't know that, do you? People with arts degrees do actually work. It's pretty old-fashioned the notion you're putting forward.'

'Do *you* work?'

'I beg your pardon?'

'Well, do you?'

'In what way is that relevant?'

'Do you!'

'No. Mrs Mountjoy, this must stop. Whether or not I work is neither here nor there. I am not seeking employment. I didn't study art history, I studied languages . . . Oh, this is absurd. If I wanted to work, I am sure there is no shortage of jobs I might have done. But I really don't have to defend the fact that I don't earn a wage in my house. Nor that I don't think studying history of art a short cut to the dole queue. I might have done all manner of work.'

'Then why don't you?'

Catharine tried to laugh.

'I'm sorry, but . . . but you have no right to talk to me like that.'

'No, Catharine. You had no right to talk to my daughter like that. To an impressionable young woman at the crossroads of her life. What *you* think was not the point . . . it wasn't for you to go peddling your idle view of life. I see I made a great mistake asking you to talk with her. I'm ready to accept responsibility for that. The fact that you've no children yourself should have warned me off. If you did have you could never have spoken to an impressionable young woman like that. Never. And to be perfectly blunt, if not a little cruel, I can honestly say that if that is your idea of dealing with children I'm glad you've none.'

'Are you really going to question the fact that I don't work and then celebrate my childlessness? That's just offensive.'

'Well, what do you do with your life?'

'A question I ask myself often. My husband and I are, without success, Mrs Mountjoy, trying to have a baby.'

To her complete dismay, Catharine found herself with a lump in her throat, and she was glad that for the moment she did not wish to follow up this assertion with any further comment, for she could not speak.

As for Mrs Mountjoy, she was eyeing Catharine distrustfully, obviously doubting she was telling the truth. Catharine guessed that the older woman dealt so often with displays of hysteria from her own daughter, that the sight of woman trying *not* to cry was a complete novelty. Valerie was shaking her head.

'Oh, stop it!' Catharine managed to say with a haughty savagery that surprised her but not Valerie.

'I'll thank you not to shout at me.'

'I was not shouting at you.'

'You can shout at me all you like. But it's an apology that's required. An apology and an explanation. And more than that — what are you going to do?'

'About what?'

'About the fact that my daughter worships the ground that you walk on. What else?'

Suddenly Catharine was speechless with pleasure.

'What did you say?'

'Eh?'

'What do you mean she worships the ground I walk on?'

'Can I be any clearer? I told you. She has set you up as the great example. She rang her father and told him she wanted to go to Paris, that she had finally found someone who understands her. You're going to lend her some books of paintings, I hear. Finally, she's thrown everything I have ever done for her back in my face. Said I was stupid. It was all you. You, you, you. I don't know who you think you are.'

'It was nothing to do with me,' said Catharine softly, marvelling.

She had the sensation of imagining pleasure through the working of her emotion, like a sunny vista glimpsed between a break in the trees seen from a speeding car. Her limbs felt heavy and full of passive strength; she felt as if she had been always chill and brittle, and now the sun had come out; now there was a stately home in the valley, a broad oak.

Now she forgave the mother the remarks about work and children; she forgave her everything. She nearly even forgave herself for her own antipathy towards Angelica. How could she not? She had done some good through no conscious will of her own. Some magic had occurred. She couldn't take the credit for it. Not in a direct way; nor did she want to. The unconscious, unknown self that Graham had seen walking pensively to the cottage had made something happen.

She could not deny the great pleasure she felt; but she was not proud. Looking at Valerie Mountjoy she felt sorry, guilty, even. She hadn't wanted to trump her. But the guilt was a welcome guilt – a guilt that sought forgiveness that she should feel such pleasure, such a thrill to have reached the obdurate heart of the unpromising girl.

'Valerie . . . please let me call you Valerie. We are going to get over this misunderstanding and be friends. I swear we are. Listen to me. I am amazed you say I have had this effect on your daughter. To tell you the truth, when you knocked at my door I was thinking that I had had the complete opposite effect. When you asked me to talk to her I thought that you might have been being a little unfair on her. It's true. But when I met her, I quickly realised that you were quite right about her motives, about her unsuitability for that kind of life choice. In fact, I thought you were wholly in the right.'

'I'm pleased to hear it. Bit late to hear you say it.'

'In listening to her I attempted to understand where she was coming from and not to be too judgemental. I wanted her to discover for herself that in trying to annoy you she was wounding no one but herself. Unfortunately it seems to have had the opposite effect.'

'It most certainly has.'

'Well, what can I say but that I am sorry? It wasn't, I promise, my intention to cause any further difficulties between you and your daughter. I can see that you're in a very difficult position, Valerie.'

'Thank you.'

But Valerie was still watching Catharine with distrust. An open apology was useless to her; she was evidently finding it hard to get any purchase on where the younger woman was coming from.

They had been standing round the kitchen table, and now Catch felt confident enough to gesture Valerie towards a chair and reboil the kettle. The other woman hesitated, and then responded to the dumb show by sitting and taking out a little white handkerchief and pressing it to her mouth. The apology had worked, and she was falling back on the emotion of the morning. Catharine busied herself with the teapot and the mugs as if she had not noticed and allowed the mother her private crisis. When they were finally both seated Mrs Mountjoy was once again imperious and looked sternly at the crockery.

They sat in silence for a few moments while the tea brewed.

Marvellous, this approbation from the teenager. A kind of miracle. Like a writer who has failed to live up to the promising critical reception of his early work, but who can at least point to a devoted audience of readers, so Catharine, in spite of what she regarded as an unsatisfactory meeting with Angelica, had the judgement of youth on her side. And you couldn't argue with that. Not least because the young were the hardest audience in the world.

Was this, in a way, the very creativity, the very artistic life that she had thought she should pursue? The moment on the stairs, by the alcove, now seemed to her such a moment of introspection as to be almost a crime. What self-obsession, to think one should live one's life in one's head. A brief phone call, a walk to the church and a chat with a girl, and she had engaged, devastatingly, with the world. Marvellous, marvellous. What you forgot, when you were alone, was the fact that you had so little control over how you were perceived – this being in the world in such a way as to have an effect on others that you could not control but which influenced, benignly or not, the open hearts and minds of those whose paths you crossed. So artists, she thought to herself, did not strictly know the effect their works would have. A symphony could be moulded to every variety of personal circumstance, and listened to and marvelled at by all sorts of contradictory personalities. The piece itself had no final meaning, it was fluid. The outpourings of the free artistic spirit flowed like the sea round the contours of a coastline, filling coves here and battering promontories there; the land accommodated it. The art was in just being there. She hadn't liked Angelica; Angelica had liked her. Catch had unwittingly provided supplies for a besieged inhabitant of the island province of teenage life.

She poured.

'Of course, it's her father, Terry. He's the trouble. It's not about her at all.'

'I see,' said Catharine.

'A bastard. A right cast-iron dyed-in-the-wool bastard. You look like you don't believe me.'

'I believe you.'

'Took what he wanted off me, and left me high and dry. When he left he had nothing, so I got nothing. Now he's a rich man, and what do I get? Nothing.'

'At least he pays for Angelica's schooling.'

'How could I say no? Should never have done it. She should have stayed at home with me. But I thought to myself he could at least do something for her. So he does. And now I hardly know her.'

'Difficult.'

'She called me ignorant. Just now. That's me speaking there.

I always speak my mind, and Angelica does too. That's pure me. Can't feel sorry for myself, then, can I? As it was me that made her like that.'

'Hard for you, though.'

'I don't mind the posh school, Catharine. What I object to is the false expectations. What does your man do?'

'Tom? He's a lawyer.'

'That's right. I did know that.'

'A human rights lawyer.'

'Ah.'

'Yes.'

'Well, that's all very well.' Valerie sipped her tea. 'Too hot.'

'All very well?' said Catharine. 'Why do you say that?'

'That's all about getting people off, isn't it? Foreigners.'

'No, not really. He works for a lot of charities.'

'Same thing, isn't it?'

'No.'

'Which ones? Which charities?'

'I don't know.'

'No, well, best not to. Keep out of your husband's work, if you've any sense. They won't thank you for getting involved. I used to do the books for Terry in the early days. Doesn't help a marriage. They need it to be kept separate.'

'Oh, I don't think that's always true, Valerie. I take a great interest in Tom's work and he likes to tell me all about it. Sometimes it can——'

'Is he allowed to do that? Talk about cases? Isn't it confidential?'

'I'm sure he'd never overstep the bounds of confidentiality.'

'Sounds like he already has. Well, you've got a good one there.'

'A good one?'

'A lawyer. You could have done worse.'

Catharine tried to smile.

'What?' said Valerie. 'I'm not suggesting you married him for the money, but it must come in handy. People are so dishonest about economics, if you ask me. What, would you rather live in my cottage with nothing?'

'I didn't say anything.'

'No, but I can tell what you're thinking. Above talking about what your husband earns?'

'Not at all.'

'Rather he was a road sweeper? What did you mean by telling my daughter she needed to break with the past? What did you mean by that?'

Catharine sighed.

'I suppose I meant . . . What did I mean? I meant, Valerie, that she should look to the future with hope. Rather than feel trapped by the past.'

'By which you mean her family. Me.'

'Perhaps.'

Mrs Mountjoy laughed a bluff, mannish sort of laugh.

'You've got a nerve. You don't have children but you think you know about bringing them up; you don't work but you think you know about what jobs everybody should do. What, you think we keep her locked up? You think we hold her back? Common village folk who don't know what it is to be young?'

'No.'

'Seems like it.'

'I'm sorry, but I'm really confused. I came over to your house to try and help out. For goodness' sake. Don't you think every child, regardless of their background – I don't know why you want to turn this into some argument about class – doesn't every child need to break with the past? I mean, you talked about the fact that your parents, or your aunt, wouldn't let you be an actress. Well, I bet sometimes you wish you'd broken with the past a bit about that, don't you? Every child has to do it. I didn't tell her to destroy her artwork, she just decided that her version of growing up seemed to involve tearing up some drawings that she maybe wasn't very proud of. I didn't know they were anything to do with an exam. I was trying to get her to forget about her grievances – that usually exist *in the past* – and stop trying to annoy everybody. Could you please just tell me what I have done wrong?'

The effect of this speech on Valerie Mountjoy was a sudden, happy complacency. It was clear she was used to swearing and things being thrown; it was gratifying indeed that she could have had such an effect on an articulate, middle-class woman as to have her pleading with her. Her palate was jaded, but Catharine was a fresh, feminine sensibility, and the older woman smiled at the easy victory she had won over the lawyer's wife's self-composure.

'I'm sorry,' said Valerie Mountjoy, not altogether sincerely.

'Are you? You have attacked me from all corners from the moment you walked into my house. I have tried to help!'

Catharine had forgotten that on first setting out for the Mountjoys' house she had been determined to play the role of revolutionary in the young girl's life.

'Attacked?' said Valerie, with the sort of mock disbelief that Catch guessed was the currency of her arguments with her daughter.

'Yes. And now I think you should leave my house.'

The Mountjoy's smile evaporated, and she looked with complete amazement at the woman on the other side of the table.

'Now look here, young lady—'

'No, Valerie. I am not your daughter and I will not be lectured. Please leave.'

'Now calm down. You can't just fling me out into the street.'

'Can't I? Watch me.'

Catch's heart was beating fast. Never had she had the sensation of sitting so high, looking down on life, bearing down on another person, imposing the will of her manner, her values, her pride. It felt like one of the loneliest things she had ever done.

'Well, this isn't neighbourly,' said Valerie, trying to control the look of panic on her face.

'Quite the contrary,' said Catharine, 'I came to you in the spirit of a neighbour. Since when you have said the most hurtful things to me. I am a stranger to you. I am not your daughter. And you cannot talk to strangers like that.'

Valerie Mountjoy quivered a little; Catharine guessed that with her daughter this was the point where she would have cried and shouted, 'But I love you!' and the daughter would have gone dumb with the silence of pure hate, which the mother would read as a concession. But in Catharine's case this option was not available, so she sniffed, lifted her large head and said, 'Strict, aren't you?' and tried a little laugh.

Catharine was horrified at her ascendancy over the older woman. It was what she had always thought would be the consequence of losing your temper and dominating someone with an outburst of feeling – a hollow, spiritual ennui, and shame.

'Only when I sense injustice,' said Catch, trying to bring the argument onto a less personal footing, but aware that she sounded like a lawyer's wife.

It was strange to look at the woman and see that victory for Valerie had become everything in her dealings with others. What she took from her husband, and now from her daughter, was a feeling of being on the losing side. Competition had become second nature to her. And she could not but assume that others operated by the same criteria. So, paradoxically, in the remark, 'Strict, aren't you?', was respect for a fellow competitor's style; it was her attempt to be a good loser. She would only really have hated Catharine if she had known the truth – that Catch felt pity, not exultation, in her victory.

'Have you ever had lapsang souchong?' said Catharine, standing rather briskly, determined to dispel the tension.

'One minute she's showing me the door, the next it's fancy teas.'

But it was without conviction, and when there was no response, Mrs Mountjoy said, 'Not sure I have.'

There was a new tone to this last remark, and, following her instinct, Catharine said, 'Valerie, please don't think me nosy, but . . . where are you from? Originally.'

'Eh?'

'Are you a Yorkshire girl?'

The accent had been very faint, but Tobias had been from Leeds. She knew it. Valerie Mountjoy went very still and stared at her with wronged, schoolgirl eyes.

'Yes, I was.'

'I thought so.' Catharine made the different tea, and tried to talk inconsequentially. 'I knew a boy from Leeds when I was at college. When did you move down south?'

'When I was ten.'

'You showed me that photograph of the school your parents ran, but you never told me where it was. So it was in Yorkshire.'

'Yes.'

'Near Leeds?'

'North Riding.'

'It looked very beautiful. Do you ever go back there? To visit?'

'Never been back.'

'You don't think of it as home, then?'

'Don't think of it at all.'

The woman had gone dull and lifeless; as if she'd been arrested and was coming quietly. Catharine had always doubted the school of good manners that sought to fill a silence with a question, to show an interest; she thought sometimes it was impertinent. But something drove her on; there was something she couldn't let go of.

'Was it very different? Down south?'

'What?'

'Different. Was it a shock? You were only ten.'

'Like to talk, don't you? This what got my daughter talking?'

'Here, try this,' said Catharine, filling the woman's teacup with the smoky brew.

'You don't think I had my daughter's well-being at heart. But if I told you what it was like for me you'd know I'd never harm her.'

'Of course, I—'

'Be so good as not to interrupt. I came down here – I'll tell you if you want to know. You asked. I came down here and I might as well have been speaking a different language. And the other boys and girls, they made my life a living hell.

Well, I learnt my lesson, young woman, I learnt my lesson, and I learnt to speak the same as them. I learnt my language as surely as if I was speaking French or German. My life depended on it.'

She looked at Catharine as if she had just been given a new standard with which to advance into battle; she looked proud and relieved, fresh from a playground she had traversed without injury. Catch realised what she had given her, what unconscious charity had been driving her on to ask the questions, and felt relieved.

'That must have been very hard,' she said.

Silence descended. Far off, high above the house, the trees were swaying, their leafless branches silently conducting the music of wind and weather.

'What will you do for Christmas?' said Catharine. 'Angelica said she goes to her father's on Boxing Day.'

'Yes.'

'We shall be with Tom's family. Well, his father and brother. His mother is dead. She was a difficult woman.'

She didn't know why she said this. Unless it was to match Valerie with a confession, or to console her that mothering was hard. She did not know. Catharine thought of Tom's mother, dead from a cancer the precise location of which she had forgotten. She had only known her six months. Whenever they had spoken she'd had the feeling the dying woman was doing her best to show an interest in her son's wife-to-be, but it had been an unconvincing performance, and Catharine had never known whether this was because she was dying, or whether she was simply not interested. She suspected the latter, but had to give her the benefit of the doubt. Tom was without sisters, and his mother always gave the impression that she regarded this less as a fact than an accomplishment. She looked at Catharine as if there were quite enough women in the world and no new one was going to win her over to them, as a species. Even her own death, being the death of a woman, was less to be lamented than if it had been that of a man. All this she sensed from the woman when she was received into the sickroom. Even when she spoke of Tom's past relationships, such as they were, she called them girls. That's right. Always girls, never women. Tom's girls. Catharine certainly never felt that Tom had been in any way handed over to her, as she imagined some mothers might have seen it. No sense of 'You'll look after him, won't you?' It was as if his mother had no notion that he might need a woman in his adult life. Not *need*. Tolerate.

She looked at Valerie Mountjoy and thought, actually, what a pleasure it was to talk to such a profane, cheerfully selfish woman. The bluntness she sometimes exhibited was just a manner; a snobbish one, perhaps, but still only a learnt thing. As she put it herself, it was a language. Behind it, however vulgar and self-serving, there was a warm personality. This, to Catharine, suddenly seemed a relief. Probably what drove Valerie Mountjoy so demented about her daughter was, in fact, less the pretension of wanting to be an intellectual and more her daughter's lack of warmth. The rich father and estuary carelessness of Angelica's manner were chilly, and neither the learnt vowels of the aspiring drama-school student or the Yorkshire girl in the playground were that; she was expansive where the daughter was inward. Catharine looked with indulgence at the slightly plump hands on the table, complacent and idle, but not malicious. She felt she would be sorry to see the woman go.

'And did you never consider remarrying?'

Valerie smiled, as if she had heard that joke before. She knew the punchline.

'Well, I wasn't without offers. You'll see, if it happens to you. When *he* left, there was a queue round the block, I can tell you. They come out of the woodwork. Men you've barely passed the time of day with. "Oh, my wife doesn't understand me," they say. Well, I understood them all right, I can tell you. There was no mystery there. Oh yes. You'll see.'

'But were none of them suitable? Or they were married, I suppose. As you say.'

'Oh, some weren't. But the ones that weren't always had something wrong with them. But, yes, most of them had wives.'

She said the word *wives* as if it were an illness; Catharine could imagine a man saying it. She certainly didn't give the impression that poaching one of these men from their partners was anything more than an awkwardness rather than a crime. For a moment Valerie Mountjoy seemed to hold in her hands the instruments of forgiveness; she seemed to imply that no sin was that terrible; that there were no crimes, really. Just inconveniences. It all worked itself out in the end. Catharine felt such relief. It wasn't up to her to proclaim the moral Word; Valerie Mountjoy didn't think her *that* strict. In her own, Catharine's case, of course, adultery was never an issue. She could genuinely say it had never crossed her mind. But this principle of not taking it too much to heart was a relief. After the thought of Tom's mother, everything Valerie said was a relief.

'But you didn't want a man?' said Catch.

'They'd 'ave been dull after Terry. And I had my girl to look after. It's not that easy, you know.'

'No, I do know that.'

'Oh yes?'

'Yes. Please don't start that again.'

'All right, young lady,' and Valerie, and laughed.

The accent had slipped again. 'Lady' was Yorkshire. But it came as no relief this time. There was no sudden awareness of an authenticity behind the manner that had first alerted Catharine to an aspect of Valerie Mountjoy's biography as yet unknown. Quite the opposite, in fact. Something about the accent, this time, struck her unpleasantly. It dismayed Catch that she should be annoyed because she had been feeling fond of the woman up to this point. But whatever had happened, Catch felt all goodwill disappear. Then she realised. Valerie Mountjoy had knowingly let her accent slide away. It was not unconscious. It had soothed her, this conscious slip into her past voice; it had been done to get a stronger purchase on the situation. She had been bullied in the playground, and doubtless felt bullied by Catharine. Now, in the complacency of middle age, over the fancy tea, she had decided to speak in her true voice. But it was too late. It was like a writer lacing his story with the too personal; or a childhood anecdote included to bludgeon the reader into tender-hearted submission by its authenticity. *My true voice*, it hinted, the voice of unselfconscious childhood.

It was a trump card, and Catch hated trump cards. She always thought what proof it was that she would have been a terrible lawyer. Tom always said to her, 'What? You'd've been a brilliant lawyer! You're so morally impeccable they'd never convict if you were defending.' And she always shook her head. Now she knew why. She couldn't have done the trump cards.

The 'Very well, Mr Smith, if what you say is true, how exactly do you explain . . . this?' pulling from an evidence bag a photograph, a hotel bill, a letter thought long burnt. Too theatrical. And the truth, to Catch, was not, nor could be, theatrical. If you needed theatre to get to the truth, it was no truth worth pursuing. Obviously you had to use it sometimes, if you had to prove something in front of a jury; but as a principle she could have no part of it. To her it would always be pulling a fast one. Let those who could do it with an easy heart do it. She thought no less of Tom that that was what he did.

That was it – Valerie Mountjoy wanted to convict the world on the basis that she had been denied her true voice as a child. And this was exhibit A.

'How long have you been married?' said Yorkshire Lass.

'Nine years. But we were together for a while before.'

'Living in sin?'

'Oh yes. Absolutely.'

And Valerie Mountjoy stretched out and gently placed her hand on Catharine's arm. Not only that, but she was looking at her with a look of gentle, motherly concern so extraordinarily unexpected that Catharine looked back with dumb amazement. She daren't draw her arm away; she was paralysed. Then Valerie patted the sleeve, sighed, and withdrew her arm.

'What?' said Catch.

But Valerie was frowning and looking at her with calm concern. Catharine wanted to shout – indeed shouted in her own head – 'What!' – but she couldn't speak again. She held the compassionate gaze, and then heard, as if from a long way off, a voice that she only dimly recognised as her own, say, 'I feel lonely sometimes.'

And before she knew it, in the same church-like distance she heard the echo.

'Is his work everything to him?'

She looked down with shame, and the dull body beneath her said, 'Yes.'

It wasn't true, so why had she said it? Catharine felt that she had been led by the hand and crossed over to somewhere she didn't recognise. Over a river, over a path. She stood on some *terra incognita* where she must speak and not know the origin of her words. And she was looking back on Tom, who was still on the side from which she had come, in all his masculine otherness, defined by his work and his social standing and his being her husband; she being his wife. He was far, far, away; as far away as Birmingham.

'I think,' said Valerie, 'that he's frightened of giving up his freedom, isn't he? That's why you don't have a child. He's not ready.'

'What? No, no. He's not like that at all. We try, but . . .'

'You have to try often.'

'Oh, we do. I don't know why I said that thing about feeling lonely.'

'Because you are.'

'No. I just wonder what I've achieved in my life.'

'Well, we're back to what choices you make as a young woman, aren't we? I hate to bring that up again, but that's exactly what I was talking about in reference to Angelica's choice. Perhaps you'll understand that now. What good are languages going to do you if you don't travel?'

'Work really isn't everything to him.'

'You said it was.'

'No.'

'I'm sorry, Catharine, but you can't take it back. I asked you if it was and you said yes. Sometimes we say more than we mean to say and it's always the truth. First answers are the true ones. You can't take it back.'

'Why not?'

'Because it's so clear that you're trying to protect him. Which is to be applauded. But in the end it's best to be honest. It is obvious to anyone who cares to look that you are deeply unhappy. When I called round this morning I said to myself there is a deeply unhappy woman. So pale and nervous. I said to myself, apart from the fact that I wanted someone to talk to Angelica, we need to give Catharine a bit of purpose in her life. A job to do. Eh? That's what you need. You've just admitted as much yourself. Do you feel lost sometimes?'

'I do feel lost sometimes.'

'There you are. Don't fight it. And don't fight your friends who just want to point out what's clear to see. You think it's all about being clever. I know women like you. But cleverness isn't everything, Catharine. There's just plain life and experience. You can't escape that. And you'll find that, you know, in the village. If you're not too proud to seek it out.'

'I'm sure.'

'I mean, what friends do you have?'

'Actually, I have a friend arriving this afternoon. My friend Maria.'

'And what does she say?'

'About what?'

'About your husband.'

'Oh.'

'What? She doesn't like him.'

'Not really.'

'For the same reasons?'

'What reasons?'

'Well, putting the affairs of strangers before his wife, for one thing. That's what lawyers have to do, Catharine. That's their job. Putting the affairs of often foreign people first. Someone has to do it, but it's tough on the wives at home.'

'She just doesn't like him. It's not personal.'

'Well, that's a contradiction, if ever I heard one.'

'They just don't see eye to eye.'

'He's jealous of your female friends. Terry was. Hated them. Witches, he called them.'

However wide of the mark Valerie Mountjoy's remarks were, and however irritating to Catharine, nothing she could say stopped Catch embracing the conversation. Quite the opposite, in fact. She felt driven to carry on, to present herself with simple, emotional truth, in the hope that *her* way of doing things, *her* way of not knowing the source of her unhappiness, if unhappiness it was, would silence the older woman. Besides, the latter was like someone who had been moved into the sunshine. From the blustery past of being bullied in the playground, her failure to gain the citadel of the Central School of Speech and Drama, and a suicidal daughter, she was now a calm Yorkshire mother, breathing easily, lulling Catharine with the soft music of misunderstood femininity, intoning, 'You're unhappy . . . you're unhappy . . .' Catharine felt powerless to resist it.

Besides, if she was truly even-handed, should she not at least consider the possibility that there was something amiss in her marriage? It didn't have to be something that was not fixable. Since Valerie Mountjoy had never even met Tom, it couldn't be personal. It was just floating the idea. 'I will not be such a snob as to think I cannot speak of my true feelings to this woman, who may, or may not, understand me,' she thought.

'I suppose,' said Catch. 'Well . . . it sounds . . . I don't know . . .'

'Tell me.'

'I . . . you'll think me foolish, Valerie. The truth is . . . I'm frightened of having children. But . . . but not in an obvious way. I'm frightened of the . . . the . . . ostentation of having a child. The drawing attention to myself. The "Look at me" part of it. Not in a self-deprecating way. I'm sure I'm no more modest than the next person. But . . . I used to play the piano. I used to read books. I loved books. I cared what other people were doing in the world. I don't do any of that any more. I don't even read the newspaper. Instead, each day, I wait for my husband to come home. And I am so lucky. He doesn't expect his supper on the table. I make it for him because I've nothing else to do. He doesn't expect me to do the hoovering or the washing – I do it because I have nothing else to do. And I do it happily. Knowing that he would do it too. He's not an old-fashioned man. He's wonderful. We are what they call a modern couple, I suppose. But why is it I don't read, I don't do anything? Because we are waiting. Waiting, waiting, waiting. For a child. A baby that I don't even know I will love. For something I have put above myself – above playing the piano, or books, or thought itself. And yet which does not even yet exist. And that seems to me terrible, and, well, yes, arrogant. Who the hell do I think I am? And it's that word I keep coming back to – ostentatious. It feels ostentatious to have a child. To hope for one at the expense of everything.'

All through this Catharine had been tracing the grain of the pine table, its long, russety synapses weaving their long lines like thought itself; she had almost forgotten the woman opposite her. As she looked up at her now, she felt the relief of having spoken at such length and gratitude towards the woman whose gentle counsel, however misdirected, had enabled her to speak so frankly. What she saw, however, on Valerie's face, was a look of undisguised hostility.

'I don't understand you at all, my dear,' she said. 'What's that word you keep using? Ostentation?'

'Yes, it means—'

'I know very well what it means, thank you very much. But I haven't a blessed clue what you're talking about. Your problem, if you don't mind my saying so, Catharine, is that you think about things too much. Yes, yes, yes. I know all about midlife crises and all that. But you talk like someone who's got something wrong with them. Having children's the most natural thing in the world. And if you can convince yourself somehow it's not, then you've gone wrong in your thinking in some way or another. What are you on about, dear, using long words and tying yourself in knots?'

'No, please, I didn't mea—'

'It's wrong, young lady. Now you listen to me. You can convince yourself of anything if you think long enough about it. I remember when Terry walked out on me I got it into my head I couldn't carry on. But I did. And that wasn't just ideas I'd dreamt up about why I might be unhappy. That was real. Honestly, I've got more sense out of my daughter this last week than hearing you talk.'

'Stop, stop. Valerie, you don't understand. I'm just talking. It doesn't mean anything. I'm just . . . just chatting.'

'You call this chat? I call it self-indulgence. The trouble is people like you don't realise how lucky you are. You and Angelica are made for each other – she doesn't know how lucky she is either. If you can't have a baby, you can't have a baby. There's no point dressing it up to sound all interesting and clever. It's a fact. We all have disappointments to bear in life and, trust me, the best way is to accept it and let life have its way.'

Catharine flushed.

'Well, I'm sorry, Valerie, but you don't do that, or you wouldn't be wringing your hands about your poor daughter, would you?'

'My *poor* daughter? Well, now we know for certain whose side *you* are on.'

'This is ridiculous.'

'Quite ridiculous.'

'I have misjudged the situation . . .'

'Quite misjudged it.'

'Please allow me to finish. I have misjudged the situation. I wasn't trying to . . . to impress you, or set myself up as an interesting person . . . I . . . I . . . don't really know what you think I was doing to so annoy you. But I was just talking about some of the thoughts I've been having, and I had no idea, I promise, that it would annoy you so much. So let's forget it ever happened.'

'Trust me, I already have.'

'Fine. I have touched a nerve, that's clear. Unwittingly. But I have.'

'"Unwittingly." You're quite a talker, aren't you?'

'Oh for fuck's sake,' said Catch softly.

'Ah . . . hmm. Hmm. This I have heard before.'

'I just don't understand.'

'There's a lot you don't understand, young lady. But I tell you this. If you attempt to see my daughter again, I will take steps.'

'What?'

'And if I can establish beyond reasonable doubt that you caused her to destroy her school work I will inform the police.'

'Valerie, Valerie, think what you are saying.'

'I'll thank you not to abuse me with my own Christian name, thank you.'

'Is it that you thought I was accusing you of . . . of ostentation in your having a child? Is that it? Did you think I was casting aspersions on you?'

'What?'

'If that's what you thought, I promise you I wasn't. I wasn't covertly . . . secretly trying to make you out to be a bad mother.'

'Make *me* out to be a bad mother!'

'No.'

'I should think not!'

'What?'

'Catharine, I'll tell you something about life. Yes? Get on with the business of living and look after yourself, because no one else will. That's what I've learnt. Oh, you think it's selfish and common, I'm sure, to say it, but it's what experience teaches you. It's the life we live. When we're not trying to have a high opinion of ourselves by thinking about things too much. Or swearing at respectable women, for that matter.'

'Right. I don't really want a sermon.'

'What, not up to your level, am I?'

'I didn't mean that.'

'Hmm. Have a higher level of unhappiness, do you? Down here.'

'Down here? My God, you mean down south. As opposed to Yorkshire. Well, Valerie, if you don't like it "down here", why don't you go back to Yorkshire?'

'What did you say to me?'

Catch sighed.

'What did you say to me?'

'You heard what I said to you. Please don't make it out to be the most terrible thing I could possibly have said to you.'

'It is the most terrible thing you could possibly have said to me! I told you what I have never told a living soul. Not even Terry. About the playground and coming to Berkshire when I was ten. I told you. What are you doing? What sort of monster are you?'

'Valerie, calm down.'

'I can barely breathe I'm so beside myself.'

'Valerie, listen to me. It was you who made a comment about southerners, about "down here". I am a southerner, if that is what you call them, and perfectly entitled to take offence at a generalisation about them. If you have a contempt for them, it is you who are guilty of a kind of racism, not me.'

'Would you tell a coloured woman to go back where she came from? Would you?'

'If she came from somewhere which she maintained had a better calibre of people and expressed contempt for the people she now lived among, I might politely suggest that it was possible she would be happy back in the place where plainly her heart still lay. Even if that place was Yorkshire.'

'If it was Yorkshire, she wouldn't be black, would she!'

'It doesn't make me a racist, Valerie.'

'Listen to you. What, did you pinch that argument from your husband? I'm going to say one more thing, and then I'm going to go. I made a very big mistake asking you to speak to my daughter, but that's in the past now. She'll get over it. But I will say one thing to you, Catharine, and it's not meant unkindly. Don't have children. If you don't think it's natural to have children, don't have them. You're doing perfectly well without them. You have a husband, you have money. But you're quite self-obsessed and you worry about things a mother shouldn't worry about. I'd be frightened for you having a child. And, more than that, I'd be frightened for the child. These are harsh words, perhaps, but they are meant kindly. You may remember them with gratitude, one day. And now, I am going to leave, as you instructed me to do.'

Catharine put her head in her hands.

'There,' went on Valerie, 'I've said what needed to be said. Thank God I've not lost *that* ability.'

She stared at Catharine's pale brown hair that shrouded the bowed head, suspended but a foot or eighteen inches above the table, completely still. A single tear dropped silently onto the pale pine; it rested there, neat and accusatory; refusing to dry in the cool, kitchen air. Valerie Mountjoy bore its presence, examined her conscience, saw nothing to doubt, and sighed. She swayed slightly towards the monumental

Catharine, half to console, perhaps, half to wipe away the obdurate tear. Catch dispelled the drop's companion on the other cheek, before it had the chance to join it, and looked up, as if the bowed head had been wholly private and unobserved. Her look saw through her tears, as if they were an allowable obstacle; she would never have dreamt of gaining capital by acknowledging them. This attitude alarmed Valerie Mountjoy; for her, tears could never be anything but precious currency.

Even more alarming was Catharine standing and stretching out her hand to shake the older woman's hand. The latter couldn't have looked with more surprise at it if it had been a gun. She also stood, took it quickly and turned away. Now she wanted to get out as fast as she could. Something about Catharine's emotion was terrifying to her. Something about the way the personality of the woman subsisted through her tears, seeing beyond them. When Valerie Mountjoy had cried in the school playground, driven mad by the taunts, the impersonations, the names – she had pulled at her own hair, she had gone red with rage and wept till she was a tangled mess of tears and snot and recrimination. She had believed that eventually, if only because she had exhausted the visible wrongs that were being done to her, they would stop, and then they would pity her. Pity had to come. But this childless woman, for all her over-educated angst and self-obsession, seemed not to want pity. She'd just wanted some weird 'chat'. Chatting? Valerie Mountjoy loathed it; must run from it.

'Would you like to borrow an umbrella?' said Catharine. 'I think it has started to rain again.'

The windows were caressed by yet another, unmerciful gust of wind.

'I will be *fine*.' Said like Mrs Lear, as if she might say, 'What? After *this*, the heath will be nothing!'

Then she scurried out, forsaking dignity, leaving Catharine at the table. The front door slammed.

Catch stood, like a prisoner deserted by counsel, jury and judge. As if by a court oversight; free to run to freedom. It did strike her as nothing short of a miracle, almost a consolation for all the wrongs of life, that someone could be asked to leave your house. If you waited long enough at the kitchen table, the offending presence would magically dissolve, like a child's nightmare at the creeping of dawn at the curtains. No questions asked. 'I would like you to leave.' They were the magic words. Said softly, like an incantation; shouted, bellowed, said laughing or said through tears; they worked. Only one in a million would require the police to enforce the command. Otherwise it was the perfect sentence. You could say it moments from death even. Even someone else's death, though they might be counting on your presence to see them through it; though they might be incapacitated in some way to make their leaving tricky – you could still say it. Was this entirely right? Was it the privilege of private property that gave you this unparalleled luxury? Was this why left-wing politics became harder as middle age advanced, because there were more and more people to whom it might be necessary to show the door, and the common ownership of capital and property might make such evictions harder? One might just have to resort to force more often. Difficult if you were a woman. Was she just a bourgeois bitch?

Of course, Catch knew what had happened with Valerie. It wasn't difficult to see the basic misunderstanding. Though the mother of Angelica had been prickly at the outset of their meeting, Catharine desperately wanted to give Valerie the benefit of the doubt and establish that she was a warm mother. Having seen the daughter and what the mother was up against, and having in her eyes failed to be sufficiently motherly herself, Catharine wanted to come firmly down on the side the older woman. So she had instinctively bared some of her own emotional life to allow Valerie's maternal side to show itself, something which seemed almost a charitable gesture given the revelation that Catharine herself had been given such rave reviews by the daughter as a surrogate parent-in-waiting.

But here, Catharine told herself, she had been guilty of a classic error. She regarded Mrs Mountjoy as a misunderstood woman, but Mrs Mountjoy didn't. Valerie didn't need to be treated warmly so as to elicit warmth; Valerie herself had no doubts that she was a warm woman. The doubt had been Catharine's and Catharine's only. So for Catch to go seeking consolation for her middle-aged angst came across not as an appeal to the beneficence of an older, more experienced woman, but the whining of a needy depressive. In attempting to recast Valerie in the domestic drama she had just ended up demoting herself to a role both unattractive and unfamiliar. She blushed at what she could not but now regard as her need to please. Had she not so badly wanted to reassure the mother that she was a good mother it would never have happened. But always she wanted to make people feel confident and effective and hated that what she knew to be her strictness would come across as arrogance and complacency. Instead she had come over as weak and selfish. She had come across as the precise opposite of her intention.

Except. It was all very well, this endless dissection of motive. Why not come clean and accept she wasn't a very nice person? So you married one person and they allegedly liked you. So what? They were one person and they went to Birmingham. Big deal. What did that prove? If someone else could dislike you, that undid what your spouse thought. Or at least, to use a legal analogy, left room for reasonable doubt. I'm sorry, but it did. So, if she was unlikeable to some people – particularly if you had a husband who was very good at seeing things through other people's eyes, nay, even made a living out of it – then Tom *would* be able to see what was unlikeable about her. And if he couldn't see what was unlikeable about her it must be either that he was stupid or equally unlikeable himself. Either way their marriage was clearly a lie. They were either hiding their true feelings for each other or they did not really know each other.

It must be the latter, not least because Catharine suddenly realised that she had no idea what Tom would have made of the events of the morning. None whatsoever. *He* might be good at imaginatively placing himself in the minds of others, but she could not work out what he would have thought of the meeting with Angelica, the meeting with Valerie, the positive effect she had had on the daughter and the negative one on the mother. It was all one to her whether he would have said, 'Poor Catch,' or sighed and said half formally, 'Catharine, what did you expect?' or worse, and most likely the case, looked away, avoided her eye and wondered at the strangeness of his wife; the gulf.

I'll tell him everything the minute he gets home, she said to herself. But you didn't tell him about the vicar's visit, did you, and the flowers in church. You don't tell him anything. You just waited for the moment to pass, with unpardonable cowardice.

'I don't know him,' she said out loud, with finality. Like a lawyer, summing up. Just like that thing they do, that pulling the cat out of the bag, that moment of theatre:

'Nor he . . . *me.*'

The finality of it, the admittance of it was such a relief. To admit you were unknown was to allow the world to give you yourself back. The self returned to sender, unopened. The morning had been such folly it was better that way by far. The vanity of walking to the church thinking youth was your special subject; then failing the girl but your heart still beating faster at the idea she had conceived an attachment to you; the crass telling of secrets to a mere acquaintance. These were things best unread. Self unread, eggs unfertilised. Lock the doors.

She offered up a quick, impromptu prayer of thanksgiving that they could divorce without inflicting a broken home on any children. That was one good thing to have come from all of it. Unless, she thought with a cold shudder, she was pregnant now. It was possible. They had had sex once since her last period, just before what she had guessed was the optimum time. Since then they had had a poor month of trying; Tom was tired, what with this Birmingham job coming up. But she could be pregnant. Why could she not have held off from intercourse when the dawning of the truth about their relationship was but days away? She had not seen it coming. She had felt no compromised desire in the darkness; she had luxuriated in his body and in his touch no less. When she and Tobias had been about to split up sex had become a foreign language and she had become incapable of understanding his advances. But with Tom she still wanted him. Cruel lust to forbid any precognition of what she now knew to be the case – that she and Tom were doomed. She must be more carnal than she knew, to have devoured, in a private, sensual feast, his maleness, whilst turning a blind eye to their failure to understand each other.

So what to do? Wait until what should have been the time of her next period and break it to him, then? Break it to him now and offer him the possibility of a termination if they had created an embryo? Stay with him if she were pregnant and see life through swiftly and silently? Ostentation? This wasn't ostentation, this was an abomination. A dereliction of all things human.

Valerie Mountjoy had been right in every detail of her analysis. You wrung your hands with middle-class, liberal angst, and Rome burned. You showed off your impeccable scruples, your sense of respect and mutual understanding, but behind the received ideas and stock attitudes of someone brought up on good novels and fragrant piano concertos you had no real intimacy. Sensitivity, such as it was, existed only for the sensitive; the effect you actually had, as Catch had just found with Valerie Mountjoy, was effectively brutal. You couldn't unite with anyone, because unification is always brutal. Valerie knew that. Look at her sensitivity about her accent. There was brutality at school, and then you learnt to speak differently. Sensitivity got you nowhere in the world. For her it might have been a private elegy to a better life, an elegy to Yorkshire. To the world it was a snuffling, snotty child having hysterics in the playground. It was entertainment.

It was fine. Catharine wanted to ring her and say that she was grateful to her for pointing out that she should under no circumstances have children. She should put her mind at rest. Maybe later. Catch's hands were shaking very slightly. She thought she should take a few breaths first. Perhaps fresh air. Go out, quickly. Get out. Besides, Tom might phone. Maria would come, but later.

It was still only midday.

Out in the lane, the track, up which the removal van must soon come to take their effects away in the wake of their traumatic separation, threatening the suspension while careering through the treacherous potholes, was empty. Valerie Mountjoy was long gone, safely stowed in her cottage by the church.

Through the narrow gap that gave onto the main road, Catch saw a car pass. Life was speeding by beyond the outpost of hedge and gate. She wandered towards it, as if in her daze she might casually find herself beneath the wheels of those for whom life was so swift. As she reached the road she looked either way, like a child looking right then left then right again. Nothing. Towards the village she could just make out the gibbet-like construction of Graham's stepladder, on the path now, turned the other way so that he could cut the road side of the tall yew hedge. No sign of Graham himself. Without thinking, she set off towards it. Something of the man's world-liness was suddenly attractive to Catharine; his certainties. Angelica was 'the mad girl', Valerie was someone about whom you could raise your eyes to heaven. He knew the roles of this village play in which Catch had been unknowingly cast, and he would definitely encourage her to a better perform-ance than the one she had so far given. Perhaps even assign her a different role.

Partly, given the fact that she had decided her marriage was effectively over, she wanted another man to talk to. Not to discuss Tom, but to *not* discuss him. It was inconceivable that she could talk of such things to Graham; there could be no second debacle of the sort that had left her crying onto the pine table. With Maria later, perhaps. Not with an older man. She was safe from a heart-to-heart. So, to her amazement, she would pay a social call, and convince herself that though the worst thing that could possibly have happened to her had happened, she was not a sociopath. The outer shape of life had to be clung to, while her feelings scalded her with self-reproach and loathing within.

The path was dusted with clippings and thin needles, like those from a Christmas tree. He'd swept up one lot, which lay in a neat pile to one side, and begun again. Where he had clipped and where not yet started was very clear; she could tell that he liked to appreciate the work as he did it. No short-cuts, no blurred edges. Something he could stand back from as he went along, aware of the pleasant progress of his labour. What had he to hurry him, after all? Presumably as you got older the imperatives got weaker, unless it be the ones to enjoy yourself, to relax, to make the most of what you had left.

She let herself in through the racing-green-coloured gate and up the box-lined path to the big white door with its immaculately polished knocker. To her surprise the door was ajar; inside she could glimpse the well-kept house, the upholstery of fine fabrics and swagged curtains; she had been there for a drinks party, the only time she had introduced Tom to Graham socially, and remembered again with what feminine organisation the house was kept in spite of the fact Graham lived alone. To have left the door open this morning seemed like an uncharacteristic oversight. Wondering whether to enter or knock, she paused in her progress, then saw Graham himself coming from the kitchen. She was momentarily afraid she had disturbed him in dressing or coming from the bathroom, for one of his arms was out of his shirt. Catch could see his sinewy arm and saw too that he held a handkerchief to it, stained with inky blood. She felt for a moment she had interrupted some private ritual.

'My dear girl,' said Graham, looking at her with undisguised appeal, 'you have come to save me. Look what this fucking senile git has done to himself. My guard was down and the shears, which I had just sharpened to within an inch of their lives, decided to slip from my grasp and wing me on their descent.'

Catch went over.

'You poor thing.'

'Thank you for saying so. It's pathetic. Go and get the twelve-bore from the gun cabinet and put me out of my fucking misery. Better still, get me a Scotch.'

'It might be an idea to stop the bleeding first. What's this?'

'What do you mean "what's this"? It's a bloody good hanky. Ruined.'

'Well, it's no good. You need a bandage. Do you have any?'

'First-aid cabinet in the downstairs lavatory. There, by the door. It's bloody hard to stop the flow on your own.'

'Go into the kitchen and I'll fix you up.'

'What?'

'Go back in there and sit down and I'll fix you up.'

'Oh my God, if I'd known you were going to look after me I'd have got into self-harm weeks ago. Where'd you get this composure, this coolness under fire?'

'Graham, just go in the kitchen.'

'I give myself up to you entirely. Keep being strict. I love it.'

'Now.'

'Yes, my dear. Don't be long.'

Catch went to the cloakroom and found bandages, lint and antiseptic. They were all neatly arranged in a little cabinet with a red cross painted on the front. She took them and went through to Graham's kitchen. It was a wide, handsome room, with flagstones and an Aga. There was a plucked pheasant on the side and a box of vegetables from the local farm shop. A cold cafetière was half full on the side, beside a wine glass stained with old red wine. Graham was sitting in a polished chair, waiting patiently, as if he were in a field hospital.

'Are my gardening days over, dear girl? You can tell me. Is it the home front for me?'

'Let me see it.'

He stretched out his arm. The blood had congealed neatly on the taut, lean muscle of the old man's arm, but the wound was quite deep and needed cleaning.

'Didn't your mother tell you not to play with knives?' said Catch, wetting some lint with antiseptic and wiping the cut gently. Graham didn't flinch, but twinkled at her from under his eyebrows; whatever pain he felt, which must have been considerable, seemed numbed by the sight of Catharine tending to him.

'This is going to hurt,' said Catch, taking a new piece of lint and pressing it against the clean wound.

'Sweeter than roses, my dear. I wouldn't have missed the spectacle of you in your splendid intelligence acting the part of ministering angel for anything. The loss of a limb would have been nothing to the delight I feel.'

'It's quite deep, you know. You must clean it again this evening. If you can't do it, I'll come.'

'Twice in one day? Cocktails at seven?'

'A cup of tea at six.'

'Do you know, I was in the army for nearly fifty years, and I was never wounded. Not once. Makes a chap feel a sham. Got the medals but not the wounds. Lost chaps. Lost friends. But never so much as a scratch myself. Why do you think that was?'

'I don't know. Luck? The power of prayer?'

'Naughty.'

'Here, put your finger on this.'

She tied the bandage.

'Nice job.'

'You can put your shirt back on, now.'

Graham made great pantomime over putting his arm back in the sleeve, whimpering and struggling, though it must have caused him little pain compared to the cleaning of the wound.

'Don't look at me like that, my dear girl. This is agony.'

'No, it's not.'

'Scotch. Over there, on the side. Then you can tell me exactly what you said to put Valerie Mountjoy's nose quite so out of joint.'

'What?'

'There's no need to look so shocked. What do you think I am, an amateur? There.'

Back in his shirt he peered again at Catch from beneath his eyebrows, laughed and stood up.

'Bugger the Scotch. Have a glass of wine. Chablis?'

He opened the fridge.

'Too early for me.'

'Mind if I do?' he said, taking the bottle from the fridge without waiting for an answer. 'Remember my position in the crow's nest. I saw her set sail, ready for immediate engagement with the enemy fleet, and I saw her return, flags tattered and holed below the waterline. What on earth did you say to her?'

'She was cross with me.'

'What was the charge?'

'That I'd provoked Angelica into destroying her A-level art work.'

'Did she?'

'Yes.'

'At your instigation?'

'Indirectly.'

'Hmm. Well, you've done it now. I warned you, didn't I? You should have come to me. There is no limit to the Mountjoy's appetite for new villains. You were fresh prey. Nothing will have given her greater satisfaction than to lay the crime at your door. Similarly the mad girl. Theirs is a currency of blame. They'll hate you. It's in their interests to.'

'But the daughter apparently likes me.'

Graham laughed.

'Better and better. I underestimated her. It seems she is finding more sophisticated ways of driving her mother insane.'

'I think it was genuine.'

'And why shouldn't it be? The whole village will find ways of suiting you to their tastes. Whether for good or bad. I congratulate you. Don't look so meek, woman. It's hardly your fault. Valerie's a bitch. How did you leave things?'

'That I was unfit to have children. Self-obsessed and neurotic.'

'My, you did get to her. Now you listen to me. Don't give what Valerie Mountjoy thinks of you a moment's thought. I am he that was put on earth to appreciate you, and appreciate you I do. I am your ally in the village and with me you can do no wrong. You should drink some of this Chablis, it's delicious. Care what I think of you. Fuck the others. She's an ignorant, suburban bitch. Pity her. Pity her and pass by on the other side. It's clear to anyone with an ounce of good taste and judgement that you are a super-ior woman fated to be misjudged and criticised by other women for being . . . I don't know . . . too good. Too intel-ligent. Too fucking civilised. For Christ's sake don't start crediting them with having any bloody insight or you'll go mad yourself. Valerie Mountjoy's a busybody. She had David's bollocks on toast years ago. She's a monster, a gorgon, a vast queen bee feasting off the drones and workers of her village hive. It's disgusting. In the good old days they'd have burnt her as a witch.'

He poured himself another glass and winked at Catch as if laughing at his own verbal excess. She smiled back. It was pleasant to see the old, dry man drinking the clear, fresh wine; she could smell its lemony scent and the glass was beaded with cold. There was Graham, bandaged up, his hearty chest still broad and his hands eloquent and strong, holding the thin wine glass, light as a bird. She liked the fact that he had taken the bottle, already opened, from the fridge; nice that it was to hand. Nice just to think that there were pleasures so easily available to adult tastes and dispositions; this was what, after all, was waiting for us after childhood, wasn't it? The man took the wine like medicine, or someone slaking a thirst years old. She would watch Graham's pleasure and partake of it vicariously. What else was she to do, her marriage over?

'What are we going to do with you, woman?'

Catharine laughed.

'What about?'

'Does he appreciate you?'

Catch frowned.

'What?'

Suddenly her heart was beating hard. Her face flushed and she felt something almost like perspiration on her forehead.

'Does he appreciate you? I'm not asking you whether he thinks as much of you as I do, that being plainly impossible and you being too modest to admit to being a remarkable woman. So I'm just asking a simple question. Does he appreciate you?'

'Why?'

'So he doesn't?'

'Graham, you can't ask such a question.'

'Why not?'

'I don't know. I don't know what you mean to achieve by asking it.'

'Don't you?'

'No.'

'What a pity. I invited you in here to have a civilised

conversation. If you aren't up to it, or cannot speak with candour to a man who appreciates you, say so and be gone.'

He was smiling as he said this, but Catch felt guilty and untrusting. She knew she should relax, knew that she was taking everything too seriously, and that in the wake of the meeting with Valerie she should appreciate being, well, appreciated.

She forced a smile.

'What rubbish,' she said. 'What do you mean you invited me? I invited myself, as I recall. The door was ajar. I'm sorry, Graham. She upset me more than I knew.'

'My darling girl, I'm not cross with you. If you don't want to talk, don't talk. I have a hide as tough as an elephant. You can't offend me. Come one, what's the story? You become Samaritan to the mad girl, Florence Nightingale to me. But remember, I saw you pensive in the lane earlier. I saw to the heart of you. What, is he having an affair?'

'You can tease me, but there's no need to cast aspersions on my husband.'

'Aspersions? He might be conducting a very good affair. Less of the prude, thank you, my dear. If the two of you are both unhappy, why stay together?'

'We are not unhappy. I am unhappy sometimes. But not with him.'

'And he may be unhappy sometimes, though not with you. So it is not a necessary untruth to say that, possibly, both of you are unhappy. Though not with each other. And yet you do not necessarily make each other happy. If you did, then neither of you could claim to be made unhappy by anything.'

'You've suddenly made being lectured by Valerie Mountjoy seem like a holiday.'

'Come on, come on, I'm just baiting you. Don't pretend to be less intelligent than you are. You provoke me, and largely your provocation is agreeable to me. Inspiring, even. But you radiate dissatisfaction and ennui—'

'What rubbish—'

'You're wasted here, that's for sure. What does a woman like you do? I mean, let's talk truths . . . You could have done anything, yes? You come from a comfortable background, of course. You have a degree. But aside from that. You are very attractive, you have charm, you are watchful and yet engaging. You are – and here I will hazard a guess that you need not agree with, and certainly not take offence at – more intelligent than your husband, and yet you do not work. You are instinctively charitable. There is nothing lazy about you, nothing indolent. Uncertain, yes. There are things in your universe which you worry about that a woman like Valerie Mountjoy not only does not worry about but has never even thought of. But here you are, reduced to counselling spotty teenagers, living in the dreaded house at the end of the lane and wandering the streets like one of the fucking Brontës. What's the story? Were you seduced and left for dead by a college Lothario? Is your husband impotent? Do you write poetry as a hobby? I want to know.'

'What do you mean, the "dreaded house at the end of the lane"?'

'Eh?'

'You heard me, Graham.'

'What? Figure of speech, dear girl.'

He was frowning and checking the knot of his bandage.

When he looked back at her he was taking cover behind his eyebrows.

'Graham. Graham, why do you call it that?'

'The house at the end of the lane. That's what it is, isn't it? What do you want me to call it?'

'Why is it dreaded? Stop lying. Why did you call it that?'

'I love your strictness. I love to be scolded by you.'

'Why is it dreaded?'

Graham picked up the glass of wine as if taking it by the scruff of the neck and took a large mouthful. He winced at the cold.

'Oh, for Christ's sake,' he said more quietly, as he put the glass down.

There was silence. Catharine felt that if she said nothing the secret would come out; only pure passivity now would make the man talk. Only silence would defuse the description *dreaded* that had now itself become the temporary fulfilment of all her personal dread.

'Not a house with a happy past,' he said eventually. 'But good God, girl, do you really care about such things?'

'Do you? It was you who used the word.'

'A house that changes hands as frequently as yours inevitably becomes subject to . . . rumour.'

'No it doesn't. It doesn't mean it's haunted, it just means that estate agents make a lot of money out of it. Why is it dreaded?'

'Last couple – the couple you bought it off – they were only there a couple of years. She didn't like it, apparently. Before that there was a family. Bit of a rough job. Wouldn't send one of the kids to the local school. Fracas with one of the teachers. Husband used to beat up the mother. Mountjoy called social services. Turned nasty. Wife scarpered and the house was repossessed. Before that was a woman on her own. Older. Died of cancer.'

'Before that?'

'Christ, woman, you make me feel like a bloody almanac. Before that, in the eighties there was another couple. Married. Chap was in the army. Bought a bullet in the Falklands. Port Stanley. She went a bit barmy. Started drinking in the Bull and Beggar. Had affairs. There, you see! That's all. Because it was down that lane, a bit cut off, a bit shady, people used to be funny about it. It's another reason I'm so bloody glad you came. Blew a few of the cobwebs away.'

'Superstitions, more like.'

'Call them what you will. Look, I used an expression I shouldn't have used, it was damn stupid of me. I was taken away by my own flight of fancy. Probably says more about me than anything about your house.'

'Why, did you go there?'

'What?'

'Oh, the army man. Of course. You must have done. Did you know him?'

'Not previously. He was young. I knew his commanding officer.'

'But you met him?'

'Of course. He was army. It would have been damned odd if I hadn't.'

'Did you like him?'

'I'm being quizzed.'

'You are.'

'Why?'

'Penance for putting a curse on my house.'

'My dear girl, there's no curse on your house.'

'What was he like?'

'Unexceptional.'

'And the wife?'

'What about the wife?'

'What was she like?'

'Highly strung. Life in barracks had driven her a bit crazy, as well it might. She was glad to get her own house. He'd been promoted, you see. He could live out. My dear, it's gone one o'clock. Would you like a sandwich?'

'No, thank you.'

'And no wine?'

'No wine. And did you look after *her*, when her husband was killed?'

Graham pursed his lips.

'My dear girl, what are you insinuating?'

'Less of the prude, Graham, as you said to me two minutes ago. This woman sat in the kitchen of my house. She went through a lot. I don't know. I'm touched by it. I want to know the truth.'

'I was touched by it, too.'

'So?'

'So, what?

'Were you married at the time?'

'I forget.'

'Did you forget at the time too?'

Graham looked at Catharine and laughed. It was a new, richer laugh; as if she had suddenly fulfilled an earlier promise.

'That's naughty,' he said.

'You have a penchant for accosting women in country lanes

and flattering them. Did you have an affair before the husband was killed or after?'

As much as there was a sense of promise fulfilled, for the first time Graham looked as if Catharine might have gone too far.

'Both. King and country, eh, woman. I told you I was no gentleman. Why aren't you shocked? I might add I also watched her successor in that house die a long and painful death. I flattered her and charmed her, too, and I don't regret a moment of it. I made her laugh. Is that a crime? My God, you've even got me defending myself. Remind me not to invite you over again when I'm sober. It's traumatic.'

'I thought you liked the banter.'

'What? Of course I like the banter. Not used to having the tables turned on me. What? Banter! Banter, woman. Christ, what else do we have to live for? Yes, I had an affair with her. I know your bedroom better than you do.'

'That's possibly more information than I need, Graham.'

He laughed again.

'When he died,' he went on, suddenly serious, 'she went a bit off the rails. It wasn't pretty. Used to threaten to do herself in.'

'Had the marriage been unhappy?'

'Hmm . . . "Had the marriage been unhappy?" she asks, knowingly demonstrating her progressive opinion that having an affair is not necessarily evidence of an unhappy marriage.'

'That wasn't my intention.'

'He was, as I have said, unremarkable. But then she was no virago. She wasn't the brightest. She wasn't you.'

He took a sip from his glass, and Catharine felt the compliment hang in the air, as insubstantial as the scent of the wine;

she endured it. Enduring Graham's flattery was a kind of trial to her; it seemed to her that we endure the good opinion others have of us just as much as we endure the bad. Both alarm; both, potentially, condemn – one by suggesting a promise which we cannot but fail to live up to, the other by denying us the grounds for an appeal.

But this lunchtime she felt more able to bear it, more able to bear Graham. This rather brutally related tale of misdemeanours committed years before didn't alarm her. Rather, she found her instinctive forgiveness of the man empowering; that it made them better friends. She felt at less of a disadvantage.

'What happened to her?' said Catch.

'After a while she went away. I never heard of her again.'

'Did your wife ever find out?'

'No.'

'Were there other affairs?'

'Of course.'

'Did she find out about those?'

'No. Have you finished?'

'What was her name? The woman in my house.'

'Louise.'

'Poor Louise.'

'You cheeky cow. How do you know how poor she was? Her mind was replete with the riches of men's crimes and iniquitous betrayals . . . she slept sound in the knowledge that we were all monsters, and I was the greatest monster of all. She was rich as fucking Croesus in what mattered.'

'And what does matter?'

'Being proved right.'

Catch thought of the kitchen she had left, thought of what

she and Tom had added to the room. She tried to remember what it had looked like the day they moved in, when it was just a shell that once had been full up with Louise's things. Personal possessions were such a thin patina to add to a house, such a weak filter. The house endured it, bore it, suffered it – the vanity of humans deftly scattering their personalities over a property. Nicer to think that the house – as presumably the church had once been in more faithful times – was a constant; a storehouse of tombs and plaques, where one lived cheek by jowl with history. Catch had failed in her imaginative transposition of herself into the teenage life of Angelica; it had been beyond her. But she felt now that should she get up and walk back to the house at the end of the lane something of Louise's history would still be available to her; she could be intimate with it. And though Louise's fate had not been a happy one, this thought was not depressing. It was weirdly consoling. However Graham might characterise Louise in unfavourable terms, she felt an instinctive solidarity with her. He wouldn't know what she, Catch, knew – the louring ceiling downstairs, the tiny windows up.

Like an actor assuming a role, Catharine felt herself move towards the thought of Louise as a creative act. A step forward, in which aspects of herself would come to the fore that had been previously hidden, current habits would become suppressed; a different era and a different history would flex her manners into something strange, her voice into a different tune. This fluidity was vastly exciting. So what if you felt defined by the cottage – to find another inhabitant of it, into whose mind you had sudden access, was to be released; you were not fixed any more by the one house because you were now part of the great continuum of human personalities. Catch felt the strange chances at work in her and Louise's life – what if your husband was not in Birmingham but in the Falklands? What if your husband was not a human rights lawyer but a duller man? What if you believed Graham's flattery? Needed it. If you don't want to be defined by the house you live in, both really and metaphorically, partake of the great imaginative leap into another person's circumstances. If I was Louise . . .

It was alarming, this imaginative flurry of images and second-hand desires; this challenge, to *be* Louise. But she could not baulk at it. Louise was a fact about the cottage. The house that had so brilliantly evicted Valerie Mountjoy could not so easily dispense with the spirit of Louise. For she too had slept beneath the tall trees and heard them creak like masts while she tried to sleep in her cabin.

But the waking dream of otherness involved not only her but the man across the table before her. Having taken the hand, as it were, of the woman from twenty-five years ago, she could not now let go; she must be led, if only in her imagination. Catharine did not find Graham unattractive. His formality answered her own, as did his playful, capricious sense of humour she found, so long as it remained well mannered, a seductive suggestion that it was universal. That were we to attend to the absurdities of life as diligently as Graham, we too would be as profane, as cheeky with the circumstances of existence in the shadow of the gallows.

His age, and the very incongruity of the idea of finding him attractive, made the question more able to be asked; it clarified the mental experiment. Why should she not find him attractive? Women had, and in considerable number. And, what's more, she had only to examine her behaviour with him since first making his acquaintance to know, if she was honest with herself, that she had partaken of the bantering, flirtatious relationship knowing full well that – her being at heart neither bantering nor flirtatious – he was chatting her up. Not with a view to succeeding with her, but by an inflation of her personality and charms to make her easy to be filed under 'women my heart has gone out to'. She knew all that. It made her uncomfortable occasionally, it's true. But she did know it. She could defend herself with the fact that she was lonely, that she was her own boss, that her strictness was such that she would never dream of leading someone on; nothing could be more uncharacteristic. But she could not deny her half of the dynamic.

So why should she not now allow her imagination the final trajectory that the gravity of their conversation was describing? She wanted the freedom to imagine Louise's life; at this midday moment one life was not enough. Her one life had foundered on the absurdity and impossibility of marriage and knowing only one person, being known by only one. She must go with Louise, who had dressed in the same room as her, suffered her husband to be away, and who had known this characterful, demanding man, younger, perhaps, but no doubt still possessed of the same cheerful profanity, the same mixture of cultural knowingness and army briskness.

Could she allow herself the thought of it, the imagining? Or was she the uptight intellectual that Tobias had called her years before? Maybe she had learnt nothing since then.

But if she imagined it, surely the imagining would bring with it the reality. That was how desire worked, wasn't it?

You wondered if something was attractive and soon your mind found its way to the heart of the thing imagined till you must have it. Have it at all costs. Except that Catch's imagination had always called on music first, not erotic adventure. She had craved CDs and concert series; she had craved vicarious recognition for Maria's talents. Thinking of Louise and Graham, she had no intermediary, no chaste go-between. It was upfront. It was, in some ways, disgusting to her. The gang of reactions that constituted received ideas of what was seemly or not squatted on the periphery of her consciousness for her just as it did for everyone else; watching her to make sure that she agreed. And for her the judgement was more potent because Louise had not been that much younger than Graham; in Catch's case, twenty odd years on, he was old enough to be her father.

She was drawn and drawn to the obscene thought as she sat opposite him. The more she tried to laugh it off, the more it claimed her. What she now thought of as the grand imperative – not to be prudish, not to be conservative in her judgements, not to be Tobias's Mother Superior – now demanded of her that she allow the possibility that she would or could find Graham attractive. After all, in matters of erotic freedom unsuitability was the watchword of a truly liberal outlook. If all things were mutable – as the foundering of her marriage since breakfast had proved they were – surely you could follow the operation of desire through to its standard conclusion before lunch. Why should you not? If there was a baby in her womb now, as there conceivably might be, and you stood on the brink of having another's life in your hands, surely you could succumb to the imperative of a mere moment of sexual frisson; besides, it was invisible compared to the real infant; it was thought only.

Forgive yourself, forgive yourself. She knew that was what she must do. And do also what Louise, from the sound of it, had failed to do – forgive Graham, too.

It was time to change course, this day of all days, for this day was her life. She had lived long enough in the wake of Maria's permissive cruise through life. The kingdom of experiences that had been divided up at some indeterminate time now required some frontier redrafting, so that she could occupy territory for which once she had no passport, no citizenship. Who had decided which paths were hers to take, which not? Suddenly the figure of Louise was a magic key. The figure herself was insubstantial, just a mannequin, and unlike the figure of Angelica, who had also come to Catch that morning as a figure tempting her to projections of revolution and vicarious adventure, Catch had no role to play in the other life. She would not founder on the unsteady raft of either adolescent vagaries or Valerie Mountjoy. She couldn't get it wrong. No. Louise was there. She was what Catharine might have been, might be or might become. The two women had two things in common – Graham and the house. Both, like theatrical producers, had cast them in the same role, and it was up to Catch, as to any actress destined to 'take over' a role, to understand, with reference to what was similar in their two interpretations, what was essentially *different*, and therefore unique to her talent and her imagination.

It was unbearably exciting finally to imagine herself as someone else. Magically promiscuous. And she knew, with that profane taste of mutability, that she would not necessarily need to see the thing through to any advanced intimacy with Graham. It had happened, her allowing of the imaginative act. Her intimacy now was with Louise. With the fact that she and Catharine shared a sisterhood. For Catharine, wary of all sisterly, feminine covenants, this was potent.

Might not a prisoner, in Brixton or Wormwood Scrubs, look out at the urban siege that besets him in his isolation, and take it as his daily work to imagine himself into the life of a passer-by who walks down the road beside the prison gates; imagine so deeply, in so successful an imaginative transposition, that in his success, when the moment of parole comes, some part of him has nothing to do with the dull machinery of release; because it had found respite more than he knew, the morning at the window, months, years before, the morning of looking down on the plane trees and the pavement, where a passer-by became freedom, became the greatest release he had, or will ever know? So Catch, suddenly sharing the world with this glimpsed other, Louise, felt that there were still communions to be had beyond the confinement of her house, of her life.

Torn as all who live with the presence in their life of a captivating but as yet unacquainted-with stranger, Catharine wanted to know more about Louise, but was also aware that she wanted no information which might compromise the liberation she felt at the mere thought of her. She wanted the fantasy, not the reality, and assured herself she need not feel squeamish about that, or accuse herself of immaturity, as she might have if it were in relation to an idealised lover, for example. There was no harm in using Louise, in that sense. And, paradoxically, not knowing more about the other woman in no way compromised the thrill she felt at embodying the thought of her. She decided on their differences, on the fact that Louise must have married an army man because she liked a certain sort of security, a certain boldness mixed with stoicism. But he must have been unromantic; unromantic enough for Graham to have charmed her with old-school rakishness. Graham had said she'd hated him at the end. Yes. Finding romance and then seeing that it was a shallow formula; what you thought you'd been missing was just an equation of words and sex with eventual disappointment. What did you do with charm, then? If you needed its operation, but disagreed with the result?

Never mind, never mind. That wasn't the point. The point was the moment of identification. It wasn't that Louise represented a philosophical advance over Catharine, it was that she was *other*. Attitudes untested, emotions untried and unexamined – this was what was obscenely attractive, this retrospective appreciation of how far an unhappy woman could go. A husband fighting for his country and she sleeps with a friend of his commanding officer; the husband dies; she carries on sleeping with him. With the same enthusiasm? With more? So alone we are. So alone. What is odd is not the transgression, but that it is not harder to transgress. That nothing but an inner, secret police can step in and stop you. House arrest is so hard to come by.

And having made the identification, and gone through in her head all that she and Louise had in common – the blustery walks up the lane, the husbandless bedroom, the glimpses of gravel drive and the creak of the tall trees – the moral aspect of their lives, the fact that Louise had slept with Graham, and committed adultery – does anyone use that word any more? – seemed a detail. Seemed inconsequential.

The point was the sensuous identification. Fucking was nothing. Fucking was the toss of a coin. The lamplit windows patterned with rain, scudding clouds above the church and watercress beds, a glimpse of blue sky, a scarf pulled tight against the wind as it gusted around the primary school as the children halloed to their mothers. These things placed Louise, for they must have been her experiences too, and suddenly Catch had a purchase on her own life; Catch was high up, looking down on her life as Graham had been, looking down on the unwitting, unconscious passer-by that had been herself.

So it was quite clear. Weather was more arresting, more important, than morality. Weather made you grab your magician's cloak, weather made you see your life for what it was. What else did you have when morality, such as it was, upped and went off to Birmingham and strode up and down the courtroom? What you actually lived, left at home, was rain and sleet and snow and the insufficiency of tea to make you happy. My God, my God, she thought – I have come to the place where infidelity to my husband would be, to me, a detail. Me, for whom every breath was morally circumscribed by curiosity and an even-handed approach to everyone. Thinking well of everyone.

'Your house is so clean, so orderly,' said Catch, brushing a strand of hair off her face and looking with pale wonder through to the drawing room at the immaculate sofas and cushions and clean windows giving onto the well-kept garden in the rain. 'Do you have someone from the village to clean for you?'

'No. I do it all.'

'Really?'

'Yes.'

'But a cleaner would cost nothing.'

'I could afford ten cleaners, but none of them would do it to my liking. I am even more particular about the duties of a cleaner than I am about the duties of a wife. And that's saying something.'

'Oh yes, Graham? And what are the duties of a wife, exactly?'

'Don't even think of pretending to some feminism, my dear. I know you to be beyond politics. I wouldn't do you the disservice of thinking you could be offended by my turning Tory on you. Let's just say a cleaner wouldn't clean to my liking, and leave it at that. I think we covered my insufficiencies as a husband in our last conversation.'

'You could tell them what you liked.'

'I could.'

'After all, you must be used to giving orders.'

'Of course.'

'Then why don't you try it?'

'I like to be in charge.'

'But you would be.'

'*Completely* in charge.'

'I see.'

'You do, do you?'

'You think you can do everything for yourself in life? That we have nothing to offer each other? By way of assistance.'

'I can do everything.'

'Then why have anything to do with anyone?'

'I don't.'

'That's not true. Or we wouldn't be . . . acquaintances.'

'Friends, surely.'

'Friends. We wouldn't be, would we? Nor, for that matter,

should you complain about sleeping alone if you value your own company so much.'

'I didn't say that there weren't some things in which a second party is not indispensable. But the fact that they are indispensable doesn't make them welcome. Merely necessary.'

'Can't you make a virtue of necessity? Otherwise it's pretty rough going on your partner in . . . in crime.'

'I quite like the rough going.'

'Charming.'

Catharine stood up, her heart beating unpleasantly. She wandered into the doorway that led to the drawing room and looked again at the neat and hoovered room, the beige carpet and the regimental photographs over the fireplace; the tall, walnut drinks cabinet and Sanderson cushions, plump and smooth as open parachutes. She was struck by the absence of any photographs of children, and she remembered Graham's dismissal of them when they had spoken in the lane.

'Your clock has stopped,' she said.

There was a pause.

'Shouldn't you be running along?' said Graham.

Catharine thought to herself that he must know how much she hated him at that moment, how she loathed a subtextual conversation like the one they were having; how it was the height of dishonesty to a sensibility like hers. His dismissal of her was a kind of revenge now. As if it should be that way round. I ask you.

'My bandage appears to have come away. You wouldn't be a dear and fix it for me, would you? Before you go.'

She turned on him and looked him full in the face. As if she might refute him by a glance. But he looked from beneath the covert of his eyebrows with complacent confidence, perfectly poised, it seemed to her, between defence and attack.

'Of course,' she said, and went over to the table.

It didn't look loose, but he put his arm out as if he were about to give blood, and pushed up the shirtsleeve. She knew he was staring at her from his position of safety, and that even as she carefully rearranged the lint and surgical tape he was taking her in, breathing steadily and calmly; breathing, no doubt, her perfume; breathing the air of his kitchen, his house, his castle. She knew she was somewhere that in five or ten minutes, away from here, after consideration, she would be appalled at having visited; the future would blush though the present held her, still pale, still insistent she see something through, though she was not sure what. She'd forgotten Louise, now. Forgotten her as much as an actor, in the execution of a scene, forgets he is playing a part; the identification complete. Fury held her there, too. Fury that her femininity was under attack; *her* femininity – he was right, she wasn't political. But she would stand up under fire, would resist. She knew it all; knew he had gone silent, knowing that more talk was futile; knew that with his stare he could prosecute her puritanism while never openly showing his hand. Knew that he knew she was attacking herself as relentlessly as he was. She knew, in short, that he had hope; knew that he was shrewd enough not to feel false hope. And that therefore his hope was not unfounded. There it was. She was as good as guilty. My God, to have hope so near the end of your life. Exhaustless Eros. If the young only knew that nothing changed, would they ever feel desire with such impunity, knowing that what they felt, so new and fresh, would live on till its newness and freshness would bring shame and unseemliness in old age? She tried to pity Graham with the imagined judgement of the young but she couldn't. Graham wasn't pitiable. Life was a cipher for desire. Nothing else. She felt how strongly desire was the proving of his life. His house was immaculate just so nothing would impinge. There must be no obstacles. No children's faces on the mantelpiece. No sentiment. And no untidiness. She must relent. If this day was her life, then this day, and her visit, was his life, too. Who was she to stand in the way of that?

She rewrapped the tape once, then twice around the soft dressing. He winced. She loosened it without apologising.

What were we if not the realisation of each other's sexuality? After all, it was the only role we were cast in with any certainty. Succumb and you absolved those who desired us of shame, of reproach; you allowed them to be right. You allowed them to be young.

'There,' she said, pulling down the sleeve over the dressing.

'Too kind.'

As she sat back, the trauma of actual physical contact over, she felt herself retreat into a temporary daze. The room lost its three-dimensional assurance; even the man opposite her looked like a cut-out or a silhouette. Organic life and the dresser behind him were all equally vibrant, equally dull; she could no longer differentiate. Was this the syndrome soldiers were said to succumb to when, traumatised beyond help, they entered enemy villages and saw in women and children mere flickering images of resistance, of what must be annihilated; as simple to destroy as tearing up an unpleasant photograph?

One look at him, in the eye, and she would set it in motion.

The transgression would be hers. Not his. It would be a relief, surely. A charity, almost, to take on the sin. Or admit that it was hers, and always had been. She had led him on. That much was obvious. So see it through. Better, in the dog days of their marriage, for it to be her. Tom would be no good at infidelity. Tom needed to be full of certainties and justice and cats that he pulled out of the bag. Tom nailed the perpetrator. Tom knew the judge. Catch was more even-handed. She saw both sides. So better she should be unfaithful and let Tom and Graham off the hook. It was far nicer to do that. Tom would have been hard on himself if he had only Catharine's vague withdrawal from their marriage; he would have blamed himself. This way he could blame Catch. And Catch could do what Louise had *not* done, and *not* blame Graham.

She would ask for nothing from Tom. Not the house, not money. If, by an extraordinary freak of nature, she were pregnant, Tom would, of course, have custody of the child. It was only fair. He and Valerie Mountjoy, perhaps, would meet in the lanes and exchange sad, knowing smiles at Catharine's disgrace, at the tragic inevitability of such a woman becoming a mother. Leaving a baby so worthy of love to fend for itself. Catharine would be, by now, exiled, having compounded her sin with other sins, just to make sure there was no uncertainty about whose fault the whole charade had been. There was shoplifting – things for the baby, maternity wear; a car accident while not paying due care and atten-tion, she having failed to pay due care and attention to many things; the attempted arson of her house, which Tom char-itably attempted to cover up as an accident whilst cooking. All these things were possible; or there was suicide. After all, if you really knew you had done wrong, you didn't need a conscience, did you? You needed a rope.

She had always assumed that the approbation of a man must constitute in some way the happiness of maturity. Not flattery, or a desperate need for reassurance – just the sense of having done well, of having done someone else's bidding, in a benign sense; answering the call of another's heart. Something not a million miles away from playing the piano to her father and her being pleased when he said, 'That was a nice one, Catharine.' Such approbation was perhaps not enough to make you a concert pianist, but it gave a bloom to the moment; it gathered up promise and hope and optimism. That's all she wanted to carry her through life. As she got older she knew that the sentiment, 'That was a nice one, Catharine,' was most likely to be echoed subsequent to the administering of a sexual favour. But she had never shaken off completely the hope that an older masculinity might still, beyond the carnal, say to her, 'Well done.' For all her beating heart and weird reveries in Graham's kitchen, she knew she had sought it of him. And now, at the least likely moment, she had a great, stubborn desire to pluck an avuncular respect from the jaws of an unseemly seduction.

'Not having a very good day, Graham.'

'How so?'

'Can't seem to shake it off.'

'My dear girl . . .'

'I really should go.'

'Of course. Do come again. You have missed your vocation. A ministering angel. That's what you are.'

'Oh, shut up.'

'What? Ah, you're smiling. That's better. You are all that

Valerie Mountjoy will never be. You never did tell me what gave her the face of a gorgon stomping back to her house. Apart from destroying the mad girl's scribbles. Another time. You turned the tables on me and got me into confessional mode. Not sure how you managed it. I shall have to put it down to your magical touch, both with the bandages and with my susceptible heart. The rain's holding off. Look how bloody dark it is. We should all be in bed. The long, bloody day closes. Go on, off you go. I shall finish this bottle and then finish off the hedge. You've got me fit for active service, at least. Patched me up. Go on. Don't mind me.'

'I won't leave you if you'd rather I didn't.'

'What? Go. Go on! What is there to keep you here?'

'I don't know.'

Still she hesitated. Now it seemed to her that to leave was as compromised, as bourgeois as to stay. If she left she was a coward, a naysayer. She had a private misgiving that her life was utterly foundering on her failure to connect, and she had the chance to put some clear water between herself and her life, to reappraise. And only something as outrageous as intimacy with Graham could accomplish that. She didn't want it, but that wasn't the point. She needed to ditch Tom's world, the legal covenant of marriage, the legal covenant of Tom himself. She knew she was in the dock already. 'I put it to you, members of the jury, that this woman was perfectly appraised of her husband's character. She could simply have waited for him to come home and then had a damn good chat about her unhappiness and straightened things out. This is the twenty-first century and this woman is no Madame Bovary, however much she might like to romanticise herself as such . . . et cetera . . . et cetera . . .'

'For Christ's sake,' said Graham very quietly.

'What? What?' said Catch, suddenly strident, almost furious.

'My dear girl, if you have something to say to me, say it.'

She was in an agony of not knowing if they were thinking the same thing.

'Perhaps it's not so easy, *my dear man.*'

Catharine stood up and Graham looked at her, brightly, as if he had come out from the cover of his eyebrows, like a woodland creature come to taste the daylight.

'Go along now, there's a good girl. Your cakes will be burnt.'

Catch turned, walked through to the drawing room, opened the front door and let herself out.

She was angry but knew she had no right to be. The rain spat down and the wind blew hair into her face. She stumbled into the road; if a car had come at that moment she would have been done for. Bloody done for. But the thoroughfare was empty. A waste of a road. In an attempt to be a more obedient woman, more moral, she took the kerb and clung to the hedgerow side for the walk back to her house.

She blamed Louise. She was allowed to, after all; Louise wasn't there to object. Louise had given her a passport to foreign territory. It had been too tempting. Unused to finding anything in common with other women, the sudden presence of this mannequin, onto whom one might project one's own thoughts and desires, had been too tempting.

She was tired; desperately tired. Brambles detained her, the hard road jolted her. Here was the empty stretch of road between Graham's and the turning to her house. To the dreaded house. The lovers' walk. This was how they must have come, either she from Graham's bed, or he from hers. No. He was married, too. They must have done it at her house. 'I know your bedroom better than you do,' he'd said. How dare he? How repellent. As if the world were just a shared playground and no corner of it was wholly yours.

She made it to the house. She turned the key in the lock and dropped her coat inside. How had she made it so far? A few moments ago the distance had seemed insurmountable. She must lie down. She took the stairs. With six steps to go from the top she had a grave misgiving. She was too tired to make it. The last six presented themselves to her, a further gang of obstacles that defeated her. She would sleep, wedged between banister and wall. There would be no shame in the unwitnessed collapse in the face of such exhaustion. The light green carpet was soft; worn but soft. At the last step, which she wanted to kick for all its arrogant certainty, she paused. Louise had thrown herself down these stairs. What? Louise had thrown herself down these stairs, to punish her lover. And to punish Her Majesty's Government for taking her husband from her bed. Louise did, but I will not. I will climb where Louise fell. That is how superior this Mother Superior is.

On the bed her shoulders shook but no tears came. Surely the physical pain she felt at her mere continued existence could not last. A body could not feel pain without just cause. She turned her head abjectly on the pillow and felt herself looking out of the window as from a sickbed, the neck twisted under the constraint of bed rest. It was raining. Raining without her. What, that morning, had been the pleasant supposition of her powerlessness was now the continual application of sensory pain, imaginary pain; pain that could carry on without her. Perhaps even beyond death.

Why couldn't it snow? It had snowed in the nineteenth century, why could it not snow now? What epochal deprivation meant that we were to be denied? Snow was moral. When it had snowed you looked back at the route you had taken from gate to door, from road to porch, and your blue steps gave to the poetry of the morning a human dimension; they showed you where you had gone, which animals had passed where you passed, where the cat had arched its neck to inspect the step for a saucer of milk; where the fox had cased the chicken coup. Perfect evidence of your whereabouts co-existed with beauty; you could give up thinking where you were, for your coordinates were logged till the thaw came.

She looked up at the ceiling. If I could die an imaginary death. If the transposition of thinking yourself into the guise of another person was available to her, why should she not think of herself as dead. Just as an experiment, so she could start again.

Then, with a pure horror, she remembered the woman after Louise; the woman Graham had said he had befriended while she died. That was here too. A sick feeling overtook her. Catch was becoming anyone. She must fight the identification as strongly as she could. It had been a great mistake to think of it. Staring at this ceiling, perhaps, as she died in agony, that woman, that nameless woman had been here too. This window had been the last thing she ever saw, perhaps. Worrying the covers, distraught at what she left, at the dissolving of consciousness . . . weakly smiling at Graham's wit in the face of calamity; grateful to him but wanting to scream *not now*.

Better to be Louise, said Catch to herself, better the mad woman. Better to fill up this smuggler's cabin of a bedroom full of a thousand thoughts of infidelity than find yourself in the mind of a dead woman. Let them all come. Let them come to me, as they came in ancient mythology, as Zeus came, as bull or swan or cloud of gold. My God what a relief to succumb to the divinely sanctioned fuck. I'll lie there and wait for the world to have me. And if a god can't fill up my womb with a child, I'll find a field or barren slope, as barren as I am, and I'll have done. I'll shut up. Finally. Shut up.

Downstairs the clock struck three. Three? What monster had eaten away the afternoon, denying her lunch? From her life she had had deducted a meal. It was unrecoverable. She could not now taste of whatever she might find in the larder downstairs and call it lunch. It would taste of something else. Of casual sustenance. Catch felt panic grip her throat. She would never be able to eat again. She would become anorexic. The thought of food threatened to make her retch. If only her head could fall further into the pillow till the white cotton depression engulfed it entirely.

Her feet felt the chill. She should have put thicker socks on. I should have put thicker socks on.

She went to sleep.

Now the mothers will be walking home from school. Catharine has checked the clock and it is a quarter to four. She has put on the heating early, and already the house is warming up. She has changed into a cardigan, brushed her hair and put it up with a comb Maria gave her for her thirtieth. Her friend is due in fifteen minutes, and though she is always late, Catharine does not give up hope that one day she will be on time.

The kettle has boiled, and Catharine would no more make herself a cup of tea before Maria's arrival than she would drink champagne before everyone was present for a celebration.

Nearly the shortest day. She never knew the exact date of the winter solstice, but she knew it was just before Christmas. Nice to think of the day, of the daylight itself squeezed to its smallest allowance, augmented by fires and the warm glow of the laptop screensaver in the alcove beneath the stairs. She liked to check emails in the winter; liked the link that subsisted despite the dark. Maria teased her, for Catch wrote messages like old-fashioned letters still; informality was a trial to her. Maria dispensed with both their names; Catharine qualified both with adjectives: Dearest Masha . . . love from your devoted Catharine. Reading anything good, Masha? Your emails.

They would send a flurry of messages and then phone each other, impatient of the written word. Then they would say everything they had written, Maria now fulsome in her affection and Catharine more relaxed, as if they had exchanged roles in the movement from the written to the spoken.

There was a knock at the door. It was well past four. There she was, standing in the rain, a slightly bedraggled diva, smiling through the weather, her cheeks slightly flushed. She held off from crossing the threshold, as if her arrival were to be made space around, like the audience of a visiting monarch. As if she wanted to take in the fact of her own devotion, marvel together at it.

But Catharine, as she had when she had heard the sound of Maria's voice on the phone that morning, felt, not disappointment, but a failure to completely recognise the late-thirties incarnation of her college friend. She was tired around the eyes, but then she had had a concert the night before. A concert and a man.

'Shouldn't you come in out of the rain?' said Catch.

Maria only laughed.

'Look at me. I'm wet through. I left the car in the road.'

'Why? Why didn't you drive up to the house?'

'Oh yes. Do you remember last time? Some of those potholes are larger than my Mini.'

'Silly.'

'It's true. Disappear and never come back. Shame the Tube doesn't come out this far. Hello, darling.'

She came forward and kissed her friend; when it was over Catch moved to pull back but Maria held her there for a second. When they detached Catch looked wonderingly, but Maria was determinedly taking off her long black chenille coat. Underneath she was dressed in a russet skirt and a velvet waistcoat. Catharine remembered the old Mini and wondered again at the characterful combination of bohemian glamour and scruffiness.

'Wanted to get here in daylight. Gets dark so bloody early. I ought to be wetter but I managed to park under some trees. Some old bloke came out and started lecturing me about parking close to the verge.'

'That was Graham, probably.'

'Like something out of the last days of the Raj.'

'Definitely Graham.'

'I told him to fuck off.'

'You'll have made his day.'

'Well, I mean, honestly. Get a lot of parking crime down here, do you? It's all go in the country.'

'No, don't put your coat there. I'll put it somewhere warm to dry.'

'I can't see you in this light. Can't see if you're all right.'

'What? It's so nice to see you. Why shouldn't I be all right?'

'It's lovely to see you too.'

'I'm fine,' said Catch.

'You sounded odd on the phone.'

'I am odd. Have you only just noticed?'

'Strained.'

'Just a weird day waiting for Tom to come home. Tea?'

'Thought you'd never ask.'

They went through into the kitchen. It was strange to see Maria there, after the meeting with Valerie Mountjoy, after the thoughts of the day. As if Catharine were reconciled to every interview being difficult; every conversation a challenge.

'How was the journey? Car still going strong?'

'Yes. But going to get another.'

'What?'

'Darling, I can't drive a Mini when I'm forty. Not one that has one green wing and one yellow.'

'I love that car.'

'I want to talk about you.'

'What car are you going to get? Can you afford it?'

'Dad's lending me.'

'How much?'

'Five grand.'

'Five grand, Masha, buys quite a nice car.'

'Dad's getting protective in his old age. Maybe it's because I don't tell him to fuck off so much as I used to do. I should have tried it ages ago.'

'You tell everyone to fuck off.'

'Except you. Never done it to you.'

'I'm deeply touched.'

'So you should be.'

'How is your dad?'

Now he's retired he's turned sort of grand. Magnanimous. It's quite annoying.'

'Well, if it's like father like daughter there's hope for you yet.'

'Fuck off.'

The two women laughed.

'You're standing on ceremony,' said Catch, 'why don't you sit down? Now. Tea. You can have wine if you want.'

'It's you. You're formal. You make me formal.'

'I've never noticed you be formal, ever.'

'Make me want to be, then. I'm only joking, darling.'

'Do you want some wine?'

'At four o'clock?'

'Nearly five, actually.'

'Shit, was I that late?

'Within the hour is quite good for you.'

'I'm getting better. Honestly. Oh shit!'

'What?'

'I had a present for you, and I forgot it.'

'What was it?'

'The new Thomas Kershaw.'

'Never mind.'

'I'm such a—'

'Sit down!'

Maria sat.

'So,' she said. 'What's the story? He not looking after you?'

'Who?'

'Who? The Pope. Your husband, counsel for the defence,

Englishman through and through, Tom. Ah, Tom. I love the sound of his name. Safe and solid.'

'There's a mad Tom in *King Lear*. And of course he's looking after me.'

'There's no of course about it. Don't look at me like that. Best friends are allowed to ask of their best friends whether their impeccable husbands have suddenly turned to beating them or having affairs. It's allowed. It would be a dereliction of duty if I didn't ask. It's in my interests in a way if he *has* turned into a wife beater, since my stock would go up terribly. You'd be on the phone to me every night. I'd be in clover. But I love you so much I don't want him to fail as a husband. I want you to be happy. My learned friend Tom and I have had our differences in the past, but I in no way want him to fail you as a husband, because then I would have to kill him, and murder is so messy. So?'

'He's looking after me.'

'What a shame. I've always fancied myself as an assassin.'

'I thought you just broke their hearts and left them for dead.'

'Why didn't you answer my email?'

'Which one?'

'The one I sent last week.'

'Oh, I . . . I didn't check them.'

'There was a link to that boy in Latvia. You must check your emails.'

'I don't like them. I hate them. We speak, we have pizza. Why do we need emails?'

'There's my nineteenth-century girl.'

'Anyway, he is looking after me.'

'Still on that, are we? Say it twice and it begins to look like you're covering something up.'

'I want to talk about you. You said you had something to tell me.'

But Maria was watching her friend.

'Oh, it's nothing. I'll tell you later. Seriously.'

Catharine put her head in her hands.

'Why don't *I* make the tea?' said Maria.

'All right.'

'And you tell me all about it.'

'I don't know.'

'Don't know what?'

'If I can tell you all about it. I'm not sure it's the sort of thing that can be told.'

'It's all right,' said Maria softly.

'Is it?'

'Yes.'

'Why?'

'Because I say it is. Have you forgotten who this is? Your old, mad Masha.'

'I'm very grateful.'

'So you bloody should be. I had a punch-up with Mark booked for tonight and I put him off, just for you.'

'I thought you saw him last night.'

'What, you can't have punch-ups on two consecutive nights? What do you think I am, a novice? Punch-ups are like sex, you have to work at it, you have to get close, intimate, seek out the sensitive areas, indulge your fantasies, be open and prepared to experiment. That's it, laugh.'

'I don't deserve your friendship.'

'Oh, is that right?'

'I'm a puritan, and a snob, and superior. And I have so much, and I'm so bloody ungrateful.'

'Right.'

'And I don't even know why I'm unhappy.'

'Well, let's look at it. Do you think it's moving to the country?'

'No.'

'Is it Tom?'

'Tom? Why on earth should it be Tom? Tom's perfect.'

'Keep taking the pills, darling.'

'It's me that's the problem.'

'You in what sense?'

'In the me sense.'

'I see.'

'Do you?'

'Not really.'

'It's no good. Can't we just talk about you?'

'Why?'

'I just think that talking about you would make it all right. If only for an hour.'

'I haven't got enough material for a whole hour.'

'Oh, the past, then. I don't know. When we were younger I just remember us talking about nothing for hours. You made me laugh. I used to laugh and laugh.'

'We aim to please.'

'I never knew what you saw in me. I never knew what it was I brought to your life. You see? Selfish, selfish, selfish.'

'You think keeping me sane with your careful consideration, your lack of judgement of me, your . . . intelligence and sort of older-sisterly thoughtfulness, patience, loyalty . . . was nothing? Grown-up-ness, most of all. And what I felt was unconditional love. Isn't all that enough to be going on with?'

'You'll make me cry.'

'So cry.'

'But what good is it all if I hate myself?'

'My God, you've got a good one going on there.'

'A good what?'

'I don't know what you call it, but I've had one myself. It'll pass.'

'What's the cure?'

'Tea. Friendship. Or a good shag. Mine's milk, no sugar. Oh, I said I'd make it, didn't I?'

She got up.

'Masha.'

'Ordinary do you?'

'Ordinary's what I like. My marriage is over.'

'What rubbish.'

'It is. You ought to be shocked.'

'If it was true, I'd be shocked.'

'How do you know it's not true?'

'My love, this is me. Tom may be a humourless, analytical, tiresome pedant, but the two of you were made for each other. Laugh, please.'

'It's not funny.'

'All right, but what could possibly be wrong between you two? Has he got a pretty new secretary?'

'Why should it be him who is tempted? Why shouldn't it be me?'

'Is it?'

'Are you mad? No, I just . . . I just don't want only one path. I don't want . . . I can't explain. I want . . . choices. Look at you.'

'Oh yes. Look at me. A picture of middle-aged wisdom and contentment.'

'What? You're wise. You've worked hard, you're a self-sufficient independent woman, you've refused to be pinned down, you're talented, creative. So what that you don't have the conventional things you're supposed to have at your age? So what if your Mini is green and yellow? You'll always be you, and it's genius.'

'Steady.'

'It is! All right, I've never wanted some of the things you've got. I'd be useless being a bohemian. But you've never yearned after things in a useless way. And you've never looked down on anyone in your life.'

'Neither have you.'

'Not in a conscious way. But I expect so much, Masha. Of myself. And expecting a lot of yourself must mean that secretly you expect a lot of other people. Otherwise who the hell do I think I am with one rule for myself and another for other people? Ambitious, Maria, you know? Looking for answers and understanding and the nature of charity. You know?'

'I'm not sure I do. Anyway, you've never looked down on me. Or have you?'

'Look up to you now.'

Maria frowned.

'So why is your marriage over?'

'We're comfortable, yes? We're middle class. We have enough food, we have comforts. Tom and I don't even have children, for God's sake. So why is it still so hard? Who the fuck am I to still find each day – this day – just a matter of survival? My God, it ought to be more than that. Marriage is just survival. Survival *à deux*.'

'I wouldn't know.'

'And if you're going to survive, at least know yourself. If knowing yourself is the problem, then do it on your own. Don't burden someone else with the awfulness of your own personality.'

'Tom didn't look too burdened the last time I saw him.'

'Because he doesn't know me.'

'Have you talked to him about this?'

Catharine just shook her head.

'I can't. We're strangers,' she said, looking down. 'This morning, I couldn't play a single note of the piano. I sat and stared at it and couldn't do so much as play a note. I just stared. I'm paralysed, Masha. I couldn't impose myself. I just wanted to be obliterated. I have to do something more than think and walk the lanes and drink tea waiting for my husband to come home. I have to.'

'Yes, you probably do.'

'You know, I remembered thinking the last time we met how much you'd spoken about our time at college and something that had happened to us, I can't remember what, and at the time I'd thought it was self-indulgent. There, I can admit it. I actually thought that.'

'Last month.'

'Yes. I'd actually felt it wasn't a worthy way to live your life, just going over things that had happened a long time ago. Like a sort of in-joke. But now I think what sort of dreadful person do I think I am? Loathsome, critical, judgemental cow. How dare I? You are my great friend. The one great constant.'

'Darling.'

'It's true.'

'I only go on about the past because I think it's what you like.'

'Oh my God, does that mean we've run out of things to talk about?' said Catch.

They laughed.

'And anyway,' went on Maria, 'I wouldn't hold my life up as anything to emulate. Do you know I once left a perfectly nice man because I found out that he had a pension fund. That was all it took to put me off him. He had been unfaithful with the Alliance and Leicester and I could not forgive him. Pretty hateful, eh?'

'Did you come clean that that's why you were leaving him?'

'Of course. I gave it to him straight.'

'What was his defence?'

'His parents had died without a penny and hadn't been able to afford proper nursing care. He'd promised them he wouldn't let the same thing happen to him.'

'Oh dear.'

'Oh yes.'

'Did you have him back?'

'I seem to remember that by that stage he wasn't that wild on me *having* him back.'

'It's a good story.'

'My hatefulness has made some good stories.'

'Masha.'

'It has.'

'I hope you never change.'

Maria smiled, but there had been a little pause before the smile.

'At least we'll always have each other,' said Catch, filling the silence.

'You really should read the latest Kershaw.'

'Why?'

'What do you mean why? Books not made it down to these here parts yet?'

'Why should I read it?'

'You just should. Everybody should.'

There was another pause. Catharine heard a voice which she knew was her own, the same voice which had said to Valerie Mountjoy, 'I feel lonely sometimes,' say, 'But I don't like Thomas Kershaw.'

'But I gave you *Albion Mansions* for your birthday and you said you loved it.'

'I was lying.'

'Right.'

'Don't be angry, Masha.'

'I don't care that you lied. But I care that you didn't like it. It's an amazing book. And he's an amazing writer. I can't believe it. Did you find the end too shocking?'

'I didn't make it to the end.'

'What? You didn't finish it? That's outrageous, darling. I gave you a book I rate in my top ten reads of all time and you didn't even finish it. We can't even have a good argument about it if you didn't finish it. And if you didn't read the end then of course none of the rest of it makes sense. None of the people are who you think they are. It's not what you think it's about.'

'I see.'

'Well, heigh-ho.'

'I'm sorry. I'll try it again.'

'Do. Give it a go. See where it takes you.'

'It's what I was telling you. I don't read any more. I don't seem to do anything.'

'Right.'

'Are you sure you don't want wine?'

'I can't.'

'Driving?'

'I'll have some more tea if there's any in the pot. So . . . you don't read any more?'

'No.'

'Wow.'

'Yes. Shocking, isn't it?'

'You don't look shocked.'

'Books seem beyond me.'

'Beyond you? What do you mean?'

'He's so rough, Kershaw. I mean, I feel it all so keenly.'

'The violence?'

'Not just the violence. Everything. His manner. Instead of getting a thicker skin as I get older, I feel it's thinner. More sensitive. I feel his portrayal of the world as a kind of . . . affront. So bold. So decisive.'

'So brilliant.'

'Maybe. But he makes me want to argue with him. To make the world not like the one he portrays.'

'That's good. He's got you thinking.'

'I don't want to be got thinking. I don't want to compete. I just want to be left alone.'

'Some would say that what he's trying to do is shock people out of their complacency.'

'I don't want to be shocked,' said Catch softly. Almost like a child. 'I had a phone call, this morning,' she went on, still quiet, almost marvelling at her discovery of the past within her, even though the past was only that morning, 'from a neighbour. She wanted me to speak to her daughter. It seems something of nothing now I look back on it, but it shook me,

Masha. You see, there was this girl – *is* this girl – in the village, the daughter of a bit of a village gorgon, and she's not very happy, and she got it into her head that she wanted to study history of art when she left school, but really only so as to wind up her mum and dad, who are divorced – the girl's in the sixth form now – and I got sort of co-opted into being the one to go and talk her out of it – to go and sort of counsel this girl. So I did, and the mother left me and Angelica, the girl, together, and we got to talking, and I made some comment about breaking with the past – that as you got older sometimes you had to break with aspects of the past that might be holding you back – you know, I didn't mean it in a revolutionary sense – and this girl went upstairs and brought down what I later found out was her A-level art coursework, and she tore it up, Masha, there and then, in the kitchen of this little cottage, before I could stop her, and she said, "There, I've broken with the past," and about half an hour later the mother came knocking at my door threatening to press charges – thought I'd incited the girl to vandalise her work.'

'Well, you had.'

'Indirectly, yes. I suppose I had.'

'But now that she will probably fail her art A-level, you have at least prevented her from studying art history at university. Or anything else, for that matter.'

'God, do you think I have?'

'Why shouldn't the girl study art history?'

'Oh, she wouldn't like it. She'd be bored. You should see her. It's just a wind-up. But you know, I found her tearing up those drawings as shocking as anything I've seen or read. I mean, talking of Kershaw.'

'You should get out more, love. Breaking with the past. There's a thought. Always thought you'd break with me, one day.'

'Masha!'

'I did. Maybe you still might.'

'Why?'

'You'll find a reason. Take a shine to this girl, did you?'

'What? No. In a way I couldn't bear her. She was all attitude. You know the kind of thing.'

'But you still wondered what it would have been like if she'd been your daughter.'

'How do you know that?'

'Darling, it's obvious. Why shouldn't you? How did it make you feel?'

'Unworthy.'

'Surprise, surprise.'

'Well, it did.'

'Are you still trying?'

'Trying what?'

'To have a baby.'

'Yes. All the time.'

'Well, from the sound of it you got through to this girl. You probably did some good.'

'The mother said she'd liked me. Which made the mother furious.'

'How funny. You should follow it up.'

'How do you mean?'

'Befriend her. The daughter. Be a good Samaritan.'

'I couldn't.'

'Why not?'

'Well . . .'

'You said you needed to do more than sit and—'

'I could manage the cool thirty-something for one meeting,

but she'd soon see through me. I don't think she'd like me if she got to know me.'

'I liked you from the start,' said Maria, 'it was you who took some winning over.'

'I didn't.'

'But I won you over to the gypsy camp in the end. By playing the violin passing well. Without the fiddle I'd have been lost.'

'Don't say that. That's terrible.'

'True, though. You wanted to be a musician and took vicarious pleasure in my quite extraordinary talent and you decided I could be your friend. I qualified because I could do something you couldn't. Why shouldn't you? I enjoyed being adopted. I was used to being wanted by boys just for a shag. I liked being wanted for something else. Nothing's that pure, is it? Seems to me.'

'Put like that it sounds rather calculating.'

'We're all calculating, aren't we? For better or for worse.'

'You can call it calculating. Or you can call it . . . call it . . . celebrating.'

'Bit too rose-tinted for me. Maybe that's what I was letting all those boys do – the ones I lured back to my room. Celebrate me. Come and celebrate me.'

'Maybe you were.'

'And mind you wear a condom while you're at it.'

'But, Masha, to go back to the thing about music. It wasn't mercenary. Music reveals people, doesn't it? I like to think I saw a new part of you when you played.'

'Don't beat yourself up about it. You were able to appreciate the music without actually having to get involved and you liked it. What's wrong with that? I, on the other hand, actually had to put in the practice. You know? Hours of it. Only to see girls with the talent and personalities of ponies walk straight into jobs with London orchestras because they toed the party line and never lifted their pretty heads above their desks.'

'Ponies?'

'Yes, I don't know why I chose that animal. All a bit pony club, I suppose. Ponies who could play in tune. Ponies who wished they'd gone to Oxbridge. Anyway, how did we get onto the past? Kershaw agrees with you, by the way. The indulgence of the past. Particularly the middle-class past.'

'I don't think it's indulgent. I was criticising myself for having thought that, remember?'

'Whatever.'

'It's important.'

'Well, maybe I'm the puritan now, eh?'

'As opposed to me?'

'That's what Tobias always called you, wasn't it?'

'He called me lots of things,' said Catch. 'I can't remember a characteristic of mine that he *did* like.'

'Other than being his one true love.'

'Most of the time he wanted me to be more like you. "Why can't you be more like Maria," he'd say.'

'What fine virtue of mine was he craving in particular, do you think? Something to do with sex, no doubt.'

'Why "no doubt"?'

'I don't know. He was always rather driven, wasn't he?'

'Yes.'

'Well, there you are. Probably no one girl could have given him all he wanted.'

'But you could have given it a better shot than me?'

'I didn't say that.'

'That's what you're implying.'

'He probably assumed I had more experience than you.'

'Which was true.'

'Which was true.'

'That's all I meant.'

'"There's a girl who knows how to have good time." That's what he said.'

'Everybody has a good time. The puritans and the head girls of this world are having just as good a time as the wild ones. They're having their own way, just as much. Pisses me off when everybody assumes the moral ones are obeying the rules. They made the bloody rules, didn't they? They're having a great time. Kershaw's good about that, too. Disapproval.'

'But you disapproved of Tobias. You hated him.'

'No.'

'You said you did.'

'I thought he was a cunt. But as your boyfriend I tolerated him. He could be amusing.' Maria scratched her eyebrow and frowned. 'He could be amusing,' she repeated. 'He said he couldn't keep up with the moral challenge of sharing a bed with you.'

'You talked about me with him?'

'Yes.'

'I didn't know.'

'You know how indiscreet he could be. When you split up with him he badgered me for a while. With questions.'

'What questions?'

'I can't remember. But he came to me, the day after you'd dumped him, I think it was. I don't think I ever told you. I even ended up in bed with him.'

'What?'

'Well, you didn't want him any more.'

'Masha!'

'Yes.'

'You slept with him?'

'Well, not when you were going out with him, *obviously*.'

'But . . . why didn't you tell me at the time?'

'I didn't think you needed that particular seduction related to you. You ought to be flattered.'

'What do you mean?'

'Are you offended?'

'No. It's just . . . we're so different. That's all. What happened?'

'He came to me. He came to my room and he just stood there and he said, "She's dumped me. She's bloody well gone and dumped me." I said, "Poor you." And he said, "Why, Maria? You know her. You know her bloody better than she knows herself. Tell me why." I said, "Because you're a cunt, Toby." And he said – I can remember it, it was quite an amusing conversation – "Ah. I see." I think he was a bit drunk. In fact now I recall, he was very drunk. "It is a possibility," he said. "It is a distinct possibility." You know how posh he got when he was pissed.'

'Then what happened?'

'Then he said – it's all coming back to me – he said, "What do you think, Maria? Am I?" And I said something like on the balance of probability he was probably part cunt, part bloke. And he said, "Which part?" Then I seem to remember we chatted in a similar *entendre*-ish sort of way, and then I went over and unzipped his flies and gave him a blow job. After which he fell on the bed and went fast asleep. Then,

226

when we woke up that morning I shagged him. Allowing him ample opportunity to demonstrate his extensive repertoire and a little showing off into the bargain. Then I kicked him out. Then, as chance would have it, you came round looking suitably haunted and guilty for having dumped him. That's right. I didn't think it appropriate to share what had just happened.'

'I was actually terrified because the last time I'd seen him he'd told me he was going to throw himself into the Manchester Ship Canal.'

'I was the Manchester Ship Canal.'

'I see. I still think you might have told me.'

'I didn't want you to think he wasn't suicidal. A girl ought to feel every once in a while that a bloke might top himself for their sake. Don't you think? You were entitled.'

'Did you think I'd be angry?'

'No. Are you now?'

Pause.

'No.'

'As I say, you ought to be flattered.'

'Why?'

'It was a way of . . . of being close to you. It was about you. Not him. I idolised you. I wanted to see life the way you saw it. You were so certain, so . . . decided about things. That was rare in those days. Now it's common as muck. Then it was . . . special.'

'Well . . . I'm not so certain any more.'

'About Tom?'

'About anything.'

'For God's sake don't start that again. Tell me you've had an affair. Tell me you've converted to Buddhism, but don't tell me you and Tom aren't destined to spend your lives together. It's annoying.'

'You slept with Tobias.'

'I knew you'd be angry.'

'I'm not. I'm marvelling at the fact that I don't care. Not only am I not angry, I don't care. That's what the past does, isn't it? Makes us not care. If enough time passes, nothing matters.'

'Believe me, it didn't much matter at the time.'

'I never felt he showed off when he was in bed with *me*.'

'Maybe he thought he had less to compete with. I mean, he knew I had past form. More to compare him with. You know how competitive boys can be.'

'Tom's not.'

'Dream on. Look at him with me. He's pure bloody competition.'

'Would you sleep with Tom if I left him, too?'

'Darling . . .'

'I'm going mad. You've got to see me through today. You're the most important person in my life and you've got to see me through it. I've taken a wrong turn, Masha. Somewhere I've made a terrible mistake, and I need you. Otherwise I'm done for.'

'What's got into you? Really, you should leave displays like this to me. I've got the hair to go with it.'

'Done for.'

'Stop saying that.'

'If I can just make it through till tomorrow morning I feel it'll be all right. I just need to shut down and have an early night and tomorrow will be different. It can't be right to live like this. Just to think in an empty house. Not if you don't have children. It can't be right. I should do something. Charity work.'

'Then do it. Then again, read Kershaw on the charity industry.'

'Charity is not an industry.'

'As good as.'

'No. Charity is *not* an industry. Car making is an industry. Agriculture is an industry. But charities are different.'

'All right, Catharine.'

'And Kershaw is not the fount of all wisdom.'

'Font.'

'The font of all wisdom.'

'Perish the thought. Though how you can say that if you don't even get to the end of his boo—'

'I want to be known, Masha.'

'I know you.'

'I want to be known. Or I'm going to die.'

'You're going to die anyway, actually.'

'Do you know me? Do you know Tom? You don't like him. I do. One of us has to be right, one of us has to be wrong. Surely.'

'It's subjective.'

'*Too* subjective.'

'My God, this is all a bit middle-class undergraduate territory, isn't it? No offence, but—'

'What do I do?'

'What? If you want to be known – get God.'

'I have no God.'

'Failing God, have a—'

Maria stopped and looked away, as if the word she was about to say had run loose in the room, eluding her and causing mischief, such that all she could do now was look after it with a look of sorry reproach.

'What?' said Catch. 'What? Say it. Go on. I know what you were going to say. Why not say it?'

'How do you know what I was going to say?'

'Because you're my friend. And I saw you make the decision not to say it, and I love you for it. But still you ought to have said it. Then it might have come true.'

'Said what?' said Maria, quietly.

'Have a baby. Failing God, have a baby. That's what you were going to say, wasn't it?

'Yes.'

'Yes. That's right. Well. Don't be sorry that that is what you were going to say. Because it's probably true, and we can bear a little truth in our lives, can't we, you and me? Crazy, isn't it? We spend all our twenties making sure this thing, having a baby, doesn't happen, and thinking one slip up and that'll be it, and then thirty-eight comes along and you can't get pregnant for love nor money. You think you know your body, but it might as well be the body of a stranger, with a set of manners and rules and ways completely foreign to you. You don't know what secrets it holds. Like cancer.'

'Christ, Catharine – kids and cancer.'

'It's true. If you want to have a child, these are the things you think about.'

'Are they?'

'Yes.'

'What about Tom? Has he been understanding?'

'You're assuming he hasn't been.'

'Not at all. I was genuinely enquiring if my great friend is getting the support she needs.'

'Yes.'

'That's good.'

'Well . . .'

'Yes?'

'Insofar as the marriage is doomed.'

'Of course.'

'Why won't you take it seriously?'

'All right.'

'When we were trying, he wouldn't address it.'

'Address . . .'

'The problem. He wouldn't formulate a strategy.'

'Put like that it's not the sexiest invitation to reproduce.'

'I mean if we keep trying and nothing happens. He wouldn't talk about what we were going to do.'

'He was probably just looking on the bright side.'

'That's all very well, but you have to be realistic. You have to evaluate your options.'

'Well, think about it,' said Maria. 'It's not very nice for a man to think he might be failing you in some way. He's probably just trying to take the pressure off both of you. Otherwise it just becomes a self-fulfilling prophecy. And you don't want an impotent husband on top of an infertile one. If that's the problem. So he's probably right to just relax and keep trying.'

'What you say is very sensible.'

'My advice would be . . .'

'Extremely sensible.'

'. . . not to put too much pressure on him.'

'Right. Why are you defending him all of a sudden?'

'I'm not. I just think that a man's sense of not conceiving a child is bound to be very different from a woman's. It's more about providing the right input. As it were. Men are used to being in control. Even men like Tom. Suddenly there's this thing over which they have no control. A fifty–fifty thing. They can't do anything to affect the result and some men find that a problem. At the risk of incurring your wrath about my favourite man of the moment, Kershaw wrote an article in the *Guardian* a few months back about the crisis of masculinity. About how hard it is for men to place themselves emotionally and economically these days. Men don't provide for women like they used to, which is more power to our elbow. But it means that when they have to provide a baby – I don't know – maybe it gets harder and harder. As it were. You're different from most women – you're able to assume your husband will treat you as an equal. But don't assume that Tom doesn't need a bit of an old-fashioned role sometimes. He's a bloke too, you know.'

'It's . . .'

'What?'

'It's strange to hear you talking . . . I don't know . . . from a man's point of view.'

'Why?'

'You were always so hard on them.'

'I just don't think you should be down on Tom. Has it ever occurred to you that in my single state that I might envy a little of what you have?'

'Often. I feel guilty that I have a complacency with respect to—'

'I don't want your guilt, Catharine. I want you to be just. Just to me. Just to Tom.'

'I should never have got married.'

'Oh shut up.'

'There was a woman who lived here, before me. Louise. She went mad. I've become her. Has that ever occurred to you? That I might have gone mad? Has it? While you sit there judging me? Have you thought that?'

'Judging you? Judging you? What are you talking about? Musicians get judged, Catharine. Friends don't. If you want me to judge you, go next door and play me a piano sonata. I'll tell you if it's any good. My hunch is that it probably won't be. That's life. I can judge you as a musician and you can have that judgement for nothing. But I will never, ever, judge my friend.'

'If I got the notes right my interpretation would be as good as anybody's.'

'My God, you *have* gone mad. If you got the notes right? You're missing my point. You know, this music stuff pisses me off. Do you know that? You have a thing about talent. An unhealthy complex about it. I'll tell you something. Talent means nothing. Absolutely nothing. You may have become my friend because I could play the fucking fiddle, but I certainly didn't become yours because of you sublime appreciation of music. OK? If you got the notes right? I love you for your humanity, which right now seems to have a taken a left turn. You didn't have the talent. You don't have the talent. Accept it and move on. It doesn't make any difference. Support your husband. You were made to be a wife, just like I was made to be a mistress.'

'What a stupid, artificial distinction.'

'Stupid? Yes. It is stupid, and I have paid for my stupidity. I have a one-bedroom flat, a violin and a clapped-out Mini. I'm thirty-eight, too, Catharine. I'm on my own in ways that you cannot even begin to imagine. If you want me to feel sorry for you and your middle-class angst, I'm afraid I can't.

In the great scheme of things it's just so much self-importance. Read Kershaw on the dispossessed cultural aristocracy.'

'Oh, shut up about that *fucking* writer!'

The branch that scraped at the windowpane, like the fingers of a corpse buried alive, tiredly testing the roof of the coffin, fathoms below the earth, and weakening, scraped still, louring in and out of the lamplight. Catharine was trembling, now, as with the cold, though the kitchen was the warmest it had been all day. Maria recoiled from the display of anger, partly from the anger itself, partly from the fact that it was, from Catharine, unprecedented.

'What on earth has got into you?' said Maria.

'I don't want writers, Maria! I want my friend. I want my friend. That's all.' She sighed. 'Just a writer,' she added, like an exhalation.

All day, she felt, she had dealt in realities – in the intransigent presence of real people in her life, in her kitchen. And now the dominant figure terrorising their conversation, her very friendship with Maria, was Kershaw. This name, perhaps because it was devoid of actuality, became a focus of uncharacteristic hatred to Catch. Not only was the constant echo of his name in their conversation extremely irritating, he always seemed to crop up in such a way as to suggest the very ideas she was trying to reject. Everything about him annoyed her. Most of all the role he seemed to occupy in Maria's life. Like an *uber*-husband, whose thoughts and opinions shadowed your own, in whose wake – as Catharine feared she lived in Tom's – you swam, your individuality traduced; shackled to a lie. This idea of the writer she wanted to take on. Maria's infatuation seemed unpardonably gauche. It smacked of Catharine's moment in the Music Room, of the absurd hope engendered in identifying with music, with expression, with fiction. Hadn't Catharine tried that today already, engaging with the real people as if they were fictional ideas, creatures of her imagination, trying to make the individual stories come out satisfactorily – Valerie and Angelica, Graham; ultimately her actual identification with Louise, ghostlike forerunner of her own misery? It had got her nowhere. Couldn't Maria see that it got you nowhere? It wasn't about you. What it was she didn't know. But it wasn't about treating life as if it were a puzzle to be solved or a game to be won with writers as the smart players.

Now, in spite of the fact that she had been goaded by Maria about her lack of talent, Catch felt able to embrace her failure in the Music Room as the greatest thing that could have happened to her. Hearing Maria talk about Kershaw, she realised that it had kept her safe from being an apostle. No communal, cultural values held her; she belonged to no congregation of like-minded people, shared no opinions; wasn't part of Kershaw's readership. If she had been a musician, this would have happened. Again and again she would have had to visit the models, the tonalities of the nineteenth century, keened over the atonalities of the twentieth century; become a cultural cipher. Having failed at art she could turn her back on it and be free. It sounded so easy.

There was just one problem. Rejecting it, you were brought into competition with it. You were either of the church, or you set up a rival church. Catch wanted neither. She didn't know what she was required to set up in its place. All she knew was that she saw in Maria's love of Kershaw an idolising of both the writer and of the sensibility that engaged *with* the writer. And Catch wanted Maria to engage with *her*. That was it. She was jealous. Jealous of the hold Kershaw had over her friend's imagination. Once upon a time Maria had regaled her with tales of the bedroom, of her lovers. These had been profoundly, profanely, entertaining. But these tales of the *writer*. They were, she realised with amazement, dull. Maria had lost her profanity, Catharine thought, and it was terrible. The look of ecstasy on her face when she mentioned Kershaw, was repellent to Catch. At least her own moment in the Music Room, ecstatic and dismaying all at once, had been reflective of the solitude of self in the face of a great example – the music. But this adoration of the writer, of ideas and opinions that were not your own. It was backward, stunted, teenage in the worst way. Be honest, Catch, she thought, it's jealousy. You never had to be jealous of those who took their place in your friend's bed. But in her *mind*? There must be no berth but mine.

So, she thought, it is quite right that the thing I seek is a child. A baby. It was right to turn from this meddling with adult roles – artist, wife, counsellor – to something real. A child. The artificial organisation of the novelist's world was so pathetically desiccated compared to this craving for a baby, however dismaying and painful that craving was. Kershaw made no cot, no haven, no crib or sanctuary to a newborn. Catch didn't need to compete with the novelist or with Maria's idolisation of him because there was, in the end, no competition. It was the one constant of the day – and this was the ratification of it – she knew what she wanted. Now there was no mistake. A child. In the dark ether of their shared, midnight bed, she and Tom were beyond scrutiny, beyond articulation.

No novelist went there. No writer could ratify their dreams and hopes, or offer succour to their monthly disappointment.

Catharine couldn't say these things to Maria. How could she? Maria had never wanted children. Best to stay silent. It was, after all, as the music had been, a private thing.

But Maria herself wasn't done.

'You know . . . I'm frightened for you. You just have to ask yourself a simple question, Catharine – are we in this together, or not? And I don't just mean you and me. We – we – humanity, the shared bit of society, call it what the hell you like. Are we meant to join together to help, to survive, to live together, or not? I used to think we cared about the same things, but now I begin to wonder. It's like you've gone to sleep. Like you just don't care any more. I'll tell you what is special about Kershaw – though I'm still bemused why his name seems to be a dirty word to you – he's a challenge. That's all. He roughs you up a bit. He takes it as read that we are in this to do good rather than bad, to challenge injustice rather than see it thrive, to be better at being human. What the fuck is wrong with that, exactly? What's wrong with you? Are you so bloody sure of yourself that you can't be questioned? Can't be challenged? You say you're not so certain about the world any more, but that's not how it comes across. What comes across is someone who is only prepared to be *un*certain on her own terms.'

'No, I'm just jealous that you're so swayed by him – *I* want to sway you! I want to be more important to you than he is.'

'Well, you've just proved that what I've said is true. Who are you? You live down a bloody country lane.'

'I'm your friend!'

'There are still things to do, Catharine. You know? You carry on as if all the battles were over. We still have corrupt government, we still have massive social inequality, corruption, chauvinism. Have you become completely complacent? You talk as if I should be ringing you up to find out the truth about the big wide world out there. It's a joke. It's like you want to turn everything into a bloody religion. As if you were the high priestess of morality. You're not. Tom's out there, making a difference. How dare you tell me that Kershaw doesn't matter? He provokes people. What difference do you make?'

'I don't want to be provoked. Not by him, not by you. It's rude. All your life you've provoked people. You've never done it to me.'

'No. You were exempt.'

'Yes. I liked it. Aren't I exempt any more?'

'Maybe not. Maybe we haven't been very good for one another. You know?'

'Don't say that. I beg of you not to say that.'

'Maybe it's true. Me always the wild girl. You the aloof one. A bit superior.'

'I liked our differences. It meant we needn't compete.'

'So what's wrong with competing? I want to compete. I'm tired of you playing the older, indulgent sister. I don't want it.'

'Then stop playing the brattish younger sister.'

'Whoa, at last, some fire. And not just a casual snipe at a brilliant writer. A challenge is finally thrown down. Finally Maria doesn't have to come up with all the tunes.'

'That is so horrible. So, so horrible.'

'Oh, listen to her. The disappointment, the sheer disdain that the world has failed to come up to her own, exalted standards. You're not jealous that I like Kershaw so much – you're just jealous of Kershaw. Because he has genius.'

'I'm not an artist! I'm not jealous of him as an artist! Don't you understand?'

'No, you're not an artist. *You didn't have the talent.*'

Catharine put her head in her hands. Then she stood up, her hands still holding her head. She swayed for a moment. She felt as if consciousness was suddenly questionable; that there might be another, preferable option; a sort of cloud that threatened to engulf her. As she tried to remember where she was, her thought was not that she had suffered psychological trauma, but that there was simply something very wrong with her physically. She wondered how quickly an ambulance could get to the house and whether it would be able to negotiate the potholes in the lane. She wondered if there were any medicines in the house that could stave off what was happening to her; if not in hers, perhaps in Graham's. She tried to remember the contents of his first-aid cabinet on the wall in the downstairs cloakroom.

Catch made it to the kitchen sink, and turned to look back at Maria, who was still seated at the table. Maria wasn't looking at her, and it struck Catharine how shut off we all are, that death or imminent dementia can come so invisibly upon us, so dramatic within, so unappreciated without. She stared at the black window, where night, too, full of wind and weather, was busy, invisibly, swaying unseen trees. Dark and blank; sealed off, Catharine thought, like being in a submarine. This was it. Consciousness, such as it was, wouldn't last much longer. One of the other ways through this would soon present itself. The thing was not to be too frightened. The worst had to be over. The *physical* would be over; that brief period. Even so, it was indescribably horrible.

'Are you all right?'

Word had got out that Catharine was not all right. People would surround her soon. She would probably be lifted, lain out; something would be administered.

'No.'

'You look weird. Why don't you just sit down and I'll make you a cup of tea.'

'I don't want a cup of tea. I feel sick.'

'What's wrong with you?'

'I feel sick.'

'You're not going to faint are you?'

'No.'

'Are you sure?'

'Quite sure. I'm fine, really. Just give me a moment.'

Maria looked away, as if she didn't want to make too much of Catharine's momentary turn, though it was impossible to say whether it was to spare her friend embarrassment or through her own scepticism as to its seriousness. Catharine made her way back to the table, sat, smiled weakly, and tucked behind her ear a strand of hair which had worked itself loose when she had put her head in her hands. Maria, who attempted to smile back, noticed that Catharine's hand was shaking.

'Are you sure you're all right?'

'Oh, don't make such a fuss. Thank you but I'm fine, now.'

'Rather melodramatic of you.'

'Yes.'

'I'm sorry. I wasn't very nice,' said Maria.

'What? I'm just overwrought. It's my fault. It's all me. I mean . . . not in an egocentric sense. I hope. Just me being . . .'

'It's all right.'

'. . . difficult.'

'Leave the histrionics to me. I told you, didn't I?'

'Yes. Next time I will. You can do it for both of us. You're my best friend, after all.'

'It's all right, Catharine.'

'I do wish you'd stop calling me that. You hardly ever call me that.'

'What else can I use? What is it your man calls you?'

'Catch.'

'Can't call you that, can I?'

'No.'

'Husband territory. What are we going to do with you?'

'Don't know.'

'Better now?'

'Much.'

'Good.'

'Well?'

'What?'

'Come on. Let's forget about whatever it was we were talking about. You said you had something to tell me.'

'Did I?'

'On the phone. You said you had something to say. What is it?'

'Oh. I'll tell you another time. Seriously. I'm not being funny. Not now.'

Catch laughed.

'Mysterious. Why?'

Maria shook her head.

'I'm adamant, actually. It's nothing and I don't want to talk about it now. OK?'

'But you came down here to tell me.'

'How do you know that?'

'I can tell. I know that you did. And I've been just what you said I was being – self-indulgent and obsessed with my thoughts, and waited till now to ask you what it was. And maybe because I've waited till now to ask you, you're pissed off with me and we've had a row, and now all I can do is beg you to make up and tell me whatever it was.' She laughed again. 'If we're friends, you'll tell me. I think it's something good.'

'I don't really know what you mean, Catharine.'

'Now you're Catharine-ing me again. Is it a man?'

'We'll talk tomorrow, darling. Please. Don't make me get cross, again.'

'It is a man!'

'It's not a man.'

'My God, it's something terrible. You're not ill?'

'No, I'm not ill. Just leave it.'

'The orchestra's finally come through with a full-time post.'

'No.'

'Mark's proposed.'

'No.'

'No secrets, Masha, just tell—'

'I'm pregnant.'

Maria looked away again, and muttered something under her breath.

Catch put her hand to her face involuntarily, and took a sharp intake of breath, then no breath at all. The hand might have been raised to stifle an inappropriate giggle or exclamation, but none came. Her breathing had stopped, as if she were taking the last steps to the summit of a hill and were waiting till she could take in the fresh air of the summit and the view all at once. Then, the moment seemingly mastered, she tried to say something, and tiny sound escaped, till she turned it to an 'Ahhh' and just managed to say:

'Maria.'

'Yes. Bit much, isn't it?'

'Goodness.'

'Nothing to do with goodness, as Mae West might have said. There, you see. It happens. I wish it was you, but it isn't. What a turn-up, eh? Say something, for God's sake.'

'Are you happy? Are you thrilled? I . . . I don't know what to say. Tell me everything. Tell me who, for a start.'

'Oh, you know. Couple of suspects. I'm being deliberately flippant, I know. It's probably Mark. Almost definitely. Whoever it is, I'm not going to tell them.'

'Right.'

'I'm going to have it . . .'

'Of course.'

Maria frowned and leant back in her chair.

'I hadn't finished what I was saying. I'm going to have it on my own, and be me, my violin and my baby. She can sleep in my violin case while I play. It's about the right size, I reckon.'

'She?'

'God wouldn't give me a boy, it'd be too cruel to both of us. I know it's going to be a girl.'

'Sounds perfect. Are your mum and dad thrilled?'

'Well, it got me a new car.'

'Oh, that's right. The new car. You told me about that. Why didn't you tell me the moment you came through the door? How could you keep it to yourself? When did you find out?'

'Two days ago.'

'Two days ago, Masha!'

'Yes. And I came straight down here to tell my childless friend all about it. Considerate soul, aren't I?'

'Is that why you weren't telling? Because you thought I'd be upset for myself?'

Maria looked at Catharine for a second, looked down, and shook her head.

'Why then?' said Catch.

But Maria just leant over the pine table and the two women embraced, staring over the shoulders of each other at the peopleless spaces of the kitchen where no one came and went. When it was over, Catharine got up, wiped a tear from her cheek, flicked on the kettle and turned to Maria with a triumphant smile.

'I want to be godmother.'

'You're not allowed to say that. You have to wait to asked.'

'Not bloody likely. No one else is doing it.'

'It's an important decision I have to make affecting the spiritual and emotional future of my child.'

'Me.'

'I need a Christian and a fine upstanding member of the community.'

'Me.'

'Of impeccable moral credentials.'

'Me.'

'You got the job. No one else would take it on, anyway.'

'And no silly names, Masha.'

'Why not?'

'Something honest and homely.'

'Like their mother.'

'Precisely.'

'Or like . . .' Maria pursed her lips, 'Catharine. Little

244

Catharine. Yes. I quite like the sound of that.'

'Don't be ridiculous.'

But Catch was blushing with pleasure.

'Well,' said Maria, 'we'll see.'

'So you haven't told Mark?'

'No. I talked hypotheticals last night. You know, what if this happened, what if . . . blah blah blah . . .'

'And?'

Maria shrugged her shoulders.

'Well, he wasn't keen. Obviously. But then why should he be? It's not what he was in it for. Be unfair to spring it on him. I was pissed and got my maths wrong. Should I hold him to account for three glasses of wine and a failed maths O level? And I don't even like him that much.'

Maria was frowning as she spoke.

'But look,' she went on, 'I'm sorry, but . . . I have to say this. I just have to. I did have doubts.'

'Doubts?'

'Yes. A doubt. A doubtful moment. You asked why I didn't tell you straight away, and this is sort of why. Look – a minute ago I said, "I'm going to have it" and you said, "Of course." But I hadn't finished. I hadn't finished the sentence.'

'No, it was about her sleeping in the violin case.'

'Yes. But you thought I was talking about whether or not I would have an abortion. And your remark, "Of course", was you assuming that I wouldn't even consider a termination. But I have.'

'It's understandable. I'm sorry I interrupted you.'

'I don't care about the interruption. You say it's understandable. Not to you it isn't.'

'Why do you say that?'

'Because I know it's not. You would never do it. You would never consider it.'

'My circumstances are different from yours.'

'Well obviously you wouldn't have one now, when it's what you want. I'm talking about whether you would under any circumstances.'

'That's one of your – what did you call them – hypotheticals.'

'Yes, it is.'

'Well, I think it's dangerous to make generalisations.'

'I had one before, you know. An abortion.'

'When?'

'When I was twenty-six.'

'I see.'

'I never told you.'

'No.'

'Why do you think that was?'

'Because,' said Catharine, her voice catching unexpectedly on the word, as if it had snagged a thought below the waterline, 'I am a disapproving, puritanical sort of person and you thought I would not be completely there for you.'

'I expect so.'

Catharine nodded, slowly.

'Then I am sorry. I am sorry I am that person and I'm sorry you could not tell me. And that I did not have the chance to be something better than you thought I was. And I am sorry that by interrupting you just now I gave you the impression that I might disapprove of you still. I am sorry for everything.'

Maria put her head in her hands.

'This is what I can't do, you see,' said Maria. 'Tell me – tell me that you are not slightly disdainful – not even disdainful

– just infinitesimally judgemental of me bringing up a baby without a man, without a steady income, alone in a flat. OK, it may be my problem. It is my problem! I'm in thrall to your respectability. It's pathetic. I don't know why I'm here telling you this. This is why I couldn't tell you straight away. I can't have you looking down like some severe sister on what I'm doing. I can't do it. You're aloof from things, so you can't know, or completely forgive, what people like me are doing. It's pathetic, but I need your approbation.'

'You have it.'

'No, Catharine. You seem to think that what you say is all that matters. I know you. I know what goes on in your heart. You know, you're good. So bloody good. I'm just not sure that you're good for me.'

'Well, you can't just dump me as if I was a man,' said Catharine.

Maria looked up at her.

'Well, you can't,' said Catch, with an edge of desperation in her voice.

'I can do whatever I like,' said Maria quietly. 'I can destroy any number of embryos I choose to. I can. And it is vital that I can. Do you understand? I can leave my best friend Catharine and never see her again. I can burn my fucking violin and be completely on my own. I can do whatever I like. I'm free. And it's vital that we are free, and that morality is . . . is real and not learnt, and that we're not in the shadow of disapproval.'

'But you cannot, if you don't mind me saying so, once you have a baby do whatever you want. Surely that, if it doesn't sound too bourgeois for your taste, you would agree with. Why are you picking a fight with me?'

'Because I'll suffocate otherwise.'

'Oh for God's sake don't be so bloody melodramatic, Maria. There's no need to shout your freedom from the rooftops. I know all about your freedom.'

'My promiscuity, you mean?'

'No! Look, there you are, assuming I'm being judgemental. Sorry, but this is about you. It's you who's judging *yourself* and seeing that you can't carry on the life you've lived so far because you have responsibilities. You're turning against yourself, not me. Well, if you think you've got to get real about certain aspects of your life, then do it, but don't blame me for it. I don't need you lecturing me about your freedom any more than I need Thomas Kershaw lecturing me about the state of the nation. You're the one who's having a baby.'

'Wow. Just as she denies occupying the high moral ground she ascends to the *summit*.'

'I don't disapprove of you, Maria. You disapprove of yourself.'

'Oh, so clever!'

'Love your baby, and spare some love for yourself and for those around you who love you and want what is best for you.'

'My God. Is this the piety you've been storing up for childcare?'

'I . . . I just don't know what I have said or done to deserve this.'

'Your attitude towards Thomas Kershaw is a perfect illustration of what we're talking about.'

'It's that bloody writer again.'

'Shut up. You live almost entirely on a moral level. So the

really spontaneous terrifies you, because you have to look at every motive, every nuance of behaviour to work out the moral dimension. So when you see a vibrant artist like Kershaw, you just suck the blood out of it, neuter it, like defusing a bomb. Drugs, abuse, violence, you don't like them in novels because they threaten you. You're so sure that they are wrong that you think, "Well, we don't need to see that, do we? It's just there to shock, it's just trendy." It's fucking life, Catharine. Not everyone lives at the end of a fucking country lane. There are real people out there, without the luxury of introspection. It's why you'd never have made a decent musician if you'd practised every hour of every day. You have no spontaneity. I'm sorry to have to say that but it's true. You think it's about talent. It's not. It's about attitude. Freedom, too. That dirty word.'

'But these so-called real people that you want to canonise for living spontaneous lives – they don't read Thomas Kershaw novels, do they?'

'So? What, you think you should only write about the sort of people who read novels? That's the most absurd thing I've ever heard.'

'No. I'm just saying that yours is an advanced superiority because you have the benefit of introspection, and get real people, as dressed up by Thomas Kershaw, to entertain you. It's like a Victorian freak show. It's sub-Hollywood fantasy real life for the chattering classes. He's not a revolutionary, Maria, he's just got an eye for the zeitgeist.'

'Oh, fuck off and finish reading one of his books.'

'This is the most upsetting day of my life.'

'For a good middle-class girl that's not saying much.'

'You're a middle-class girl, too, Maria.'

'Well, Tom's not middle class.'

'What?'

'I know what you're going to say. But he's not. Not in essence. He's got hypocrisy too nailed to be called that, of all things.'

Catharine stopped. She was dumbfounded. This sudden concession to her husband was so arresting, so much an answer to an unspoken prayer that for a moment she wanted to cry, or embrace Maria and kiss her across the table. Just to have introduced Tom into the argument was to grant her an ally, a long-lost partner in crime, who would be a salve to the pain of the discussion. It was a masterstroke of Maria's to retreat like that, and in the face of such generosity Catharine could not but lay down her arms and come quietly. She felt ashamed now, to have met Maria's stridency with stridency, fire with fire.

'I know what you mean,' said Catch, aware that her own generosity should come from her not remarking too much on Maria's, lest it come across that she found it too remarkable that Maria should be generous at all.

'Glad you grant him something,' said Maria.

'Masha, I grant him everything. When I said it was over, I meant it about me. Not him. I never doubt him.'

'Who are you talking about?'

'Tom.'

'Kershaw?'

'What?'

'I'm not talking about your husband, Catharine. I'm talking about—'

'Tom.'

'Tom Kershaw.'

'What?'

'Thomas Kershaw.'

'You call him Tom.'

'It's his name.'

'But you don't know him.'

'I've met him once.'

'And you called him Tom.'

'I was encouraged to, yes.'

'By who?'

'By him.'

'But I thought you were talking about my husband.'

'Obviously not.'

'But I don't call Thomas Kershaw Tom.'

'So?'

'So why are you calling him that to me? Especially when there is such potential for confusion.'

'You see? Just when I think maybe I'm being too hard on you for being a moralist you start this. OK. If you think I'm showing off, there's nothing I can do about that. Everyone who knows him is encouraged to call him Tom. He hates being called Thomas. Apparently. So, in an unguarded moment, just now I called him what I was made to call him when I met him, briefly, at a reception, two weeks ago. I call my mum Mum when I talk about her. I don't expect you to call her Mum, but I do expect you to know who I'm talking about. I know Tom Kershaw. End of story. Get over it.'

'I don't understand. I just thought you were talking about my husband.'

'You have this thing about famous people. I've noticed it in you before. You want – you *have* to make them like a separate species. Like the music thing. It's something other people do. Like weird father figures that you can't approach. If we call them by their first names we've crossed some kind of Freudian line in the sand, and some great edifice of . . . of authority's going to come toppling down.'

'And you're still clinging to some adolescent craving to rub shoulders with people of significance and let everybody know about it.'

'Fuck off.'

'You've always done, it, Maria. Catching tutors out at college with details of their private lives. Being over-familiar with famous conductors. Always having to *prove* that they're like everybody else. If you need to prove it so badly then it's *you* must see them as being fundamentally different. Can't you see that? And now you know Thomas Kershaw. Well, congratulations. Do I have him to thank that my friend has turned against me? Has your ambition finally nailed a person of importance? Freedom? You're not free if you care so much about a bloody novelist. Can't you see that? He makes the world an ugly place, Maria. What's the point? I'm asking you—'

'Calm down.'

'No. No! I won't! You've done this. You see what you've done to me. I won't. I won't. Agh! I was thrilled for you that you're pregnant. Thrilled. But now . . . now I just . . . I just . . . hurt. Hurt, hurt, hurt.'

She could feel and hear her voice starting to change, and the words were becoming like a song, as if they had taken leave of their basis in actual sense, becoming music, but a horrible, abstract, sickly music that whirled in her head, like a nauseating fairground ride. Maria had begun to say something about the fact that she had real responsibilities now that she was going to have a baby, and that she was realigning her life. That there might be casualties, but that it was the only honest thing to do. Then Maria called Catharine *Catch*, but in a sarcastic manner, and Catharine begged her to stop, though the appeal was also like a song and involved the repetition of the word *beg*, used in many different ways. Then Catharine reminded Maria that only two minutes previously Maria had implied that she, Catharine, might be godmother to her baby; at which point Maria said something along the lines of that being no longer possible. Then the song stopped.

It may be she glimpsed the kitchen window as she passed it, for she was aware of the silence existing beyond the kitchen, beyond the gravel drive outside, aware that the pure dark extended higher than the roof and trees, up to the fitful spaces of clear sky, where the cool blue stars held their gazes in spite of the wind. These things she guessed and momentarily longed for. Then she was overcome with shaking, though she was neither cold nor sick. All speech or song had now become impossible. She thought no more of any medication in either her or Graham's house, only of enduring what was happening to her. She saw her hand, as disembodied from her sense of physical wholeness as the branch at the windowpane was from the trunk that bore it. This hand rose up and made it to her cheek, and felt the dead face. Then, instead of her own hand against her face, she felt it replaced by the cold kitchen flagstone floor, which magically came up to meet her. Then she closed her eyes and saw nothing but darkness: darkness unsocial and unjudgemental, and she suddenly felt in the flagstones and the hard carapace of the kitchen the same relief and delight she felt when she climbed between the cool white sheets of her bed, from which she had been exiled that morning, that unimaginably distant time in the past. Everything seemed soft

and gorgeous except the terrible pain that was in some inde-
finable place beside her, in that vessel called her body.

Then she knew herself seated on the sofa in the living room,
a blanket over her knees. There was someone in the kitchen,
out of sight, fussing. Such terrible fussing. To reciprocate she
started to rub her cheek with a gentle sawing movement, and
then found that she could not stop. She forced herself to be
still. Something she recognised as pain drew her hand to the
spot where her forehead had kissed the cold flagstones in her
fall, and when she took her hand away she saw a little badge
of blood on her finger, like a telltale menstrual sign; as sweet
and hopeless as her barren body's blood, incongruously vivid
at the hopeful month's end. She sighed and shook her head,
saw the piano and found herself smiling at it. Then she
proceeded to pull at her hair till it hurt. This occupied half a
minute or so. Then, as if she must make a decision, she got
up, went to the cupboard under the stairs, took out her coat
and slipped out of the house.

In the lane, now, the wind had stripped the sky of clouds.
While her arms wheeled like a child as she shot them through
the arms of the old coat, she caught sight of the stars, closely
packed, glistening harbingers of the frost that by morning
would glisten with winter reciprocity. Coat on, she took a few
breaths of the freezing air and laughed, it caught her throat
and tickled her. Her eyes smarted with tears from the chill
and from the emotion that flowed warm beneath her skin,
like a stream beneath its icy overcoat.

She would walk till morning. Catch reasoned that if she was

careful not to actually stop moving she could not die. The road that ran through the ford out of the village she reckoned was due south and that was the way to the coast. The frost would soon freeze the muddy lanes and she would have a surer footing. By morning she would find herself on major roads. It wasn't that cold. Rumours of an imminent freeze were bound to be exaggerated.

The road climbed slightly towards Graham's house. The instruments of his labour had been tidied away and beneath, in the lane, she could just make out Maria's Mini. Behind the yew hedge she could see the Georgian windows of Graham's house in yellow squares as regular as neat battalions.

From here through the village there were street lights, bracingly modern and strangely comforting, their yellow patina casting an urban confidence on the road; they reminded her of the city lights she had left behind earlier that year. She felt a child's wonder at the darkness beyond the concentric pools of light beneath each lamp post. It was pleasant to blind yourself momentarily by staring hard at the neon and then look at the billowy dark, peopled with the temporary aurora, the eyes' sense-memory of the lights.

The post office was shut up. Again she felt the gravity of the dip that led down to the watercress beds and the way to the church. It wasn't her way. She oughtn't to succumb, but one last indulgence would be hers and hers alone. No one need know. Besides, she felt sure of herself on the slope, as if she could ride gravity like one expert in it. She guessed where the hawthorn covered the path and the lane wound round to the church; guessed it from the absence of stars above her. Then she plunged forward into the darkness, knowing that she must suffer a short distance in complete darkness before coming out on the pale gravel of the path to the Mountjoy cottage and the graveyard. She plunged in, blithe.

But something had entered the darkness from the other side, for she knew something was before her, and a collision was unavoidable. A rough coat caught her cheek and the weight behind it, barely halting in its progress, pushed her back.

'What the . . . !' said the shape. 'What damn fool . . . ?'

'I could say the same of you,' said Catharine.

'What?'

'Graham?'

'Eh?'

'It's me. Catharine.'

The shape retreated, as if considering.

'Graham?' said Catch again. But the man stayed back. 'Are you all right? Graham?' Still neither sound not movement. 'Why don't you say something?'

'Bitch,' said the darkness.

'What?'

'I said . . . bitch.'

Then she smelt the wry scent, the intensity.

'You're drunk,' she said.

'Where the fuck are *you* going?'

'To the church.'

'Not tonight, my dear. There's no place for you there. You hear? I've marked their card as far as you're concerned, once and for all. Just so there's no mistake. You needn't go there with your Lady of the Manor prickteasing manners tonight. Or any other night.'

'I don't know what you're talking about.'

'I told you not to spend yourself on them, didn't I? You could have been with me. You tart. The Mountjoy woman got hold of Louise and you're halfway over to her camp, too. Couldn't have that. I've marked their card. *Tu comprends, salope?* Have neither of you rather than lose you, too.'

Then she felt the dark breathing closer to her, the ugly, warm, scented breath. There was contact, from which she recoiled, and she sensed an arm in the dark, though whether it was to claim her or push her out the way she could not tell. She threw out a hand to keep herself apart and felt some kind of return blow which pushed her to the floor.

'Bitch!' said the voice again.

Catch lay in the dark for a moment, while the figure moved on up the hill. She waited till there was silence and then she got herself to her feet and walked on. Soon she came out into the faint starlight of the path and saw the brighter, planetary security of the distant living-room window of Valerie Mountjoy's cottage.

Careful not to illuminate herself, she moved closer to the window, stealthily creeping over the frosty ground that was becoming fixed and intolerant of any movement. The wind had dropped, too. As she got closer she could see right into the living room and the kitchen beyond; the kitchen where she had talked to Angelica and where the girl had destroyed her drawings that morning.

At first it seemed impossibly bright, her eyes having grown accustomed to the dark. Then, in the frame of the window, she saw the scene, glowing in orange light, the rich browns and reds of the sofa and furnishings, the yellow kitchen behind. There, in a chair, its back turned towards the window, sat the mother, and at her feet, her head cradled in her lap, was the daughter; Valerie was stroking the head of the girl, with her bejewelled, fat hands, caressing it with infinite

tenderness, her own face looking upwards, but wholly atten-
dant to the younger head rested in the crook of her body.
And Angelica clung, her thin wrists laid on the body of her
mother like a creeper on stone.

'There, my darling,' said the mother, 'my love, my darling.
It's nothing. You cry it out. It'll pass. It will. I promise you.'

'I'm sorry.'

'What? What, girl? There's nothing to be sorry for. You're
never as much trouble as I was when I was your age. Trust
me. Being young's hard, love. You cry. Stupid woman. We don't
need her, do we? We don't need her sort.'

'No.'

'No. You cry it out. And we'll get on. It's Christmas soon.'

Catharine turned from the window and back into the darkness. Further along the path was the silhouette of the church,
cut out of the starlit sky and, beneath, the jagged outline of
crosses and tombstones; a little forest of the dead. From this
too she turned and walked back up towards the road. It was
bitterly cold now. She must get indoors.

As she took the path by Graham's house, high above the
road, she saw a figure beneath her, in the lane. It was Maria.
Catch watched, safe from her vantage point, as her friend
scoured the road and the darkness, searching for her. Up and
down she walked, evidently unsure whether to continue her
search or not. She said something indistinct, which Catch took
to be an admission of defeat, or impatience, and the keys
turned in the door of the Mini. The door opened, slammed
shut, the engine started and the lights of the car temporarily
illuminated the tunnel-like lane of bare trees and frosty verges.
Then it disappeared into the night.

Well, why shouldn't she go? said Catch to herself. I'm on my way to the coast now. What are we but water in each other's hands, unrealisable, impossible to keep? The responsibility engendered there ends only with death; the preparation for which had been immaculately rehearsed by Tom in his going to Birmingham.

Catch waited, the key to her house still nestling in her magician's raincoat. In spite of all the cold, she waited till the grass around the path, the branches of the trees and the path beneath her feet were all as rigid and unyielding as the tombs which the frost surrounded in the graveyard. Colder and colder. But she waited, moving up and down the high path, walking more easily, moving with grace over the ground as hard as a palazzo's marble floor. The certainty of the frozen ground beneath the stars made her feel as if the earth itself turned on perfectly carved trajectories, as if, if she looked up, she would perceive a new, unexamined elegance in the turning of the spheres.

The lights went out in Graham's house; Orion bestrode the hedges. Still she waited, without admitting what she waited for. Half an hour passed. Forty minutes. Then, along the gulley beneath her she saw bicycle lights and heard the faint crackle, like radio interference, of thin tyres on the frosty road. She waited another five minutes and set off for home.

When she had let herself in, she went through to the living room and saw, on the sofa, a coat which she herself had bought for another. On the table was a whisky.

What should she do? Utterly strange the shape of history, of her heart, that she could now climb the stairs and lay her body beside the mystery of another. How were such things accomplished? Weird and contradictory. But not, it seemed to her, unnecessary. Her heart beat faster. She paused at the foot of the stairs, till Catharine should be Catch, and then went up.

In the morning, she was first up. Before the central heating had warmed the air, she came downstairs, her dressing gown held tightly round her neck.

At the alcove at the turning of the stairwell, she paused. There was her little theatre of objects, the ballet dancer, the Chinese man and box, brightly lit this morning by the frosty windowpane behind, marbled with ice. She remembered what she had tried to accomplish by her scrutiny of this little scene the day before; remembered the quality of *waiting* which she had endured. And only now, now that the waiting was over, was she able to recall the heightened sensibility of that part of her which had waited, as tender as the precious surface of a bloom, finely filamented as a flower, the face of her inner self, brought up to the face of one who loves it, to daylight, to rain. And she was now able, now that the day of waiting was over, by necessary and inevitable extrapolation, to rechristen that one day, *her life* – the constantly shifting attitudes, the fragile allegiances and failed friendships, all that could not be pinned down. Crowned by this one extraordinary phenomenon – the return of daylight to the little alcove, as if the one characteristic to be added to the miracle of creation itself was repetition; that there should be *another* day.

She looked at the ballet dancer, and the missing part of her face. Yesterday it had traumatised her. This morning she noticed that, indeed, the missing segment seemed catastrophic, having wrought a devastating disfigurement. And she could not, as the nervous systems of those who lose a limb are said to do, offer up a phantom sensation to fill the void and make from something broken the illusion of wholeness. But she recognised what she had not seen before – that the poise of the dancer, cheap and kitsch though it might be – forbade, in its fixity, the diagnosis of an accident or vandalism. The poise remained. Nothing could destroy the tilt of the head; no part of the figure could have been said to be without some of the desire to please, to present; to bask, *a point*. It was indestructible. Catharine wondered how much of the alabaster figure would have to be destroyed before the attitude perished, or whether, like the smile of the Cheshire cat in *Alice in Wonderland*, it could survive annihilation and live on, objectless, in the freezing, morning air.

Once she had noticed the figures, and seen again the flawed deportment of glaze and artistry, she was struck by the detail of a speck of dust on the crown of the ballerina. She saw the crumpled tutu, the spidery tracery of dye around the Chinese man's eyes, the grainy rust on the clasp of the little box, and behind the perfect arc of ice that led from the casement to the shelf below, the minutely shaded whitewash of the wall, the neon blue of the light that glowed through the glass: a colour that told her that snow had fallen in the night.

She stood back. Before she need go down to the room with the piano in it, there it was. There. With what technical brilliance the world presented itself. What accomplishment. What unfailing accuracy. The shades, the finely wrought detail. Brilliant. It was brilliant.

Years before she had been frightened when she played music that to concentrate on the technicalities would destroy the beauty of what she was attempting. She was frightened of losing the larger picture. Never mind. Now the world was before her, the virtuosity of its presentation, of what she stared at, was its own larger picture. It was magnificent. The speck of dust, the dumb secrecy of the box from

Clermont-Ferrand, all rendered in the most exquisite detail. It was brilliant. *She* was brilliant.

The world was played. Played with the sureness which she had always dreamed could have been hers if only she could have mastered the notes. Now she didn't need to. The world itself was presented to her as a consummate performance, a perfect balance of technical accomplishment and emotional engagement; the almost molecular detail of what she saw left her aghast with admiration, the breathless command both dazzling and humbling. The world was virtuosity; the world was virtuous. Full of grace, poise, physical ease; it was soulful, human, merciful and full of humility; extravagant and proud, exuberant, spirited and deft; the inexhaustible adjectives must eventually silence her, or leave one only to define the greatness of the performance.

Lived.